Praise for *Whenever You're Ready*

"Rachel Runya Katz has done the :
She's written a contemplation on gr
summer road-trip adventure, and a
It was an honor to join Jade, Nia, ar
history of Jews of color in the Sout
with one another. I fell in love with the beautifully grounded characters, the celebration of queer and Jewish joy, and the oh-so-satisfying
romance. Poignant, tender, and swoony, *Whenever You're Ready* is an
instant favorite from an auto-buy author."

—Alison Cochrun, Lambda Literary Award–winning
author of *Kiss Her Once for Me* and *Here We Go Again*

"This book is sexitragic at its finest hour. Reader, you aren't ready, nor
could you ever possibly be ready, for this level of exquisitely painful, precisely witty, perfectly calibrated hornysadness. *Whenever You're Ready*
will lovingly rip your heart out and set it on fire, then leave you aching
to read it all over again from the beginning." —Jen Comfort,
author of *What Is Love?*

"*Whenever You're Ready* is a deeply felt meditation on the intertwining
of grief and love: how both can weave our complicated webs of friendship, family, and romance. Jade, Nia, and Jonah's road trip is a complex
journey of personal and cultural history, and the miles they travel bring
each of them closer to the courage they need to fully embrace that love,
both for one another and themselves, even in the midst of the grief. A
moving, singular read." —Anita Kelly, author of
Love & Other Disasters

"Is it okay to say that Rachel Runya Katz's characters are always so hot
to me? The slow-burn tension between Jade and Nia in *Whenever You're
Ready* was off the charts. But more than that, Katz always creates such
believable, relatable friend groups, grounded in their relationships with
one another and their relationship to the world around them. I adore
this author's mind!" —Alicia Thompson, *USA Today*
bestselling author of *Love in the Time of Serial Killers*

"*Whenever You're Ready* cements Rachel Runya Katz as one of the freshest
and most electrifying voices in romance. Nia and Jade's lived-in inti-
macy and searing connection will have friends-to-lovers fans swoon-
ing. I can't wait to shove this book into the hands of everyone I know."
—Ava Wilder, author of *Will They or Won't They*

ALSO BY RACHEL RUNYA KATZ

Thank You for Sharing

Whenever You're Ready

Rachel Runya Katz

ST. MARTIN'S GRIFFIN
NEW YORK

First published in the United States by St. Martin's Griffin, an imprint of St. Martin's Publishing Group

WHENEVER YOU'RE READY. Copyright © 2024 by Rachel Runya Katz. All rights reserved. Printed in the United States of America. For information, address St. Martin's Publishing Group, 120 Broadway, New York, NY 10271.

www.stmartins.com

All emojis designed by OpenMoji—the open-source emoji and icon project. License: CC BY-SA 4.0

The Library of Congress Cataloging-in-Publication Data is available upon request.

ISBN 978-1-250-88833-4 (trade paperback)
ISBN 978-1-250-88834-1 (ebook)

Our books may be purchased in bulk for promotional, educational, or business use. Please contact your local bookseller or the Macmillan Corporate and Premium Sales Department at 1-800-221-7945, extension 5442, or by email at MacmillanSpecialMarkets@macmillan.com.

First Edition: 2024

10 9 8 7 6 5 4 3 2 1

In memory of Sonya Essaadi.
Loving you with all my heart, always.

This story centers around the main characters' grief over the death of their best friend. Because it takes place on a Southern Jewish history road trip, white supremacy, including anti-Black racism and antisemitism, primarily in a historical context, is discussed. Please read with care.

PROLOGUE

My Dearest Darling Nia,

I begin with the obligatory greeting: HAPPY 29TH BIRTHDAY!

God, the number of times I've written the words "happy" and "birthday" today is obscene. I never want to see them again. Though I will, many more times over the next couple of days, because I'm counting on you and Jade having many more than three more birthdays. It's a three-person group chat. Two of us dying tragically young would just be gauche. This is MY thing, Nia. Neither you nor J are allowed to copy me. Nor even J the second.

Twenty-nine is kind of an odd one, isn't it? Thirty is momentous, because it ends in a zero and symbolizes the demise of youth or whatever, but twenty-nine is rather blah. I have a way to make it not so blah: cross the last item off the bucket list.

I know the point of a bucket list is to do it before you die, but alas, the brain cancer growing in my lungs has other plans. Yes, still counts as brain cancer, because that's where it started (also, it sounds way more metal. I had a tumor in my BRAIN and was still the wittiest and coolest and sexiest [and humblest] person any of you knew).

You don't even know yet. Because your Preliminary Exam is on Tuesday, and I really don't want the D-word (and not the fun one) hanging over your head. For what it's worth, Jade hated being the only one to know and begged me to tell you, so I hope you weren't too mad when you found out she kept the secret. You know how she is. As it turns out, making it to Rosh Hashanah was overly optimistic. Dr. Sandoval says end of June, if I'm lucky. Which means that even if I'm around then, I'll be in no shape to travel. I know you put so much work into planning this road trip, which is why I want you to go this year. Before you and Jade turn thirty. And Jonah, too. From how often I have to tack him on at the end of a sentence in these letters, you'd think that our favorite barista is right and the three of us are a throuple and he's just incidental. (Jonah is, basically. The concept of a boyfriend when you've only got a couple months left is ridiculous. Don't tell him I wrote that.)

Maybe I've got it wrong, and you're reading this thinking, Michal, we took the trip last year, what the fuck are you on? Well, first, nothing. I'm dead, and I'm pretty sure no psychedelic is strong enough to overcome that. And second, great! Sorry this year's birthday letter is completely useless. I've got to fill the space somehow; I'm planning on you getting very old. But I know you well, and I don't think I will be wrong. Neither of you will be ready next year, maybe for the next two. And then you'll want to go but be too afraid to ask Jade.

Ask her, please. If it's too much to think of it as part of my bucket list (or post-bucket list? tipped bucket list? I have, presumably, already kicked it), then make it a goodbye to your twenties. A beautiful sendoff for the decade of debaucherous young adulthood. I'm kidding of course, you nutjobs chose to spend most of it in graduate school. Side note—do you both have PhDs now? That's absurd. The things I've seen . . . they'll give those to anybody, I guess.

Anyway, feel free to chop off the Savannah portion if you don't have time. I've been talking to my avuela, and she's told me stories and showed me pictures. I'm sure she'd be happy to show you and J², too. Go to Charleston, though. The twins should get to learn about their family in person. And the beach, and Atlanta, because those parts will probably be more fun. Besides, it's not much of a road trip if there's only one stop, right? Change the itinerary as you must, but please just go. I think it'll be a good thing. I've enclosed our original brainstorming sheet. I know you have the Google doc, and I'm sure that is much more practical, but something about the chaos here is more inspirational, no?

Are you surprised I'm not insisting you talk to Jade about something else? I bet. Don't worry, that's going to be 90% of Thirty.

That's all I have for Twenty-Nine. My hand is already cramping, which is concerning. Like I said, I've decided that you and Jade will die very, very old, which means there're a lot more of these to go. Though the later letters will be shorter. These first few are for you guys, but also for me. The rest will be just for you. Promise.

Loving you with all my heart, always,
Michal

*FINDING OUT WHERE I CAME FROM BEFORE I FIND
OUT WHERE I GO ROAD TRIP*

Note: change title, too long

and it sounds too much like the lyrics of "Cotton Eye Joe"

Southern Jewish History Road Trip

Note: Nia's titles are BORING

First stop: Savannah, GA

*Mickve Israel, my avuela says this is the oldest synagogue in
the South. I think my family was there until WWII*

*There's supposed to be some pretty sick gothic architecture
and a house that at one point was haunted by an antiques
dealer*

Note: switch to second stop, makes more sense with route

second stop: charleston, sc

my aveulo says kahal kadosh beth elohim is the oldest
synagogue in the South lmao *Oooooh the girlies are fighting*

my family was there until just before the civil war I think.
will check w/ avuelo.

we should bring jonah if we're doing this   I agree

nice beaches nearby

Note: switch to first stop

Final stop ATL?

Add in Jewish civil rights tour? *i'm down*

General good food and city things

*THIS IS GONNA BE SO COOL!!!!! ONCE WE HAVE A
BETTER NAME!!!!!!!!!!!!!*

CHAPTER ONE

march

There is a mouse in the kiln room.

Jade knows there is a mouse in the kiln room because she is sitting on the floor, back against the wall, legs extended, and said mouse just ran across her foot. It startled her, but not nearly as much as she startled it by going from statue-still to shrieking in a matter of seconds. Poor thing probably isn't long for this world—whatever instincts led it to a foodless room that'll be pushing one hundred and five degrees as soon as Jade gets off her ass do not bode well for long-term survival.

Then again, Jade decided to check her ex's Instagram at work, so perhaps her own self-preservation instincts leave just as much to be desired. Atop Toni's "effortlessly" (read: painstakingly) curated feed sits a picture of two left hands linked at the pinkie, matching emerald-cut diamonds on the adjacent fingers glittering in sharp focus. Blurry in the background, but still distinguishable: Toni and Cheyenne's faces, linked at the lips. A perfect ménage of browns and caramels and corals and rusts and every other godforsaken golden hour hue imaginable, the very quintessence of Toni's social media color palette. Hashtag engaged. Hashtag queer love.

Hashtag swirl. The last one would nauseate Jade if the rest hadn't left her feeling like she is floating outside of her body, unmoored from this earthly plane.

Jade saw the fingers that once memorized every inch of her body (and, concurrently, Cheyenne's, as she later discovered) and promptly sank to the cracked concrete. Damned be the hundreds of custom plates for a Thai place on the Upper West Side that await firing. And she sat there, staring at a divot in the floor, not sure if she was even blinking, for a scientifically indeterminate amount of time. Until, of course, the mouse.

It's not a particularly recent breakup, though the haziness of Jade's last three years tends to obfuscate the passage of time. At first, there were many drunken two-in-the-morning pity parties and several meltdowns on the floor of a tissue culture room, but those are long gone. And not just because Jade hasn't set foot in a lab in two and a half years. No, the stabbing force between Jade's lower ribs is from the realization that the woman she once thought she would be with forever—that *everyone* in her life thought she'd be with forever—is choosing to irrevocably belong with someone else.

If there's any silver lining to finding herself single, graduate degree–less, and in physical contact with a Brooklyn-bred rodent on the day of her ex's engagement, it's that Nia's text message seems far less daunting than it had this morning. **Do you think this June?** came in at 9:08, and it's past 7:00.

For most of their friendship, a ten-hour delay wouldn't be unheard of. But that was when they talked regularly—or rather, never stopped talking. Text threads, DMs, the Three Witches One Coven group chat (named by Michal) held conversations with no particular start or end. That couldn't be understood from text alone because they wove between spoken and messaged, the reply to the last of a late-night conversation often coming the next morning during a hug *hello*.

Now, though, they haven't seen each other in nearly three years.

It wasn't supposed to be like that. Maybe at first, when Nia, or really both of them, needed a cooling-off period. But then Nia got busier with her PhD, and her dad moved full-time to the place he bought back in Jamaica, so she didn't have much reason to come to New York. Jade, on the other hand, never has much reason to leave.

They still talk, sometimes. Texts sent in staccato bursts, replies arriving in rapid fire. Like they're both worried that if they don't get back to one another quickly enough, they'll lose what's left of the friendship completely.

Jade knew this message was coming. Maybe not this year, but it had to come eventually. Plane tickets need to be bought, rental cars reserved, Airbnbs booked. None of that can happen without the instigating decision.

But she can't make the decision without talking to Jonah. Her twin brother is a part of this, too, like every other aspect of her life. At least there's a chance of using him as an excuse to put it off another year.

So, Jade peels herself off the ground and turns on the row of kilns. She pushes through the beaded curtain that divides the firing room from the shelves of bisqueware. Whispering a soft prayer of luck to the mouse, she strides toward the cubby labeled JWP.

Later, Jade boards the M, hands fisted in the pockets of her oversized denim jacket, hoping she can spend the entire ten-minute ride to Bushwick staring out the window and pretending she never looked at her phone.

NIA HAS BEEN running up her screen-time average all day. Staring at her phone as she eats. Reaching out of the shower, soapy water dripping onto the case as she flips it to check for a notification. Running to the bathroom so often that her students and advisor alike must think she has a UTI. Now, burning the shit out of her grilled cheese and Jackson Pollocking her phone screen with tomato soup.

Maybe if Nia had said the real reason it needs to be this year, her phone would have pinged with a response already. She feels guilty for omitting the truth, but she'd feel more guilty telling it. Jade has to want this, and not just out of obligation.

Jade has always been good at that. Obligation. Loyalty. It's an admirable quality, but there's a line past which it becomes self-destructive. A line that Jade lives to toe.

Nia will tell her about the letter when she needs to. Really, she will. Just not yet.

She sits down with her grilled (absolutely fucking charred) cheese and a mug of soup, folding her legs under herself. The couch takes up a sizable amount of her studio apartment but is well worth the sacrifice. And besides, four months from now, she'll be a struggling graduate student no more. Exactly where, she's unsure, but the money she makes will be classified as "income" rather than "stipend," and that means she'll probably be able to afford a living room. At least that's something.

Two of Nia's students canceled their appointments for the month, informing her they'd made the March Madness tournament. So, she's been watching (i.e., googling the rules every two minutes) and has discovered that she is the on-campus therapist to two of the best women's basketball players in all of the NCAA. Like, headed-straight-for-the-WNBA best. She flips to the Stanford vs. Wisconsin game, feeling rather disloyal as she roots against her alma mater in the Final Four. Or *almost* alma mater. She left Madison almost a year ago, but she won't truly be Dr. Chin, PhD, until her professional internship is over.

She nearly drops the tomato-softened burnt bread when her phone chimes. **Sorry**, Jade says, followed by the typing ellipsis. *Shit*. She should've just asked to call. But they don't really do that anymore.

The typing bubble disappears. Nia waits, staring. It doesn't reappear.

What if Jade says no? "Sorry" plus typing bubble seems like "sorry for the delayed response," but sorry minus typing bubble . . .

She'll give it another minute. It's fine. Even if Jade says she can't this summer, it's not the worst thing in the world. After June, it's still six months before Nia turns thirty. There'll be a fall break and, worst case, a winter one. She can make it work. She can convince Jade. She hasn't failed.

The Google doc they'd used years ago is pulled up on her laptop. It's marred with comments—Jade's asides about what her grandfather had told her about the synagogue in Charleston, what Michal's grandmother said about Savannah, Nia's reminders that they need some fun plans, and should they tack on Atlanta, too? She remembers how fun it'd been then; how sure she'd been that she could make this trip perfect. Now the open tab is threatening her from the coffee table.

That typing ellipsis still hasn't come back. Her chest tightens, anxiety dripping from her throat down to her stomach. What if she *can't* convince her? What if it's just been too long?

So, Nia does what she swore she wouldn't do ever since she opened Michal's letter in January: she types out **Michal said she wanted us to go this year, before we turn thirty**, and sends the message before she can convince herself not to.

The moment it swooshes away, messages from Jade arrive. Quick succession, each sent as a text and then repeated verbatim as iMessage, the hallmark of shitty cell service.

Stoney Baloney

toni and cheyenne posted.
got distracted. meant to
reply earlier

they are engaged. #swirl

like come on

and there was a mouse at
work and it TOUCHED me

fucking at&t. i'm sorry
you're gonna get like fifty
notifications from all of this i
forgot about the dead spot

Nia moves to turn on airplane mode, but it's too late.

Stoney Baloney

oh

okay, yes. i can do june. i'm
almost home. i'll ask jonah
then

Okay, Nia types out, heart racing. **Let me know what he says.**

After she hits send, she tosses her phone to the other end of the couch as though the message might burn her and plucks her sandwich-shaped lump of coal from the coffee table. It proves inedible. Lonely tomato soup it is.

Nia stares directly at the TV, trying to will her phone

out of existence for the remainder of the game. She folds and unfolds her legs beneath her, lounges horizontally like a Victorian woman draped in malaise and chiffon, sits back upright when she finds herself unable to eat in this position, scrapes the dark, wavy hair off her neck and into a haphazard bun. Even as Stanford wins, securing her students' position in the championship game, she can't dim the intense awareness of her phone sitting silently half underneath a throw pillow. Worse, the awareness of what she's just done.

Because Nia always knew that the instant the words "Michal wanted" left her lips (or pinged across a few cell towers), Jade would say yes, no questions asked. No matter how much the trip would eat her up inside. Whether she was ready, or not. Whether it was the right thing for her. It feels tantamount to coercion. Which is why the afterburn of this interaction is like a boa constrictor winding itself around her rib cage, slowly squeezing until she pops.

That, and the fact that Nia has never been Good At Bravery when it comes to Jade.

JADE POCKETS HER phone as she turns the key in her apartment door. Jonah reclines on the couch in gray joggers and a mismatched gray hoodie, scrolling through Instagram while the original *Candyman* plays on their living room television. Jade shields her eyes as she hooks her keys by the door and removes her Docs and denim jacket.

"It's March, Jonah, really?" she says.

"It's a classic," Jonah replies in his dry cadence, not looking at her. Well, she can't actually *see* that he isn't looking at her, what with her hand covering her face, but she can hear it in his voice.

"Did you take Luna out?"

"Yes, she tired herself out at the dog park, now she's curled up in your room, as always. Even though I'm usually the one cleaning up her shit. Makes no sense that she likes you better."

At least someone does, Jade thinks. "It makes perfect sense, because I'm not the dumbest dude in Brooklyn." The TV safely out of sight, she drops her hand and peers into her room. Sure enough, there's Luna, asleep at the foot of her bed, feet gently twitching, still at the dog park in her dreams.

Jonah looks up at Jade, face blank, the scene where the graduate student discovers that she decapitated her own dog in a fugue state having no apparent effect on his emotional well-being. She sees her blood-covered form reflected in his glasses and shudders. "You're annoyed, and home late. Something happen?" he asks.

"Toni and Cheyenne are Instagram officially engaged." In response, Jonah snorts.

"What?" asks Jade.

"That girl looks nothing like you. It's funny."

No acknowledgment of Jade's feelings, but Jonah has never been particularly emotionally intelligent nor particularly fond of Toni, so it's no surprise. She wishes he were wrong, though. Cheyenne is all heat-formed blonde curls and flowing dresses, not a tattoo or freckle in sight. High femme, cottage core. Jade is . . . not. "Also, Nia texted, so we need to talk," she says.

He hits pause, sitting upright. "About what?"

"We need to do the road trip this year."

"What road trip?" He makes his eyes wide and innocent, then a shit-eating grin.

Involuntarily, her arms fold across her chest, jaw jutting forward. "Jonah, come on. When it was the four of us, you were supposed to go. Which means you need to be able to have a serious conversation about it."

"Are *you* ready to have a conversation about it?"

"Just look at your fucking schedule, Jonah. Last week of June," she says.

He raises his hands in surrender, ever the victim in the wars he himself started. "I'm just saying, I'm not the one who isn't ready. You never even say 'Michal' out loud."

She turns, halfway through her door. "Oh, I do. I just never have a good enough reason to talk about her with *you*. Schedule. June. Let me know tonight." And then she kicks the door shut.

Luna stirs, yawning, and for this, Jade feels a pang of guilt. She lies down on top of her bedspread, reaching out to rub Luna's belly. The dog rolls over, too-big-for-her-face chocolate brown ears curling against the blanket, tongue hanging out in delight. Jade's heart swells. Two weeks ago, she told Jonah she didn't want a dog in their apartment. But Luna is clearly the best thing that's happened in years. The most perfect creature in existence, and Jonah, of all people, was the one to pick her out.

Jade rolls onto her back, sighing. The abstract 1970s lamp she thrifted at Housing Works casts rings of deep orange onto the ceiling. She finds herself here, staring straight ahead, unmoving, with a higher frequency than she'd like to admit. At least with her hand couched in the fur of Luna's stomach, she can pass it off as an actual activity. She's *petting her dog*, see? Could someone existing outside their body move their hand? No. It doesn't matter if hours pass by like minutes.

Her right index and middle fingers press against the fifth rib on her left side. The ink there is long healed; there's no raised skin for her to feel. But she traces the outline anyway, inhales, presses back against her breath.

The buzz of her phone forces her upright, and her hand falls away.

JWP II
I can do the last week of
June.

She swings her legs over the side of her bed and makes her way to the tiny corner table (unsure what era, it was found on the street, along with their coffee table and a knife block estimated to be worth over five hundred dollars), where she keeps her incense and the other things she likes to burn. Jade loads her grinder, twists, turns, sprinkles, rolls, seals with her tongue. She changes into a sweatsuit to rival Jonah's and emerges from her bedroom, peace offering in hand.

Her brother looks up from his phone, the ending credits rolling in his glasses. She waves the joint. Wordlessly, he sits up, making room for her on the couch, and hands her a lighter extracted from the depths of his pockets. She joins him, sitting with her legs crisscrossed on the cushions. He never says the words "I'm sorry," but he turns on *Insecure* while she takes the first hit, so he apologizes all the same.

Jade passes the joint and swipes to her messaging app, hovering over the thread labeled **NOT LONG NIA**. She closes her eyes, inhaling deeply before she lets her thumb touch down on the screen. **Yeah,** she types, **end of june works for us.** And right after she presses send, she finds herself typing **it's been a long time** and sending that, too. Like it's not the dumbest, most blatantly obvious thing she could have said.

Nia replies anyway: **I figured it was the lactose intolerance.** And then she sends a picture of Jade in a triangular orange cheese hat, from when she visited during fall break in their third year of graduate school.

"You good?" Jonah asks, and Jade realizes she's curled in on herself, knees drawn up close to her chest as she carefully cradles her phone. She straightens her back, cracks her neck, plucks the joint from his outstretched hand.

"Yeah," she says, and takes a deep drag before passing it back.

NOT LONG NIA
You know, since you didn't
come back to Wisconsin

Yeah, she deserves that. It was possibly the worst message she could have sent. Not just throwing stones, but shooting a BB gun in a glass house.

Jade
you haven't been back to
Brooklyn

NOT LONG NIA
Or to Palo Alto.

Jade
or . . . still Brooklyn

NOT LONG NIA
I applied to a position at
NYU, actually

Jade
really?

NOT LONG NIA
Yeah. A bunch of other
places, too

Jade rubs her hand over her mouth, unsure the best way to respond. When the three of them dispersed across the country after college, they all swore they'd end up back in New York. It was something she'd held so tightly, cherished. She didn't know it was still on the table. She hadn't known how to ask. But if it is, if Nia's still committed to the plan, maybe she feels this way, too. Like what happened between them excised another part of her. Just a minor one, like an appendix or pinkie toe—something she could learn to live without, but she still notices the scar every single day.

Maybe Nia wants to have this again just as badly. Not as it was before, Jade knows that's impossible. But something like it.

Jade
it'll be good to see you

NOT LONG NIA
I know, J. It'll be good to see you, too.

CHAPTER TWO

april, may, june

Stoney Baloney

i just realized i forgot to tell
you that we got a puppy

or, jonah got a puppy. but
she's definitely mine now,
too

Nia blinks down at her phone screen. Jade has never
had a pet in her life, unless you count taking care of Nia's
aquarium during her family trips to Jamaica growing up (you
shouldn't). She has, in fact, expressed extreme wariness about
ever letting an animal live in her home. Surprisingly, this was
not one of the tension points in her relationship with Toni—
Jade's ex had always said that being a veterinarian, she spent
more than enough time with animals at work.

I need a picture, Nia types back. She presses send, then
immediately brings her thumb to her mouth to chew on an
already ragged nail.

It comes in quickly, like Jade was already composing the
message when she asked. The dog is some sort of mutt, her

short fur the color of a Hershey's bar except for a lily-white belly. Her eyes are wide and bright, her mouth even wider, and her floppy ears are far too large for her head. It almost looks like she's smiling. She is truly and thoroughly adorable.

Nia

I LOVE HER

Stoney Baloney

me toooooooooooo

Nia

Okay, now I need a name

Stoney Baloney

luna. nia she is so perfect you can't even imagine

Nia

Well please tell Luna that I love her

Stoney Baloney

i will

on a related note, are any of the places you were looking at for the trip pet friendly?

on a related related note, would you consider letting me find new ones if they aren't?

Nia

Hold on, I'll check

We're good on Charleston and Savannah but not Atlanta. But don't worry I'll just do a new search. I think Airbnb has an option to look only at pet-friendly places. You said J2 wanted to be near Piedmont Park?

Stoney Baloney

nia

i will find a new one

but are you okay with us bringing a dog along? she's kind of young to board, but if jonah asks mom to watch her she's not gonna say no lol

Nia

Yes!!!!!! I would love to meet her!!!!!!!

Not if you asked her?

Stoney Baloney

i mean probably, but it's a better shot with jonah

Nia

Yikes. Have you told them about the trip yet?

And I already found a new place that allows dogs 😊

Stoney Baloney

not yet. i think we're going over for shabbat next week so maybe then

i'm gonna have to go rogue and set up the synagogue tour without telling you aren't i?

otherwise you're going to
do this entire thing without
asking for any help

Nia

Text me after if you need

And you don't have to do
that. I have our old Google
doc so it's hardly any new
work for me. I emailed
the one in Savannah this
morning and I'm going to
contact the one in Charleston tomorrow

Stoney Baloney

that was a test. i called kkbe
yesterday and set up a tour
for friday morning

Nia

Jade!!

Stoney Baloney

nia!!

Nia

I would've done it

Stoney Baloney

i know

but you shouldn't have to do
ALL of it

Nia

I like planning

Stoney Baloney

i know you do, but you also
have a big kid job. and jonah
and i should pull our weight,
too

or i should. literally all he has contributed is offering to have his friends from business school take us to bars in atl

Nia

You have a big kid job, too

Uhhhhhhh do we have to?

Stoney Baloney

you know what i mean

no lmao we definitely do not

although seb and leo are pretty okay as far as jonah's friends go

Nia

Okay, maybe we could do it the last night? Like a pre-birthday celebration

Or I guess, during-birthday celebration because I'm sure we'll be there after midnight.

We can play it by ear

Stoney Baloney

yes, we can. and please let me plan more of it

Nia

So, when you say that, is it like a "I don't want you to have to do all the work" kind of thing or is it more of a "I really want to make more active decisions in

it and will feel left out if I
don't" kind of thing

Stoney Baloney
why

Nia
Please answer

Stoney Baloney
it's the former

why

Nia
I've kind of already planned
the whole thing?

The only thing I had left
was to contact KKBE

Stoney Baloney
nia!!

Nia
Jade!!

* * *

NOT LONG NIA
How did it go?

When she and Jonah got back from Shabbat dinner at
their parents' place, Jade had stayed inside only long enough
to shrug on her denim jacket before taking both Luna and a
joint for a walk.

So, she's doing better than she was about thirty minutes
ago, but still not great. That's why she texted Nia—because
she wanted her to ask. And yet she doesn't know how to
respond. She hadn't really thought that far ahead.

They talk a lot now. Daily isn't even the right word; when Jade pulled open the thread to text Nia, the entire screen was messages from a single hour this morning. It's not like they ever really stopped texting, but it's gotten to a place where it feels almost exactly like it had before.

The thing is, this is the kind of conversation they used to have over the phone, which gets her stuck on the obvious problem that she hasn't heard Nia's voice in a very long time. And she misses it.

She stares at her screen, paralyzed by indecision, for long enough that another message appears.

NOT LONG NIA

I'm guessing from the lack of response that it wasn't good

We could call, if you want

No pressure tho

Before she can second-guess herself more, she clicks on Nia's contact and presses call. It rings only once, and Jade holds her breath.

"Hey," Nia says. Jade's stomach clenches. It's so familiar, but her memory didn't have it exactly right. It's smoother, maybe. Soft in quality, not in volume.

"Um, hey," Jade says. She laughs out a single, uncomfortable *ha.*

"So . . ." Nia trails off, and Jade wonders what she's doing right now. It's only seven in California; maybe she's getting ready to go somewhere for dinner. Or maybe she's tired from the week and is settled in with a glass of wine and a podcast Jade would find too stressful to get through. Jade finds herself rubbing at her throat, as if to massage away the completely nonphysical blockage she feels. "You were there for Shabbat . . . ?" Nia prompts.

Jade swallows. "Yeah, um. We go maybe once a month now. Jonah travels a lot for work, but he's almost never stuck over a weekend. My mom's getting pretty good at six-strand braiding the challah."

"That seems nice," Nia says, and it sounds kind of like *this isn't what I was asking, but I'll indulge you.*

"This is kind of weird, huh?" Jade blurts. Nia hums, and Jade isn't quite sure what to make of that. "I mean, we just haven't . . ."

"A little, maybe," Nia says. "I don't know. I meant it when I said no pressure. But maybe I shouldn't have offered. We can go back to texting, if you want."

"No, no. I'm the one who called." Jade sighs. Part of her does want to go back to texting—it's safe. She knows they can do that. But she's going to be packed in a car with Nia and Jonah and a dog in only a matter of weeks now and if they can't even handle a phone call, that does not bode well. She clears her throat. "Well, we told them. Mostly to ask if we could do our family Shabbat a different weekend for June."

"And because you wanted to see how they'd react?"

Jade laughs. "That, too. Dad put his hand on Jonah's shoulder and said we should call if we needed anything, but he was looking right at him. Eventually, he grabbed my hand, but like two minutes later. And then when Jonah was in the bathroom, Mom cornered me and asked me to make sure he was okay, and got all teary and said, 'I know it'll be hard for all of you, but I just can't imagine losing a girlfriend at that age,' da da da da. The usual."

"Fuck, Jade. That sucks. I'm sorry that they've ever been

like that, and I'm really sorry that they're still doing it. I kind of hoped that they would've gotten past it. Or, like, maybe Jonah would've said something by now."

"Sometimes he'll roll his eyes at me over someone's shoulder, but that's about all I get. And it really could've been worse tonight. I think I'm just kind of sensitive about it."

Nia laughs. "Sure, but being sensitive to something doesn't mean it's wrong for it to bother you."

"You really are a therapist now, huh?"

She can hear Nia sucking her teeth, can picture her eye roll. "I'm not *trying* to make you my patient," she says, and Jade is relieved to hear amusement in her voice.

"I'm joking. You've always been good at that." Jade shifts, lying back against her pillows. "What are you up to?"

"So get this," Nia says. "I'm sitting on my couch."

"Nice."

"In my pajamas," she continues, and Jade *ooh*s. "And a face mask." Nia's putting on a sultry tone, selling her evening to Jade like she's the narrator of a luxury car commercial.

"Tell me more," Jade says, trying not to laugh.

"There's a glass of the most steeply discounted Oregon pinot I found at the grocery store this week on my coffee table. And until you called, I was listening to *5–4*: a podcast about how much the Supreme Court sucks."

"That sounds so *relaxing,*" Jade says. "I can't believe I didn't think of it."

"Gotta unwind after a week of trying to help my students work through their stresses and traumas. Saturday evenings are when I actually have fun."

"Yes. And nothing says 'unwind' like a podcast about the United States Supreme Court," Jade says.

"Right," Nia says. "I'm glad you understand."

* * *

Nia

There is a strange man in
my apartment

Stoney Baloney

????

extremely ominous text to
receive with no follow-up

Nia

Sorry, strange man is
named Gene and was
brought by my mother. And
now I have to go to dinner
with them

Stoney Baloney

wait is helen dating someone
new??

Nia

Apparently

Stoney Baloney

and she brought him across
the country to visit you
without communicating this
beforehand??

Nia

YES

Stoney Baloney

omg

please update me after
dinner

Nia tucks her phone away, puts on a smile, and calls the artisanal pizza place she'd made a reservation at to ask if they have room for one more.

An hour later, between bites of arancini, Gene says, "I've never been a stepfather before."

She nods, takes a sip of her drink, and hopes her eyebrows didn't lift as much as it felt like they did. *I'm not sure this counts,* she thinks, but she makes a vague assenting hum. "Please excuse me, I need to use the restroom," Nia says. She fully intended to wait until she's home and her mother and Gene are back in their hotel, but they're only on appetizers and she feels like she's going to start screaming if she has no place to vent.

Thankfully, the bathrooms are home-style and not stalls. She locks the door, pulls up the thread with Jade, and holds down the voice note record button.

"Okay, I am currently in the bathroom of a fancy pizza place so I'm going to try to be quick," she says. "But, J, oh my God. Oh my God. She has been dragging her feet on turning her separation from Matt into an actual divorce, which I'm pretty sure is because she wants the option to go back to him when the time comes, but I haven't seen her in four months and she brought this guy I've never even heard about! Last week, she texted to say that she was going to stay in a hotel instead of at my place but, like, that's the closest thing to a warning I got. And then, you actually won't believe this, he said, 'I've never been a stepfather before.' Like? I'm twenty-nine, I don't think that's what this is? And I want to be open-minded because Mom is generally stable about other parts of her life even if she's a bit, uh, tumultuous with men, so, like, who am I to judge? But what the fuck? What the fuck! This is an entirely new level."

Nia releases the button, checks that it's sent, sets her phone next to the sink, and sits down to pee. She can see the typing ellipsis pop up on the screen ten seconds later, and it gives way to a message as she washes her hands.

Stoney Baloney

oh my GOD

helen what are you doing

stepfather???????????

> **Nia**
>
> I'm going back in. Pray for me

Stoney Baloney

i am

call me after?

Nia has to steel herself to return to the table, but the flutter in her stomach isn't about the prospect of nodding and smiling through another course. It's that last message. No hedging, like her oh-so-casual *no pressure tho* from a few weeks ago. Just a normal thing to send now.

Not that she wouldn't have told Jade about this if it happened in February—they never truly fell out of touch in that way. The most important updates were still shared. But she wouldn't have tucked herself in a restaurant bathroom to send a voice note, and Jade certainly would not have suggested that they call.

She makes her way back to her mom and Gene, reminding herself to smile. But through the rest of the meal, she finds the call with Jade in the back of her mind. She's participating, but part of her is cataloging each moment as it happens, storing and discarding as needed for the debrief later.

By the time she gets home, it's after midnight on the East Coast, so she types out a quick **Are you still up?** before changing into her pajamas. The reply is immediate: **yes, and waiting with bated breath.** She presses call.

"Oh my *God*," Jade says, not even bothering with a hello.

"I *know*," Nia replies. "Like, I'm pretty sure it's still only a separation with Matt, because they're still in contact and they've had ample time to file the papers if they actually wanted to. But she met Gene in a running club three weeks ago and she brought him to Palo Alto to see her only child?"

"I think she may have out-Helened herself this time," Jade says. "You okay?"

"Yes? Honestly, I don't think I've processed it yet. I had actually no warning. She just texted me that she was here and when I went to let her up, he was there, too."

Jade's laugh filters through the phone. "Wow," she says.

Nia flops down onto her couch, setting the phone down on the coffee table so she can wrap her arms around a throw pillow. "Gene's fine, though. Seems nice. He's white," she adds, without really planning to.

"Matt and Mike were, too, right?" Jade asks. "And John, actually."

Nia nods. "Yeah. Everyone she's dated since Dad has been. Or at least everyone she's felt serious enough about to introduce me to. Reversion to the mean, I guess?"

Jade gives a short laugh. "Maybe."

"I don't know. I guess it would be weirder if she somehow exclusively dated Afro-Chino-Jamaican men. But truly, *all* of them are white," Nia says. "I think I'm a little offended on behalf of my dad, maybe. I'm not sure that's a reasonable feeling."

"It's okay if you feel some type of way about it," Jade says. "Now who's the therapist?"

"Still you. I can't believe she didn't give you any warning."

Nia groans. "God, me, neither. It was so unbelievably awkward. I'm never going to be able to go to that restaurant again."

"Is the Bay Area short on artisanal pizza joints?"

"No. But it's the *principle*," Nia says.

JADE ADJUSTS THE T-shirt on her bed, making sure it's flat enough to read the text on the front, before snapping a picture and sending it to Nia.

> **Jade**
>
> started packing. look what
> i found

NOT LONG NIA

Oh my god ha ha

The pinup cowgirl was such
a choice. I can't believe we
wore those in public

> **Jade**
>
> we wore matching shorts
> and cowboy boots too. at
> disneyland

NOT LONG NIA

I know. Think we could get
another one made for J2 last
minute? It's really a shame
they've only been worn once

> **Jade**
>
> speak for yourself
>
> it's my favorite fit for shab-
> bat with my parents

NOT LONG NIA

LMAO

I would pay genuine American dollars to see Jonah in that though

> **Jade**
>
> i don't think either of us could afford his hourly rate
>
> is there anything special i need to bring?

NOT LONG NIA

A swimsuit for the beach and maybe an outfit for going out. But I think you knew that

I think mostly just casual clothes for hot weather

> **Jade**
>
> ugh yeah i checked the weather. we're gonna be sweating our tits off at every stop

NOT LONG NIA

Yeah :/

> **Jade**
>
> i'm really excited tho
>
> for the trip. and to see you

NOT LONG NIA

Yeah

I'm really excited too

CHAPTER THREE

thursday afternoon, june 26

The line at Raleigh-Durham International Airport is interminable. There's no rush, really—the North Carolina Botanical Garden doesn't close until five, and they weren't planning on getting to Charleston until just before bed. But Nia was so nervous about being late that she arrived twenty minutes early, letting her pea-soup-green Kia Soul (the tragic lone rental car left in her price range when she'd gotten in four days prior) idle long enough for the line monitor to yell at her.

At least it took her mind off seeing Jade for a moment. They've exchanged roughly the same number of texts since March as they had in the two years prior. They've spoken on the phone three times. A good thing, obviously. But her stomach is turning inside out with equal parts delight and anxiety. And now, after her obligatory lap, the number of cars seems to have tripled. Her phone has pinged with two separate **we're outside** texts, and she finds herself inching her way toward the arrivals' lane at a snail's pace.

She cranes her neck out the window, spotting the three Pardos in the distance. Jonah has the strap of a duffel bag slung diagonally across his torso, each fist wrapped around the extended handle of a roller suitcase. Jade holds Luna in her arms—seemingly struggling to keep her there—and what is presumably the dog's empty carrier hangs from the crook of her elbow. Nia's heart triples its size in her chest.

From afar, Jade and Jonah don't look all that much alike. Jade is by no means short, but Jonah towers over her, broad shouldered and muscular. Nia knows they have the same pale brown skin, but from here, the freckles that cover every inch of Jade make her look a full shade darker than her brother. Jonah dresses like a guy who was in a frat at Columbia (which he was), and Jade has this sort of stylish-but-lazy tattooed Brooklyn lesbian thing going (which she is). And there's the hair: Jonah's cut into a fade, tight, auburn curls spilling onto his forehead, Jade's shaved so close to her scalp each curl barely has the chance to circle itself. Up close, though, they have the same deep-set, ever-so-slightly upturned eyes and perfectly straight seam between their lips. The top one a full, deep brown—the exact shade of Jade's freckles—and the bottom one slightly thinner, a near bubblegum pink.

They look, for all intents and purposes, exactly the same as she remembers. There's a flash of a memory, then: Jade's face, drawn and sullen, looking away from her on a bench in Prospect Park. She shakes it away.

A silver sedan pulls away from the pickup lane and Nia takes her opportunity, waiting until she's curbside to get their attention. She hauls her entire upper body out of the open window and does a two-arm, excited wave. They tilt their heads to the left, squint, and nod back almost perfectly in sync, obliging when Nia beckons them over.

"Sorry," she shouts the moment they're in earshot. "I'd wait to get closer, but I've been yelled at by the traffic director once already and don't want a repeat. Here, lemme pop the trunk."

"S'all good," Jonah says, wheeling the luggage to the back of the car.

"Sweet digs," Jade calls, pursing her lips to hold in a smile. She's never mastered the deadpan delivery; any words she finds funny enough to say tumble out with an amused twist of her mouth. Exactly as Nia remembers. She feels like she could split in two with happiness. It pushes down the dread.

"Why, thank you," Nia replies, seductively running her fingers, bitten nails and all, along the dashboard. "It's the finest Enterprise Rent-A-Car has to offer. I thought we'd want to travel in style."

The car shudders at the slam of the trunk. "I call Luna," Jonah says from out of view, and Jade whips her neck toward him, careful not to jostle the dog.

"Then I call shotgun," she says.

"My legs are longer." An understatement; as he circles toward the side door, taking the dog from his sister, Nia barely catches view of his waistband.

"You don't get both," Jade insists.

Nia shakes her head, settling back into the driver's seat. "I was hoping y'all got the bickering out of the way on the plane," she says.

In answer, Jonah shifts Luna into one arm, bends low enough to rest his elbow on the open passenger-side window, and winks. "Never."

"Less than a week in this country-ass place, and you're already drawlin' and y'allin'." Jade hip-checks Jonah out of the way, swinging the door open. "We gotta get you back above the Mason-Dixon."

"Calling the Research Triangle 'country' is like calling

Westchester 'the city,' " Nia jokes, but she bristles underneath it. Her Monday-morning talk at the University of North Carolina had ended in a job offer, as she'd admittedly suspected it might, and the rest of the visit had been a three-day wine and dine. NYU still hasn't gotten back to her, but even if . . .

A problem for a different day. Jade climbs in, shutting the passenger door with a *thunk*. "Also, hi," she says, teeth sinking into her cotton candy lip as she starts to smile.

"Hi," Nia replies on an exhale. Then Jade leans over the console, gearshift and parking brake likely digging into her thighs through her Carhartts, and wraps Nia up in a tight hug. Her left arm traverses the width of Nia's back, fingertips brushing against the exposed skin of her shoulder.

"It's been a while, huh?" Jade's words tickle just below her ear, and she fights the urge to scrunch, goose bumps trailing down her neck.

"Yeah," she says. Jade smells like spice as always; she's started every day since middle school burning incense. For some time, it was dulled. Something about working in a lab—maybe the sterilizing agents, or the frequent handwashing, she's not sure. But now, it tangles with the faint, earthy scent of clay, and Jade smells more like herself than she ever has before. It's amazing how deeply the scent imprinted on her, like it was carved directly into her olfactory cortex, a physical part of her cerebrum that exists just for Jade. "It's good to see you."

Jonah clears his throat from behind, and Jade releases her, adjusting the seat and buckling herself in. *Maybe all of this is going to be all right,* Nia thinks, and it's like the catchiest chorus ever written on loop in her mind.

As she watches Jade, Nia feels a gentle nudge on her right arm.

She turns over her shoulder, flashing a smile. "Hi, Jonah."

"Did you miss me, too?"

"Of course," she purrs, patting his cheek. "You're my third-favorite Pardo, how could I not?"

He furrows his brow for a moment, then gives her an unimpressed look. "I'm below the fucking *dog*?"

Jade's peals of laughter echo out the window as Nia pulls back into the flow of traffic. Her stomach is still inside out, but entirely in delight.

They pull over twice before they get to the North Carolina Botanical Garden. Once, because Luna is about to vomit in her carrier. The second time, because she *already* vomited, permanently decommissioning Jade's tastefully tie-dyed bucket hat.

Jade discovers that Jonah's Nets cap was in the same pocket of the duffel, and there's a moment when Nia thinks they'll come to blows. Jade elects to flick Jonah on the forehead instead, and the three of them dissolve into laughter. At her big age of twenty-nine, Nia isn't sure that anywhere feels as much like home as the middle of a Pardo twins spat. And with Luna's carrier, it's harder to notice the empty driver's side backseat. They all notice it, though. Nia's eyes stray to that spot in the rearview several times during the ride, and each time she flicks them back to the road, she catches the movement of Jade's or Jonah's traveling from the same direction.

They disembark, Jonah hooking a no-longer-carsick Luna up to her polka-dotted leash. Jade stretches her arms over her head, pulling the hem of her ribbed tank top high enough for Nia to catch a glimpse of their matching tattoo. Just the bottom of it, a nonsensical sequence of zigzags and looping lines. Next to it, in the center of her torso, is her favorite tattoo of Jade's: a chamsa filled with wildflowers, the fingertips disappearing up toward her sternum. The outline is perfectly symmetrical, but the flowers are not, and Nia has always found that to be poetic somehow.

"So," Jade says, eyes trailing to where Luna is yanking Jonah onto a path. "How did the talk at UNC go?"

"Really good," Nia replies. "Better than I could have expected, honestly." Jade looks at her, and Nia knows she expects her to say more. But she doesn't know how. She feels her cheeks flushing under the beating sun and starts toward the path.

"You know," Jade mutters as she catches up, looping her arm through Nia's. The gesture is casual, like it's something she does all the time. And it was, once. *Maybe all of this is going to be all right.* "Sometimes I think you're more embarrassed to be getting a PhD than I am for quitting one."

"That's nothing to be embarrassed about. You didn't want that degree anymore."

"Maybe I was tired of competing for favorite child, so I took myself out of the game entirely," she says, and Nia turns to the side so that she can see the way Jade's eyes light up as she chuckles. "But really, I wanna know how the job search is going—Jonah! Luna should *not* be eating that," she interrupts herself, peeling away from Nia's side.

Jade makes it to Jonah, and the ensuing bickering gains her control of the leash. He looks down the path at Nia with an exaggeratedly aggrieved sigh. All she can do in response is shake her head and laugh. He smiles, too, dimple popping, before turning back to Jade as though he's thought of a new retort. But Jade is already three paces ahead and, unsurprisingly, completely engrossed in conversation with a mustachioed stranger.

* * *

JADE AND LUNA cross a footbridge to rejoin Jonah and Nia, who sit on a wooden bench staring into a pond of lily pads. The water lilies are in full bloom, magenta and snow-colored petals unfurled around yellow centers. There are even frogs sitting among them, and as Jade approaches, she spies one extending its tongue to catch an unsuspecting fly. Jonah sits comfortably spread over two-thirds of the bench—legs wide, arm slung across the back—while Nia sits holding herself with slight discomfort, her ankle propped on her opposite knee, the majority of her thigh exposed by the rip in her jeans. Jade knows she'd prefer her legs folded under her, and she wonders whether it's the stickying, humid heat or the slats of the bench that prevent her from doing so.

"What'd they want?" Jonah nods in the direction from which Jade came.

"My new, very dear friend, Andy, wanted to give me some goodies for the road," she replies, raising her brows and tilting her head.

"Naturally." Nia laughs, moving to sweep the loose curls off her neck and into a claw hair clip. The heat then. The two locks in front are too short to stay put, and Jade knows the moment Nia stands up they'll fall forward to frame her face, bisecting her straight, full brows.

Jonah leans forward, resting his elbows on his knees, letting one hand drop to scratch between Luna's awaiting ears. "I swear you have 'give me weed' tattooed on your forehead."

The dog bounds toward some tall, grass-like plants, letting the stalks tickle her belly. Jade tightens her grip on the leash. "You smoke plenty," she says.

"But strangers never strike up conversations with me that end in a baggie of edibles."

"It's bud, actually." Jade smirks.

"That's because you look like you smoke out of a grav-ity bong. Jade gives off more of a 'my blunts have lavender in them, too' vibe." Nia looks back up at her, thick strokes of eyeliner thinning into soft, feminine flicks under her hooded lids, her dark eyes glinting with a smile. She's done her makeup virtually the same way since early high school, and Jade mostly stopped noticing it. But now, after almost three years away, everything about her is either an obvious change or carries a memory. Her watch, for example: a brown leather band and gold-rimmed face that Jade has never seen before. She's never seen Nia wear a watch, period. But the eyeliner reminds her of ninth grade, lying on their stomachs on the floor of Michal's bedroom and pouring over Eyeliner to Suit Your Eye Shape YouTube videos for hours on end. Nia perfected hers in three tries, Michal in five, but Jade never could get hers to look right on her own.

"See, Jonah, she gets it," Jade says. "Andy is an ally. He supports girl blunts only."

Her brother dramatically pinches his brow, sighing. "I don't know how I'm gonna get through this week alone with the two of you," he says.

It's meant to be a joke, Jade knows that. But she stiffens, and so does Nia, and the silence that falls among them is not a comfortable one.

There's a beat before Jonah notices. When he does, he clears his throat, his hand falling gracelessly to his lap. "Um, I—" He pauses, fiddling with the drawstring of his sweat-shorts. "Do you need me to take Luna?"

They all look to her, happily curled in a spot of shade, tongue out, tail wagging, leash slack. In other words, no, she doesn't need help with the dog. "Sure," she says, and hands him the lead. "Where to next, tour guide?" She nudges Nia's toe with her own.

"We could go into Paul Green's Cabin, if you want."

Jonah stands, dusting off the back of his shorts. "The *In Abraham's Bosom* playwright?"

"I'm genuinely shocked you know that. *How* do you know that?"

"I read, Jade."

"That's news to me!"

He rolls his eyes, starting in the direction of the footbridge.

"It's the other way," Nia says, and fails to look sufficiently apologetic as Jade busts out laughing.

The cabin is small and dim, the low ceilings making Jonah look almost *Alice in Wonderland* oversized, ducking to avoid stray beams. It's remarkably preserved and has that feeling of importance in its creaky floorboards. That sense of *something of note happened here.*

They read about Paul Green's work as a playwright, his commitment to civil rights and economic equity, the near teardown of the cabin after his death and the subsequent movement to preserve his writing retreat, leading to its eventual home in the garden. Then they push into the sun-warmed outside air, untie Luna's leash from a pole, and walk the rest of the Mountain Habitat. They traipse through the Coastal Plains section, the Piedmont Habitat, cross the Education Center to Courtyard Gardens. And then it feels less like they're visiting the botanical garden and more like they're delaying the inevitable, so they stop in the restrooms and make their way back to the car.

It's not a decision they discuss, really, they just exchange a few looks and know it's time to head to Charleston. There's truth to twin telepathy, Jade thinks, but it's learned, not innate. Since middle school, she's felt like she could anticipate Nia and Michal's thoughts and emotions just as well as

Jonah's. It's comforting to know that she still can, after all this time.

So they climb into the car, buckle their seat belts, and crank up the AC. Jonah puts Luna on his lap, hoping that if he holds her himself, she won't be able to move around and nauseate herself as easily.

It works—for the first half hour of the drive. Luna struggles against Jonah's arms, trying to jump up to see out the window. Jade tells him to hold her still, and he tells her he's *trying* and she says he's not trying hard enough, and Jade can see Nia doing her best not to laugh from the driver's seat. Luna wiggles, and then starts to salivate uncontrollably, drool darkening the fur around her mouth from brown to black. By the time Nia has found a suitable place to pull over, the dog is heaving. Cars whir by, Jonah rubs her back while muttering "poor baby," and Jade and Nia huddle around their phones, asking Veterinarian Google what to do for a carsick dog.

"It seems that the options are to knock her out with Benadryl or give her Dramamine to ease the nausea," Jade says.

"Does she seem anxious, too?" Nia asks, brow furrowed as she looks down at her screen. A curl hangs forward in front of her face, obscuring Jade's view of her nose. "Or just motion sick?"

"I don't think she's anxious." Jonah pulls out her portable water dish and fills it, and Luna laps happily, ignoring the pile of vomit next to her. "Dogs are supposed to grow out of carsickness when they get to about a year old."

"Are you suggesting we stand on the side of the road for the next six months?"

"Ha, ha, Jade."

"I think we should get the Dramamine. I'll route us to the nearest drugstore, but it says to call a vet to find out the proper dosage." Nia and Jonah exchange a look.

"You can't be serious!" Jade says.

Jonah sighs. "You'll probably get an answer faster than if—"

She shakes her head vehemently. "No, no. Toni's not Luna's primary care veterinarian! For a reason! I have her actual doctor's number saved. I'm calling now."

Nia reaches out to squeeze Jade's shoulder, her hand warm and light. "It's after five, J."

It's ringing, she mouths, pressing the phone to her ear. And ringing, and ringing. *You have reached the Neighborhood Vet Bushwick. If this is an emergency, please contact a twenty-four-hour emergency clinic. Otherwise, please leave your name and number after the tone, and we will get back to you during business hours, which are Monday*—Jade hangs up. She closes her eyes slowly and takes a deep breath. Fine. This is fine.

"It *is* fine, Jade. Just a quick call."

Jonah looks up. "I'll do it if you want."

Jade snorts. "Yeah, because that'll go well. God, four fucking hours into this trip and we're on the side of the road and I have to call *Toni*. Is it too late to put it off another year?"

Nia stills, drops her hand, and frowns, and Jade knows she's said the wrong thing. But she's already tempted to lie down on the gravel shoulder and stare up at the sky instead of dealing with all of this. So she doesn't bother figuring out how to apologize. She just sighs, finds the contact that says Do Not Call If Drunk (a helpful hint from Jonah two years ago), and hits dial.

CHAPTER FOUR

thursday evening, june 26

"This doesn't faze you at all, huh, little one?" Nia whispers to Luna, offering a readily accepted treat. "You're doing just fine." She lowers herself to the ground beside Jonah, leaning her weight back onto her hands, gravel poking into her palms.

"How'd she sound?" Jonah nods toward Jade. She's turned half away from them, staring blankly out into the road. Her left arm is wrapped across the front of her ribs (where her underwire would be, if she ever wore a bra) and her right elbow is propped on her wrist, phone pressed to her ear. Everything about her says Straight Up Not Having A Good Time Right Now. Nia forces herself to look away.

"I dunno, I left as soon as she called. I don't . . . I never liked hearing her when she's talking to Toni." Nor does she like being reminded of the last time she talked to Jade *about* Toni.

Jonah shakes his head. "When they broke up, I felt like I could've killed her, you know?" Nia looks to him, and there's a deep crease in his brow. "Not that I was going to actually do anything, but I just . . ."

"No, I know what you mean. It was so soon after the shiva." Two weeks, to be exact. Nia sighs, glancing over to where Jade is rubbing the back of her neck.

"Well, she's a vegan. So good fucking riddance," he says, and they both laugh.

"What's so funny over there?" Jade calls from where she leans on the front passenger-side door, left hand in her pocket, right hand still clutching her now idle phone.

"What a piece of shit your ex is and how you're an idiot for ever dating her," Jonah replies with a grin.

Nia holds her breath, waiting for Jade to pin her to the ground with a *are* you *really joking with him about this* glare. It would be deserved, probably. But she doesn't. Instead, Jade rolls her eyes, and Nia laughs without meaning to. "I wouldn't put the first part like that, and I wouldn't say the second at all, but—"

"But that's pretty much the gist of it, huh? I hate *y'all*," Jade says, opening the car door. "Come on, I got what we needed. Walgreens and the other Carolina await." She slips inside.

Jonah and Nia exchange a look of relief. After this many years of running in overlapping circles, it makes sense that Jade would have learned to handle it well. But Toni once had a way of torturing Jade so skillfully that Nia was convinced it was intentional, so she wouldn't judge her if she hadn't.

Jonah stands, dusting off his pastel green shorts, and offers Nia his hand to help her up. She blinks before taking it, one of the many moments she's stunned by Jonah's chivalry. It's woven into a tapestry of Consulting Bro and General Tool, but Gentleman is also a fundamental thread of his personality—one she often forgets.

They make it to Walgreens with little time to spare—Luna's pre-puke drool is already well underway—but all fashionable hats in the car remain unsullied. After Luna out-smarts a spoonful of peanut butter three times, Jonah loses rock paper scissors and has to hold her mouth shut while Jade strokes her throat to force her to swallow. It works, eventually, and they wait a few minutes to watch for any adverse effects. None, unless you count the excited licking that narrowly misses Nia's open, laughing mouth.

So they pile back into the Kia Soul, Jonah in the back with Luna on his lap, Jade's feet up on the dash in a very Road Trip kind of way, playing DJ on her Spotify account. The backseat passengers are asleep before the signs lining I-95 warn of the approaching state line, and Jade graciously turns the dial down, the bumping music flattening to a hum.

"There's not enough Pop Smoke on this playlist," Jade says.

Nia briefly takes her eyes off the road to look at her. Jade's gaze flicks to her phone, her teeth dragging over her bottom lip. A familiar tic that leaves her lip plump and glistening, and trails a flush of heat up Nia's neck. She forces herself to look back toward the skipping white line on the ground ahead. "Wasn't he, like, very homophobic?"

"Sometimes things that are bad are very good, Nia," Jade replies, and Nia snorts. She nods ahead, what looks to be a water tower shaped like a sombrero coming into view. "Like whatever that is."

Nia smiles. "Bad but very good," she agrees. But they get closer, and they see a sign that says South of the Border adorned with a caricature of a man in a hat matching the water tower. "Or maybe bad and very bad," she amends.

"Yet another reason you should rejoin the Union."

Nia straightens in her seat. "Jade—"

"I know, I know," she says. "It was only a research talk, racism exists outside the South, I'm being extra. It'll just . . . it would be cool for you to be in New York again."

Nia is silent for a moment, and she can feel Jade looking at her, brow furrowing deeper with each passing second. "I haven't," she clears her throat. "I haven't heard back from NYU still. I have no idea if I'll even have that option."

Jade sighs out a low note. "Oh," she says slowly. "Do you think you'd take that option if you had it?"

"It's what I always dreamed of," Nia says, and it feels like a lie even though it technically isn't. "But it isn't just what I want, there has to be a job for me."

"In academia."

"What?"

"There has to be a job *in academia* for you," Jade says. "You can be a therapist anywhere."

"Well, yeah. I want to do both."

"Would you really live somewhere you don't like just for the job?"

"No, I wouldn't." But that doesn't seem like a problem she's going to have, even if her only offer at the end of the day is UNC. She wouldn't have to live in a college town if she didn't want to; Durham—with mixed neighborhoods she might actually be able to afford a home in and old-school hip-hop and New Age folk music and breweries and local coffee roasters and legions of folks who dress just like Jade—is barely twenty minutes away. And Kayla, her informal mentor from her first couple of years in graduate school, connected her to a queer- and BIPOC-run therapy center there, which is exactly the kind of place where she'd want to do her community work. Maybe she hadn't envisioned herself in North Carolina when she started her PhD six years ago. But that was six years ago. "Things just don't always go as planned."

Jade laughs. "Really? I, for one, was certain I'd be a potter when I started my neurobiology doctorate."

"But do you regret how that turned out?"

"Not one bit." She sighs. "I get it. I just . . . I hope you'll end up back in New York."

Right, The Plan. The one they'd made with Michal before they scattered across the country for various graduate programs. She didn't realize that Jade still had an attachment to it. She should have realized though; Jade is excruciatingly good at keeping promises.

But then Jade adds "with me," and when Nia glances her way, she finds her gaze fixed perfectly on the road. Nia swallows, telling herself the race of her heart is incidental, that there's nothing special about those two little words.

Except she finds herself fixating as they fall quiet around Pop Smoke's impossibly low tenor, wondering if "with me" means a fraction of what she thinks it might—that this extends beyond Jade's usual sense of obligation. That this is something she truly *wants.* Nia can almost convince herself of it. Because why say that, otherwise? Why not leave it at New York? Jade has to feel it, too, the bone-deep loss of the past three years.

Then again, Nia has been wrong before.

THEY ARRIVE AT the Lodge Alley Inn at the tail end of dusk, overfull on drive-through food, simultaneously antsy and exhausted. The candy-coral walls that match the rest of Charleston's French Quarter are colored sunset lavender by the dimming sky, interrupted by jutting black balcony rails and gray-white columns. Jonah takes Luna for her bedtime walk, leaving Nia and Jade to load themselves up with luggage and check in.

At the front desk, Jade watches Nia drum her fingers along the black granite. Her nails are bitten to nubs. Which means she was either lying about the talk at UNC going well, or she's been nervous for the trip. Three years ago, she would have reached out to still Nia's hand with her own, held eye contact, and just waited until Nia told her what was wrong. But the space between them is tender now, bruised. So they pile into the elevator in silence, Jade sending off a message to **JWP II** with their room number and directions.

The main room of their suite is half exposed brick, half sage green, and all curved wood and upholstered furnishings.

"This place is very On Theme," Nia says. She has a way still of giving you the sense that certain words are meant to be capitalized.

"Very," she agrees. "I guess the one with the queen is me and Jonah's and the one with the full is yours?" Jade looks between the open bedroom doors.

"Oh, um. Yeah." Nia looks down, trying to fit the hairs that escaped her claw clip back into place. "You can take the bathroom first, I gotta unpack." Jade just nods, smiling. They're only here for two full days, but Nia couldn't live out of a suitcase for a single night if you paid her.

In the bathroom, Jade scrubs her face with cold water, letting the faucet run longer over the pulse points of her inner wrists. Even with the sun nearly faded, the humidity is oppressive, and dragging suitcases over two blocks of narrow sidewalks replenished the sheen of sweat that had evaporated under the car's AC.

She disrobes and steps into the shower, relishing the freedom of the water rushing against her scalp and dripping down her brow, knowing it'll dry long before she goes to bed. A simple pleasure she's yet to take for granted since shaving her head. *Quite the statement,* her mom (who hasn't worn her hair natural since the seventies) said when she went to her parents' house in Queens for Shabbat that first weekend, a single eyebrow raised. *Yes, quite,* she replied, prickled at the fact that nobody had commented on Jonah's equally nonexistent hair. *It says, "Michal is starting treatment,"* she wanted to say. But if she had explained, it would've been a whole thing and most likely ended with Jonah receiving profuse commendation for joining in, even though, at that point, it was only Nia and Jade who were close to Michal. He'd mostly done it on a whim in solidarity after the three of them had returned from Jamaica in all their bald-headed glory. Jonah had looked at her from across the table, like he knew what she was thinking, and nodded. And then it didn't feel so bad that she couldn't say it out loud.

Jade emerges from the bathroom in boxers and an oversized shirt from some fraternity event Jonah blackmailed her into attending in college, a cloud of steam billowing behind her. Jonah barrels past her before she has both feet firmly planted on the hardwood. "Jonah!" she calls, even though the door is already shut behind him. "Nia was gonna wash up, come back out here!"

"Can't," he says over the rush of the water. "Already naked."

"Jonah, you're so fucking rude. You can wait, like, two minutes for—"

"It's fine," Nia says. The door to her room is only a quarter open, but Jade can see most of her in that sliver of space. She's standing at the foot of the bed, refolding clothes that were presumably already neatly folded, and grinning.

Jade finds herself smiling back as she crosses the living area, her annoyance with Jonah dissipating.

God, is it good to see her. Jade had felt sick with nerves on the plane, worried that maybe when they saw each other in person, it would turn out that Nia hadn't forgiven her after all. She's still nervous, maybe, but mostly hopeful.

When she gets to Nia's room, she leans her head on the

doorframe and folds her arms across her lower ribs. "You sure?"

Nia toes the door the rest of the way open, nodding. "I'm sure. Besides," she says, "when has it ever taken me any less than forty-five minutes to get ready for bed?"

Jade pretends to rack her brain, tapping her chin with her index finger. "There was one time when we were twelve, maybe? Glad some things stay the same," she says, trying to ignore the wistfulness she hears in her own tone. Nia rolls her eyes in response, but an amused smile plays at her lips as she tucks a stack of shirts into an open drawer. Jade shifts a little, leaning farther so that the skin from her shoulder to her elbow presses into the wood grain. "Thank you, Nia," she says.

Nia freezes halfway between the bed and the dresser, looking up at Jade. "For what?" Her cupid's bow barely dips, and when her face relaxes like it does right now, her lips part just slightly, forming a little ellipse of space between the top and bottom. Almost perfectly symmetrical along both axes. When Nia looks at her like this, Jade has trouble looking anywhere but that oval gap.

She lifts her head from the doorjamb, gesturing with it in a noncommittal circle. "Finding this place. The whole trip. Asking us to go this year."

Nia tucks one of the front locks of hair behind her ear. It immediately starts to slide forward. "I mean, you set up one of the synagogue tours," she says, and Jade fixes her with a look. "A lot of the itinerary was from the first time around, so I didn't have to do much."

Jade laughs. "You did most of the work the first time around, too."

"That's true, I guess. I liked planning it, though."

"Yeah." Jade nods, swallowing. "You wouldn't be our Nia if you didn't." In the background, the sound of running water cuts out, followed by Jonah's footsteps and a creaking door. "I'll let you get started on the fifty-step routine."

"Ten!" she exclaims, reaching for her travel toiletry bag. One of the ones that hangs from a towel bar and unfolds to a wall of tiny compartments for every imaginable item. "And that's if you include brushing and flossing."

"Good night, Nia," Jade says, pushing herself back fully upright. "See you in the morning."

"Night, J," Nia replies, scooping a matching sleep set into her free arm. "And," she says when Jade's almost to her and Jonah's room, "you're welcome."

Jade nods, and feels her smile stretch from ear to ear.

It doesn't last, though, when she finds what looks like a month's worth of menswear strewn across the floor. "I must've missed the tornado warning."

Jonah looks at her blankly, already in bed. "My pajamas were at the bottom of the suitcase."

She doesn't feel like engaging, so she climbs in her side of the bed and picks up her book. At that exact moment, Jonah turns out the light on his nightstand, yawning.

"I'm so tired, Jade. Do you have to read now?"

"I guess not." She sighs, switching off the lamp and curling onto her side. *It has been a long day,* she thinks. *And it'll be a longer trip.*

Within five minutes, Jonah's breathing evens. Within ten, he starts to snore. By thirty, it's loud enough to cut through the pillow Jade smashes over her head. Fortunately for Jonah, it seems to muffle her groan so well that his peaceful slumber goes undisturbed. She's lived with him for their entire lives (with a brief respite for freshman year of college, when Jade finally had the requisite unrequited-crush-on-a-straight-girl experience with her roommate), but it's been more than a decade since they shared an actual room. A decade that seems to have done untold damage to Jonah's nasal passageways. Hours pass before she finally drifts off to sleep.

CHAPTER FIVE

february, nineteen years ago

Nia sat with one leg folded over the other, looking at the floor as she unfastened and refastened the Velcro of the rented shoe on her left foot. Little bowling pins with technicolor shadows dotted the carpet, its color so dingy and muted that she would have bet it was older than she was. Her right foot was starting to fall asleep, but she wouldn't release it. When she'd first sat down, her legs dangled, swinging. Camilo S. was in the same lane as her, and his feet touched the floor just fine. She hated how small that made her feel.

What she also hated was how the birthday girl herself had insisted she stay there, not moving a muscle, because she'd *be right back*. It was Michal's tenth birthday, and everyone knew that's one of the biggest ones, so Nia had listened. The enormous, glowing clock above the pins at the end of the lane told Nia that Michal had been gone for five whole minutes. She felt Camilo S. staring at her, and she wanted to shrink inside herself.

She smoothed the Velcro strap back in place one last time and looked up, prepared to ask Camilo S. about his favorite dinosaur (a go-to whenever she had to talk to a boy she didn't really know), when Michal came bounding toward her. Michal never walked. She often bounded, occasionally skipped, sometimes ran, seldom shuffled, but *never* simply walked. Following closely behind Michal were a boy and a girl Nia hadn't met before. Siblings, she guessed, judging by their matching clouds of auburn hair, light brown skin, and tall, long frames.

"I've been dying for you to meet each other! I wanted to do a playdate with all of us, but my mom said I couldn't invite you both over at the same time unless you met first. So now you met, and we'll all be best friends. Do you want to do a playdate next weekend?" Michal rushed out.

"Um," Nia said.

"You didn't introduce us yet," the girl said.

"Oh, yeah!" Michal pressed her palms into her cheeks. "Oops." She grabbed Nia's hand and shoved it into the girl's. "Nia is my best friend from regular school, and Jade is my best friend from Hebrew school. Jonah is her brother, and my mom said I couldn't invite Jade if I didn't invite him since they're twins and it's a big party. So he's here. But she said that if I had a playdate with just you two, I didn't have to invite him."

Jonah stood there, looking like he was about as excited to be there as Michal had been to extend the invitation. "Hi, Nia," he said.

"Hi, Jonah," she replied. "Hi, Jade. You have a lot of freckles."

Jade beamed. "There's one on the inside of my lip!" And then she rolled it down to show her. Sure enough, there it was. Nia had never seen so many freckles on a single person before. *Wow,* she was freckled, like, were they . . . Jade blinked. Yes, they were even on her *eyelids.*

"I have a birthmark by my bellybutton that looks like Hawai'i," Nia said, and lifted her sweater to show Jade.

Jade's smile grew wider. "Cool!"

"I knew you'd be friends!" Michal shrieked. "Please ask your parents about a playdate on Saturday. I wanna go to the zoo." *It's way too cold for the zoo,* Nia thought.

"Are you Black?" Jonah asked, his head tilted to the side. Jade pinched him on the shoulder. "*Ow!* What?"

"Mom said you have to stop asking people that!" She looked at Nia, biting her bottom lip. It was very pink, like she'd just been sucking on a strawberry lollipop. "Well," Jade said quietly. "Are you?"

Nia laughed. "Kinda."

"What do you mean, 'kinda'?"

"My dad is from Jamaica," she said. At that point, Nia's answer to any question about her ethnicity was a rehearsed speech. She was only ten, but she was pretty sure she'd been asked ten thousand times. "My grandpa's family is Chinese Jamaican, and my grandma's family is Black Jamaican. And my mom is white."

"Oh. That makes sense," Jonah said. "Our mom is Black and our dad is white and Jewish."

"Sephardi, like me!" Michal said.

"Oh." Nia nodded. "That makes sense."

Jonah looked at Camilo S., whose lucky feet were still planted firmly on the ground in front of the purple, plasticky booth where he sat. "I'm gonna hang out with him," he said. "Come get me when Dad's here to pick us up." With that, he walked off.

UNSURPRISINGLY, JONAH HAD abandoned Jade for the very first boy he saw at the party. Even though he and Jade knew exactly the same number of kids here: one.

Jade and Michal liked to play pretend before their Hebrew

school classes. Every Tuesday and Thursday evening, they got there early so they could sneak into the sanctuary and conduct full interviews with the always-on microphone on the bimah, asking each other what it was like to be famous for discovering the world's first mermaid (Michal) or being the youngest detective to solve a grisly murder (Jade). Sometimes, they whispered swear words—"motherfucker" was Michal's favorite, while Jade liked "ass" for its simplicity—just because they knew it was empty and they wouldn't get caught. After, they always stumbled to the fourth-grade Hebrew school classroom in the far wing of their synagogue, laughing so hard that tears leaked from their eyes.

Needless to say, neither had made any other friends. So Jade and Jonah (who Jade was rarely allowed to leave the house without) were the only kids from Hebrew school at the bowling alley. She hadn't wanted to spend the afternoon glued to Michal's side, preventing her friend from playing with the other kids.

But from the way Michal gripped tightly onto Jade with her left hand, Nia with her right, and dragged them both to the lane opposite Jonah and the other boy, it seemed that gluing Jade to her side had been the birthday girl's plan all along. Michal only let go to shove Jade and Nia down onto the curved booth, the shiny kind that squeaked a little with every movement. Jade was thankful that Michal had been born in February instead of a summer month when she would have had to suffer the plastic seating on her bare thighs.

Michal left them to punch their names into the machine, a painstakingly slow process. "It's the only thing she's not good at," Nia said.

Jade turned to look at her. Nia's legs were folded criss-cross on the bench, and she kept fidgeting with one of the straps of her bowling shoe. Her hair was jet-black and curly, not a mixture of kinks and coils like Jade's and Jonah's, but long waves that ended in fat, loose ringlets. It was parted in the middle, the top half pulled into two pigtails, the bottom cascading most of the way down her back. Jade had the strangest urge to reach out and touch it. "What is?"

"Typing," Nia answered. "She's good at every other subject in school, but she still types with just her pointer fingers. I'm trying to teach her." She smiled proudly, and Jade thought it was a very pretty smile, possibly the prettiest she'd seen. Maybe she wished her smile looked like that.

She must have looked at her lips for too long because Nia went back to playing with the strap on her shoe. "I'm not good at typing, either," she said. "Maybe you could teach us both at our playdate on Saturday. It's too cold to go to the zoo."

Nia laughed. "That's what I thought!"

Michal whipped around, only halfway through entering Jade's four-letter name. "It's open! I had my mom check on the computer before I asked."

"It's still too cold to go. And one of the best parts of the zoo is getting ice cream, and it's *way* too cold for that," Jade said.

"*Way* too cold," Nia agreed.

"How come neither of you are on my side? It's my birthday!" Michal complained. Her pout lasted barely a second before it gave way to one of her wide, teeth-baring smiles.

Just then a deep, booming voice came over the bowling alley's PA system: "We'd like to wish a veeeeeery happy tenth birthday to Michelle in lane seven. Happy birthday, Michelle! Welcome to double digits!"

Jade and Nia winced in unison. Michal tried to hide how her face fell, but they both saw it. "I'm sorry, Michal—"

Nia was interrupted by the sound of Debbie Sarfati's six-inch heels angrily smacking against the ratty carpet. "I told that motherfucker six times," she said, not quite under her breath, hustling as quickly as her pencil skirt would allow toward the counter below the hanging microphone. "I made him repeat it back to me. *Michal.* Not Michelle. It's Brooklyn, for God's sake, he's never met a fucking Jew before?" They couldn't hear what she was saying by the time she made it to the announcer, but her animated hand gestures told Jade that if she could, she'd probably learn a few more choice words from Michal's mom.

"She's so embarrassing," Michal said, pressing her hands into her cheeks. It was what she did whenever she was overwhelmed, embarrassed, or clumsy—so she did it almost constantly. "It's not a big deal."

Nia grabbed hold of Michal's hand, pulling it away from her face. She dropped the other one, and Jade took it in hers. "It is, though," she said, her voice coming out soft and soothing. "Maybe she didn't have to, um, to say all those words"—she flushed deeply—"but it's your birthday. They're supposed to get it right."

Michal's right, Jade thought in that very moment. *We'll all be best friends.*

CHAPTER SIX

friday morning, june 27

Nia wakes to the sound of scratching. Then wetness. It takes her a few moments to register that she isn't dreaming. When she opens her eyes, she finds her right arm hanging over the edge of the bed, a pit mix lapping happily at her fingers.

"Luna," she says through a yawn. "Has anybody taken you out yet?" The dog stands on her hind legs, pawing at the bedsheets. Nia takes that as a no. She feels around on the nightstand for her phone. It's not yet seven in the morning, and their tour of Kahal Kadosh Beth Elohim isn't until 10:15.

Nia feels mild annoyance at having been woken up early—she's not the type to easily drift back off to sleep after being disturbed—but it's quickly replaced by a balloon of flattery inflating in her chest. Of all the people in this hotel suite, Luna chose to wake *her* up.

She stumbles out of the moderately uncomfortable bed with the too-soft mattress and into denim cutoffs and a T-shirt. Her steps are soft as she finds a leash, some treats, and the requisite plastic bags, but any attempts at quiet are undercut by

Luna half-running, half-jumping in circles. Nia pauses, but no sounds escape from the other room.

When they return from their walk (which lasted about half an hour longer than Nia intended thanks to a particularly enticing throwing stick and an unearthed tennis ball at the nearby park), Jade is leaning against the countertop sipping iced coffee from a to-go cup. Purple half-moons bruise her undereyes. "I got you one," she says, handing over one of the two other cups lining the dark-stained wood.

"Is it—"

"Oat milk latte, one pump vanilla. Hot, because you're an absolute heathen and still take your coffee like that in the summer."

Nia shifts Luna's leash to her left hand and takes the drink, the scent of bitter, smoky espresso mingling with the floral sweetness of vanilla nearly enough to make her fall over with pleasure. "Hey, I already get oat milk! If it were iced, I'd be a walking bisexual stereotype."

Jade laughs, throwing her head back. Nia stares at the long line of her neck, the olive branches inked under her clavicles. "You could never. You're an excellent driver."

"I'm genuinely not. You just don't have a license," Nia says. Jade bites her lip, averting her eyes. "What?"

"I got one last fall," Jade says.

Oh, right. Three years. Nia works consciously to keep her smile in place.

"Jonah decided he finally wanted to learn how to drive," she continues. "And it seemed like a good idea."

"Or maybe you would die before letting him lord it over you for the rest of your life."

"Maybe so," Jade says, bringing the straw of her iced coffee to her mouth to take a sip. It presses into her bottom lip, making a white stripe in the strawberry skin. "Thank you for taking her. I'm sorry she woke you up."

"I'm not," Jonah says, emerging from the bedroom for, judging by the durag, the first time today. "I *am* sorry that I seem to be her least-favorite person here, even though she's known Nia for eighteen hours."

"That's because she has taste, Jonah. Or maybe she just can't stand your snoring, either."

"Aw," he says, pouting. "Fuck off."

Jade drops her jaw, aghast. "I bought you coffee!"

"Oh," he says, loping toward the cup in Jade's extended hand. "Sorry. I meant 'fuck off!'" he exclaims, his tone overly cheery.

Nia snorts.

"You're supposed to be on my team!" Jade complains.

Nia feels her face go soft with fondness. "I missed *y'all*," she says.

JADE CALLED KAHAL Kadosh Beth Elohim two weeks ago to inquire about the possibility of bringing a well-behaved (she hoped) young dog for the museum and cemetery tours, since she didn't want to leave Luna in the hotel room for so long unattended. The answer, understandably, was a polite but firm no. So she did exactly as her avuelo instructed her to and told them who she and Jonah were. Or perhaps more specifically, who their great-to-the-eighth grandparents were. It felt dirty, almost, and she spent the entire conversation wishing she had forced Jonah to make the call. But, as Avuelo promised, it worked. Luna still wouldn't be allowed to tour the sanctuary museum, but she was welcome on the walk through the cemetery. KKBE was more than thrilled to provide a pet sitter when the pet in question belonged to the estranged descendants of one of the congregation's founders.

This must be what celebrities feel like, Jade thinks as she hands Luna off to a cherubic redhead who introduces herself as Sarah, the synagogue's teen programing director. She doesn't look like she could be much more than a teen herself.

"Welcome back!" Sarah says before bending to plant a kiss on the scruff of Luna's neck.

"Thank you, but it's our first time."

Sarah waves her free hand around. "Oh, I don't mean, like, *literally.* Y'all are Pardos, though, so this place is kind of yours, you know? So cool. I wish Benji could see y'all, it's crazy!" Jade, Jonah, and Nia all nod along like they have any earthly clue who Benji is. "Just inside, to your left. Enjoy the tour!"

Nia brushes her fingers along Jade's elbow, and Jade feels hairs stand on end in their wake. It's this weird reaction she's always had to her. Like, no matter how much her mind knows it's just Nia, her body screams, *BEAUTIFUL GIRL! BEAUTIFUL GIRL IS TOUCHING YOU!* "You ready?" she whispers, leaning up toward Jade's ear. Goose bumps pinch along her neck.

"I think so," Jade says.

Jonah turns, walking backwards for a step and a half. "You can hold my hand if you get scared."

Jade rolls her eyes but says nothing. Mostly because they're approaching the guide. And, even if they're mostly here for the attached museum, they are technically in a place of worship.

The guide is tall, somewhere between Jade and Jonah's height, and has wild, wiry, silver hair with a pair of reading glasses acting as a makeshift headband. Her slightly down-turned mouth gives any facial expression an undercurrent of disinterest, even as she excitedly taps her sensible footwear.

"Are y'all here for the tour?" she asks, voice deep with age and honey sweet, accent thicker than anybody Jade's spoken to in Charleston thus far.

"We are," Nia says.

"Right on time. We're waiting on a couple more to join us, I think. I'm told they're descended from one of our founders, so maybe they'll have some family stories to add to the tour!"

Jonah clears his throat and plasters on the smile he always uses to charm old ladies (a bit toothier than the one he uses to charm young ones). "That's us." He extends his hand, and she accepts, looking flustered. "Jonah Pardo. My sister, Jade. Our friend, Nia. Nice to meet you, ma'am. I'm sorry to disappoint, but I'm not sure we'll have any stories to add."

"My apologies, I didn't expect . . ." she says, appraising the three of them. Jade waits for the shoe to drop. The *I didn't expect you to be Black* that their father had warned them might come before the singular summer they spent at Michal's Jewish sleepaway camp in Wisconsin. They were insulated at their Reform temple in Queens—there were many families of color, bi- and monoracial alike. Sure, there was the occasional weird comment from a non-Jewish kid at public school. But in their Jewish spaces in New York, nobody blinked at them. Maybe it would be different if they were Ashkenazi, or had grown up in a smaller or whiter place. It's hard to say. Regardless, it's not an armor she's used to wearing and she doesn't quite know how to fit herself into it. Jonah slathers himself in charm, but Jade always just kind of . . . stands there. "I thought you would be much older." She pulls her glasses down her forehead to rest on the bridge of her nose and unfolds the paper in her hand. Even with the readers, she squints at the text. "I think I have the wrong number of generations here. You're eight removed?"

Jade's shoulders sag with relief. "Ten. David Pardo was our eighth-great-grandfather."

"Ah, well, wires crossed! I'm Shirley. Where's home for y'all?"

"Brooklyn," Nia answers. Jade smiles, looking at her, wanting confirmation that she means what Jade thinks she means—that she's not *just* from there. That it's her home, present and future tense, not only the place she grew up. But she must not feel Jade's eyes on her, because her gaze remains steadily fixed on Shirley.

"Aren't they all from Brooklyn?" Shirley laughs, straightening the hem of her longline white button-down. The three of them exchange a *do you have any idea what she's talking about?* look. "Let's get started."

The first stop is the main sanctuary. It's grand, with intricate molding on the ceiling and enormous stained-glass windows lining three of the four walls. To Jade, it doesn't look all that different from the older synagogues in New York: bimah at the front, with seven-candle menorahs flanking it. The abbreviated Hebrew ten commandments above the ner tamid, which hangs before an elaborate wooden ark. Beautiful, certainly. But something feels . . . off. She's not sure what she expected.

Shirley holds up a laminated sheet of paper, a black-and-white rendering of a similar sanctuary drawn in the perspective from which they stand. "This," she says, "is what the sanctuary looked like before the first building burnt to the ground. The bimah was in the center, as was Sephardic tradition, and there were separate levels for men and women to pray, since the synagogue was originally Orthodox. Or, rather, was founded before there was anything other than the most religious sect.

"If you look at the floorboards in the center of the room,

you can see that when this version of the sanctuary was erected, there was still a Sephardic bimah, but it was later reconfigured and moved to the front of the sanctuary, in keeping with the rest of the Reform movement, which by that time was largely Ashkenazi. The history of KKBE is a constant pull between conforming to external forces and pioneering our own vision of Judaism. But I'm getting ahead of myself." She winks, mouth still downturned. "Don't want to spoil too much of the documentary!"

She leads them next to the Barbara Pearlstine Social Hall to show them two midcentury murals protected behind chin-high Plexiglas. The first depicts the congregation's founders—the five men foregrounded in prayer, one blowing a shofar, one reading a siddur, one holding a Torah, one leading services, and one whose mouth is open in song. "That one"—Shirley points—"is David Pardo, the congregation's first cantor. I can see the familial resemblance."

The style of the mural is cubism-adjacent, and the graying men in it look nearly identical. But with the neutral frown on Shirley's face, Jade isn't sure whether she's supposed to laugh. "Looks exactly like Jonah," she says. "Just a touch paler."

Shirley finds this downright hysterical.

After she talks them through the symbolism of the mural, how one side shows the burning of the original steeple (built in the style of churches of the time), and the other shows the Greek Revival architecture that was constructed in its place.

"And here," Shirley continues, walking backward across the room in true docent fashion, "Is *The Founding of Beth Elohim*'s twin brother, *The Patriots of Beth Elohim*."

Jonah, Nia, and Jade freeze in varying shades of shock. Because the mural across from them, in the same scale and cubism-adjacency as the mural of the founders, contains both a cartoonish Indigenous American with completely blacked-out eyes and a Confederate soldier.

"This congregation was founded in the 1740s, so its members have fought in every single war this country has had. The first Jews in the US were primarily Spanish and Portuguese Sephardim who escaped the Inquisitions. So, when they were allowed to practice freely, they felt extreme allegiance to the land that allowed them to do so. Particularly in the colony of South Carolina, where Jews were given full white status." Her eyes sweep from Jonah to Nia to Jade, a sympathetic tilt to her head, but she only pauses for the duration of her inhale. "The man on the left represents those in our congregation who served in the World Wars. The soldier holding a siddur is Abraham Alexander, who served both as a lay rabbi for the congregation and as a soldier in the Revolutionary War.

"Now, what I'm sure y'all really want me to explain is these three fellows." She gestures to the center and far right of the painting. Something soft brushes against Jade's left arm. Nia's hand, sliding down, interlacing their fingers. "It's about exactly what it looks like. This one on the horse is Francis Salvador, the first Jew to serve in any American legislature and the first to die in the Revolutionary War. He's facing off against a Tory-aligned Cherokee with a bow and arrow. The artist's rendering does nothing to highlight the humanity of the Cherokee soldier, and the choice to depict him but not a redcoat is notable. And this other one is a Confederate soldier with a broken sword, representing the Lost Cause of the Confederacy, a completely ahistorical mythology which insists that the Civil War was about Southern state sovereignty instead of protecting the institution of slavery."

Shirley looks at them, waiting. Nia squeezes Jade's hand.

Jonah clears his throat. "Why is . . . if you acknowledge the, uh, *problems*—"

Jade snorts. "That's one way to put it," she mumbles.

"—with the painting, why is it still up?"

Shirley clasps her hands. "You know, I'd have bet your sister would be the one to ask. Someone always does. This building we stand in was constructed in 1948, and the murals were commissioned contemporaneously. They're a part of our history, even if tied to an ugly part, and so we believe they should be preserved. Maybe if they were canvas paintings, they'd be in our little museum, or in the Jewish Heritage Collections at the college, but they're murals, so they can't be moved." She sighs, rocking back and forth on her heels. "I personally think it would be worse to pretend we were never on the wrong side of history, but I know that it can be hard to look at. You've never seen this in a Reform temple in Brooklyn, huh?"

"Um," Nia says. "It definitely . . . is hard to look at."

"No," Jade says. "We have not."

"Well," Shirley continues. "The next stop is the documentary. I'll warn you, there's going to be more—what is it you kids say—*problematic* content. Some good things, too. This is a very old congregation. It predates this country, and its members chose to assimilate into whiteness, with everything that entailed. It's also the birthplace of American Reform Judaism, and therefore the earliest adopter of egalitarian practices like mixed-gender prayer. But I'm getting ahead of myself again—we'll debrief in the museum after the film. Y'all ready?"

Not at all, Jade thinks, and follows Shirley down the hall in complete silence.

They take their seats on a wooden bench, Jade sitting

closer to Nia than is strictly necessary. But she can already feel herself wanting to float away, and the gentle press of Nia's knee against hers is a comfortable anchor. *If this is difficult,* she thinks, *what is Savannah going to be like without Michal?*

As Shirley promised, the documentary is a lot to take in. It washes over Jade, discrete bits of information passing through her.

The founders were descended from or were themselves religious refugees, she learns. They saw themselves as Maccabees of sorts, and they used that imagery to represent their "patriots." They fought against colonial Britain, espoused the words of the Declaration of Independence as inherent truth. They bought and sold human beings like chattel. After the original building burned down, prominent congregant David Lopez won the bid to rebuild it. He was a slaveholder. Kit and George, two enslaved African carpenters, were instrumental in its construction. The celebrated Greek Revival synagogue was built entirely off stolen labor. It is the oldest sanctuary in continuous use. The oldest American synagogue in continuous use was built by enslaved Africans. KKBE's rabbi in the 1960s was committed to the civil rights movement and was a prominent local activist. He was ultimately ousted by powerful members of the congregation for his politics.

The oldest American synagogue in continuous use was built by enslaved Africans.

Avuelo told neither Jade nor Jonah this. He told them it was the birthplace of the Reform movement. He told them why their branch of the family left in the mid-nineteenth century. He told them that their family helped found one of the oldest congregations in the South. Everything he told them about their history in Charleston was said with pride. He did not tell them *this.*

The credits roll. "Do you think Dad knows?" Jade asks.

Jonah shrugs and shakes his head at the same time.

"Do you think Mom does?"

Jonah doesn't move. Both he and Jade have the same thought: *No.*

Shirley leads them to the museum, leaning against a wall with her resting grimace as Jade, Nia, and Jonah weave their way through glass cases of Judaica. They move slowly, quietly.

"Most Jews who tour want to know if there were abolitionists in KKBE or Charleston's broader Jewish population. Particularly Northerners. As Jews, we tend to have this idealized notion of our relationship to race in America—we're a culture of immigrants, we've been persecuted ourselves, and we were fierce allies in the civil rights movement. So, if we were in the South during slavery, many or most of us must have been abolitionists. The truth is that there is absolutely no evidence to support that notion." There's a weary sadness in her tone, enough to offset the undercurrent of disinterest. "Anybody who didn't want to partake in the system left." Shirley makes intentional eye contact with Jade, then Jonah. "Though I suppose I don't have to tell the New York Pardos that."

Her words settle around them. Nia squeezes Jade's upper arm, and Jade catches a whiff of coffee and vanilla.

"Is KKBE always this . . . forthcoming on tours?" Nia asks before Jade has a chance to wonder. Jade seems to be processing a bit slower than she is. But she would have gotten there, eventually.

Shirley gives a wry chuckle, tucking a few silver strands behind her right ear. "I think it depends on the tour guide. We thought that y'all would be able to handle the big guns." She checks her watch. "Well, I have a lunch appointment, so that's the end of our time together. If you have any questions, don't hesitate to reach out. I'll have Sarah give you my contact information."

They thank her, and she leaves.

"Do you guys want to get some fresh air?" Nia asks, but she's looking directly at Jade.

"Yeah. Fresh air would be great."

"So how was it?" Sarah hands Luna's leash off to Jonah. Nia can tell the moment their fingers brush because the prominent apples of Sarah's cheeks flush crimson.

"It was a lot," Jade says.

Sarah nods soberly. "The cemetery tour will be a little less intense, I think. I mean, there are some Confederate graves but it's not"—she circles her splayed hand in the direction of the Greek columns—"all of that. Y'all really lucked out with Shirley, though; she's a total superstar. Before she retired, she had dual appointments in the Jewish and African American Studies departments at the college. And she was a really big part of the push to put in the monument and acknowledgment out front a few years ago."

Nia nods. "That makes sense."

"Thank you for watching Luna for us," Jade says.

"Oh, it was my absolute pleasure! Do y'all need to use the restroom or anything before Fred takes you over to Coming Street?"

Jade tilts her head. "Jonah?"

He looks taken aback. "Why me?"

"I don't know, maybe because you got up to pee like three times on a two-hour flight yesterday?"

Nia shrugs. "Cis men are notoriously bad at holding it."

He pouts. "*Y'all* are always attacking me."

"I'll text Fred," Sarah says, laughing.

Maybe it's that there's a little less to it, maybe it's that Fred is certainly no Shirley, or maybe it's just the hot sun and occasional heavenly breeze on her skin, but the tour of Coming Street Cemetery feels like an emotional breath of fresh air.

But before the tour ends, Fred takes them through the center of the graveyard, coming to a halt in front of an unassuming headstone lying flat in the ground. "Usually, we only show one of the Confederate soldier headstones, because, well, after one you get the idea. But I thought you'd want to see this one. 'Here lies Bechor Pardo,'" he reads, "'who fought and died valiantly for these Confederate States after his brother defected to the Union Army.' Y'all come from the brother. Vidal, according to our records."

Jade nods. "Our great-great-grandfather." She frowns. "Our avuelo's avuelo," she says slowly, like the closeness of the relation is just hitting her, and Nia wants to grab her hand again. But it's soupy-hot out and she knows that sometimes Jade needs her space. She fiddles with the band of her watch instead. "We're not that far removed from slaveholders," she says, looking at Jonah.

He doesn't meet her eyes, only furrows his brow, staring at the headstone. "Maybe some of them disagreed with it—"

"Shirley just told us that wasn't likely," Nia says gently.

Jonah nods, head still hanging downward. "But, I guess, given the circumstances of the time, maybe they didn't, or, or . . . *couldn't* know better."

"They owned *people*, Jonah!" Jade spits, eyes wide. "They owned people who looked like Mom. Who looked like us. They were Jews who did Passover Seders every year, *while enslaving people.*"

Anger radiates off Jade. Fred absorbs it and reemits palpable discomfort.

"He's just processing, J," Nia whispers.

"Are you seriously on his side about this?" she says without any trace of the humor in her similar complaint this morning.

Of course she isn't. But she's mixed, too, and no stranger to intergenerational racial strife, and this is not the kind of information you process in a single morning. Certainly not when you're Jonah, who sometimes seems to lack a single introspective bone in his body. For all their similarities, Jade's and Jonah's minds work very differently. And yet they often expect each other to think the same. "I'm not on a *side,* Jade. I think we need to give him a minute."

"Can you, like, not be a therapist about this for a second?"

"Don't bring Nia into this," Jonah says, looking up for the first time in the conversation. "It's not her problem or her business."

Nia feels a pang in her chest. A tender spot that hasn't been pressed in a while. She was always the only one of their group that wasn't Jewish, and it was this thing the other three had, this string between their chests, tying them together. She knew Michal first, was friends with her longer, but sometimes she has this tiny seed of worry that she wouldn't ever know her as deeply. She knows it isn't rational, and she's talked through it many times with her own therapist. But that seed is still there, even if she refuses to let it sprout.

"That's uncalled for, Jonah," Jade says, folding her arms across her chest, Luna's leash threaded between them. "She is just as much a part of this as you or me."

Fred shifts anxiously on his feet. "Looks like sibling rivalry is in the Pardo blood," he jokes, gesturing at the headstone.

The three of them turn to him in disbelief.

"You're not," Jade says carefully, "seriously comparing my brother to a Confederate soldier, are you?"

"Uh," Fred says.

Luna, perhaps sensing the shift in energy, stops chewing on a dandelion and barks at him.

"I think it might be time to get lunch," Nia says.

"Yes, lunch!" Fred agrees, clapping his hands. "Wouldn't want to keep you all day!" And then he walks them to the gate (with more purpose than he exhibited the entire tour) and says his goodbyes.

It's like the tension in the air is directly tethered to Fred; all animosity disappears with his retreating form.

They stop at a burrito place with a wafting scent that Nia swears is speaking directly to her soul. Jonah goes inside to order; she and Jade wait outside with the dog. Jade sit-leans against a bike loop, bringing her closer to Nia's height.

She drops her head to Nia's shoulder. "I'm sorry, Nia," she says. "I know we're a lot."

Nia shakes her head. "No, don't apologize. I've known you guys forever," she says, swallowing. "I knew exactly what I signed up for."

She lets out a loud yawn, and Nia laughs, feeling Jade's head bob along with the movement of her shoulder. It's a little too warm for this much touching, but at the moment, she doesn't really mind.

"Didn't sleep much?"

"Jonah's fucking snoring. The schnoz on that boy, I swear to God, Nia," she says, rolling her head to look up at her. Her eyelashes are short but naturally plush, her undereye circles even more prominent and deep from this angle than they looked this morning. "Can I sleep with you tonight? I really don't think I can handle it again. Not unless I get Toni to prescribe me some doggy Ambien." She sighs. "Please?"

Nia hooks her pinkie through Jade's. "Of course, J. Mi cama es tu cama for the rest of the trip."

CHAPTER SEVEN

friday afternoon, june 27

Jade lies back on the grass, her hands folded behind her head, while Nia and Jonah finish their burritos. Her stomach aches a little from how quickly she ate, but Jonah already made fun of her for it, so there's not enough money in the world to make her admit her discomfort.

"Ooh, Jonah, looks like you have an admirer," Nia says. Jade looks up and sees Sarah from KKBE cutting quickly toward them.

Jonah smirks as she approaches, and Jade throws a fistful of grass at him. "Be nice."

"Hey, y'all!" Sarah says, a little breathless, somehow looking mainly at but also avoiding eye contact with Jonah. Luna runs a circle around her feet, and Sarah steps out of the winding leash, hardly glancing down. "I'm glad I saw you sitting here. I wanted to ask if you'd come to Shabbat services tonight? It would be so nice to have you there."

Jade sits up a little, propping herself on her forearms. "Oh, we don't—we're not really that religious."

Sarah nods. "Our Friday night services are, like, twenty-five minutes, max. Especially in the summer. But no pressure! I totally understand if it's just not your thing."

"It's okay, Jade," Nia says, placing a hand on her arm, right over her bumblebee tattoo. Jade realizes that she had shifted forward, inserting herself between Sarah and Nia, her shoulders squared protectively. "I've been to synagogue more recently than I've been to mass. I'll be fine."

"Do you think . . ." Jade starts, but she refuses to finish the thought, even as she feels everyone's eyes settle on her.

After a pause, Sarah says, "You don't have to decide now! I'll see if I can convince Benji to come and we'll save y'all seats, but no worries if you can't!"

"Thank you, Sarah," Jonah says, and then he does his full smile.

Sarah looks like she might pass out, stammering through her goodbyes and running off before Jade has the sense to ask her who Benji is. Boy-space-friend, she hopes, or he's not going to enjoy the way Sarah looks at Jonah at KKBE tonight. She yanks up another clump of grass and tosses it limply at Jonah.

"Hey! What was that for?" He carefully pats through his curls, plucking out each individual blade.

Nia clears her throat. "*Thank you, Sarah,*" she imitates, her voice dropping half an octave and coming out smooth and sultry, her lips pouting out every syllable.

Jonah tries not to grin and fails. Jade laughs until she coughs, and Nia hands over her water bottle.

It's the same one she's had since college. Stainless-steel, undented, covered in what has to be six layers of vinyl stickers at this point. Jade uncaps the narrow spout (Nia can't drink from a wide-lip water bottle without half of it ending up down her shirt) and tries not to think about what it means that she doesn't recognize a single sticker as she takes a few gulps.

"It's so *humid,*" Nia huffs, leaning back a little to gather her hair and twist it up into another claw clip. A single curl stays behind, stuck to her neck in a perfect *S.* Jade has the urge to fix it, but she knows it'll just fall back out. And the touch probably wouldn't be welcome, anyway.

Or would it? She thinks of Nia's finger along the crook of her arm before the tour, her knee against hers during the documentary.

But Jade had *needed* that touch, and that's why Nia had offered it. If Jade reached out now, she'd be doing it solely because she wanted to. She's not sure she's earned that yet.

She passes the bottle back to Nia and is momentarily transfixed by the bobbing column of her throat as she sips, the glistening oval gap as she pulls it away from her lips.

"What?" Nia asks.

"So, we going?" Jonah asks before Jade has to answer her. "I don't have a kippah."

"It's a shul, Jonah. They have literal baskets of them." Jade turns back to Nia. "We really don't have to," she says.

Nia shakes her head. "I told you I'm fine, promise. Do *you* want to go? I know being there this morning was a lot."

Does she?

Not exactly, no. She doesn't really want to be back in that building. But now that she has the invitation, not going would feel like she's missing something, somehow. Or running away, and she promised herself she wouldn't do that on this trip.

So she nods her head yes.

"You'll probably have to put on a shirt that isn't cropped," Jonah says, and Jade feels her face heating. "Did you even bring one?"

"This one isn't even that . . . it's hot out."

"You just want people to look at all the doodles."

"There's at least a band's worth of *doodles* on my stomach! Maybe they should."

"They're *very nice* doodles," Nia says, batting her eyelashes.

"Made by the most talented fourth-grader in the class," Jonah says, and Nia snorts, slapping a hand over her mouth like she can't help it.

Jade flops back on the ground. "I have a full-length shirt. I'm pretty sure," she mumbles under her breath.

"You can borrow one of mine if you need."

Jonah laughs. "Are you also going to give her a bra to stuff to make it fit?"

This time, Nia throws the grass.

NIA ENDS UP keeping all her shirts (and bras) to herself. Jade unearths her singular non-crop-top, a black-sateen nineties bowling uniform with pink trim and breast pocket embroidery announcing that it formerly belonged to *Ricky*. Apparently, tonight is the first time it's ever occurred to her that it could be buttoned instead of thrown on open over a cropped tank. Enough of the bottom buttons are left undone to tuck one side into her pants. She doesn't bother with the top three, either, revealing the olive branches below her clavicles and the חי pendant that lies flat against the thorax of the butterfly inked on her sternum. *God,* sometimes . . .

"What?" Jade asks. "This hits, like, midthigh! Or, shit, should I button it up more?"

"You look fine."

"Yeah," Jonah says. "Shirley probably wears jeans to services."

And Tevas, it turns out. She nods at them in acknowledgment

as they enter, and the bald man seated beside her smiles and waves.

Nia answers Jade's brief head tilt with a gentle eyebrow raise. Jonah says, "Oh, her husband's Black!" Jade smacks him on the arm, and a very crisp image of ratty bowling alley carpet flashes across Nia's mind.

Thankfully, Sarah waves them over to the second row from the back, profusely apologizing for her boyfriend(?)'s absence as they approach. As it turns out, Friday night services are a small enough affair to be held in folding chairs set up in the social hall rather than in the grand sanctuary. Unfortunately, this means that they're sandwiched between the mural with David Pardo and the . . . other one, and Nia can practically feel Jade's effort not to look at them.

The services themselves are uneventful, nothing different from what Nia has tagged along to before, and Jade's entire body seems to exhale as the minutes tick on. Sarah barely takes her eyes off Jonah, which Nia understands, at least in the abstract. He does absolutely nothing for her now, but during the time between ages twelve-and-three-quarters and thirteen-and-a-half (and a much briefer stint at eighteen) that smile alone could make her feel warm all over.

Sarah makes her way over to them after the Kiddush, just as they're finishing their torn chunks of challah and getting ready to leave. "I'm really glad you were here tonight," she says.

"Yeah, me, too," Jade replies easily, and Nia feels herself exhale, too.

"Anything else I can do for y'all during your visit to Charleston?" Sarah directs the question to Jonah's left shoulder. Jade covers her chuckle with a sip of Manischewitz.

"We're only here until Sunday morning, and we were

planning to go to the beach tomorrow. I guess we hadn't decided which one yet, or where to get breakfast," Nia says. "Any advice?"

"My favorite is Folly. Not as many kids—Benji and I usually go there after the teen service on Shabbat."

"Y'all should join us then." Nia thinks she can see Jade's barely restrained eye roll before the words are fully out of Jonah's mouth.

Sarah blushes. "Oh! Well, sure, yeah. I mean, we'd probably run into y'all there anyway. And go to Callie's Biscuits! I'll text Benji—his shift ends at nine thirty, if you show up then, he'll have them ready and you won't have to wait in line. Any dietary restrictions?" They all shake their heads.

"Thank you," Jade says. "You've gone out of your way a lot for us today, and we really appreciate it."

"It's nothing, really! Y'all're practically extended family here. And Luna is a complete angel. See you tomorrow!" The last bit, specifically, is directed at Jonah's right pectoral.

"What now?" Jonah asks after Sarah turns away. Something passes between the three of them, much like it did at the botanical garden. The familiarity is a relief, warm and almost painful, the soothing sting of Tiger Balm rubbed onto her cold-addled chest by her father's strong hands. It's been a long day.

They fill up on pizza, give Luna one last walk, go through their respective nighttime routines. All the while, Nia's promise to Jade hangs over her like a small rain cloud—the looming anticipation much more threatening than the rain itself. Around step seven, as she's pressing a retinol serum into her face, goose bumps erupt across her skin like a crack of lightning.

Honestly, it feels a little pathetic. It's just Jade. They've shared beds too many times to count.

Except, until yesterday, they hadn't seen each other in person in three years. Why pretend everything is as it was before? It isn't.

When she opens the bedroom door, Jade's in the same ratty tee and boxers from the night before, durag on, climbing into bed. And she turns to Nia with her small smile and a head tilt that makes her want to keep pretending a little longer.

"You getting in?" Jade asks.

"Trying to get over the déjà vu."

Her lips do that amused twist. "I don't talk in my sleep anymore."

Why is Nia's first thought, *I wouldn't even mind if you did*?

She laughs a little and stiffly tucks herself in. Out of the corner of her eye, she sees Jade pick up her murder mystery novel—even as age and political awareness killed her dream of becoming a detective, she never kicked the habit. Nia opens her sudoku app and completes a single puzzle before succumbing to one of her worst habits: checking her email right before bed.

To: Nia Chin <niachin@stanford.edu>
From: Chair Chapman <echapman@unc.edu>
RE: Committee Interest

She doesn't have to read the body to know exactly what kind of committee he means. She has to give UNC kudos, at least, for trying to solicit her extra labor after the offer was made. Most of her other interviewers mentioned it before they even got to lunch.

Jade slides her bookmark back into place and turns toward her.

"Yes?"

"You groaned. What's up?"

Nia sighs. "Well, I just got . . . you know what? I'm sure you don't want to hear about it. Go back to finding out whether it was the brother or the butler."

"It's almost definitely the brother this time. There're never twins unless one is evil." She nods her head toward where Jonah is passed out and (presumably) snoring on the other side of a couple of doors. "Obviously. Anyway, I do want to hear about it. That's why I asked."

Nia shakes her head. "No, you don't. It's just academia bullshit."

Jade's brows raise a few millimeters. "I have a master's in academia bullshit."

"You have a master's in neurobiology."

She circles her hand as if to say *same thing*. Then she sits upright. "Do you think you can't talk to me about this because I quit?"

Nia feels her face heat. "No, I—it's not . . ." she trails off, inhales. "Maybe?"

"Nia," she says. Her voice is low, gently rasped, quiet. Somehow both hurt and admonishing. "Do you think I can't handle it? Is that why—"

Nia sits up, too. "No! No, I think you might not *want* to handle it, but it's not even just that. It's like—you know when you have a friend who, like, *constantly* complains about their partner? After a while, a part of you almost wants to shake that friend and say, 'just break up with them already, or if you're not going to, please fucking shut up about it.'"

Jade laughs a little, hollowly. "Are you admitting that you and academia are in a toxic relationship?"

The air chills. "*That,*" Nia bites, sweeping out her hand

to underline the words that seem to hang in the air, "is the other reason."

Jade winces. "Fuck, that came out wrong. I didn't mean—"

"Didn't you? You've never been particularly secretive about your feelings on the matter."

"*My* feelings have nothing to do with you! How am I supposed to be there for you if you won't talk to me about it? I'm so fucking sick of being treated like I'm fragile."

"You know, your palpable resentment for my career can feel suspiciously close to judgment of *me*," Nia says.

"I don't judge you, and I don't even resent your career!" Jade fires back.

"I don't think you're fragile!"

It's hard to imagine that only yesterday, the thought she latched onto was *maybe all of this will be all right.* Now, *how am I going to get through this trip?* is bigger, stronger.

Their chests heave in unison. They don't break eye contact. Maybe they're both aware, deep down, that they are lying, just a little bit. To themselves, to each other. Because as her own words settle around her, Nia knows they aren't quite true. She doesn't want to think of Jade as fragile. She knows she isn't. But she's spent the last three years, and maybe a long time before that, deeply afraid of breaking her. Even after it felt like Jade had broken *her*, Nia treaded carefully.

"I'm sorry," Jade says.

"Me, too," Nia replies, everything in her softening.

They go quiet.

Jade looks down. "It wasn't for me, but that doesn't mean it can't be for you," she says. "You're right that I resent the academy—my experience in it, its foundation, everything. But it's not going away anytime soon. You want to do research; this is where you can do it. You're aware of the problems.

You'll be good at the work. And you'll be kind, and it won't fix it, but it'll make the difference for some people. I won't let myself judge you for that."

Nia swallows thickly, fighting off the trembling sob threatening to overtake her.

Jade lies back down, curling onto her side. She looks up at Nia, low light reflected in her dark eyes. "Now, do you want to tell me what the groaning was about?"

Nia lies down to face Jade, pulling the covers up over her shoulder. "They're already asking me to join a diversity committee." Jade rolls her eyes emphatically. "I haven't accepted a position yet, and it's like"—she adopts a 1940s mid-Atlantic accent—"'how can we make our shiny new colored person fix the institutional white supremacy we've ignored for generations? I hear she's an Oriental *and* a Negro, we've really struck gold!'"

Jade laughs, and then Nia does, too, and soon both are wiping at their eyes.

"That . . ."

"Sucks?" Nia supplies.

"Real bad. The DEI committee I did was nearly the last straw," Jade says.

"I remember."

"Maybe you should cross them off the list?"

Nia shakes her head. "It's happened everywhere I've applied. UNC has actually been the most tactful."

"Ah," Jade says. "Not sure why I assumed otherwise."

They fall quiet again.

"Thank you for telling me," Jade says.

Nia nods. "It didn't cause too many war flashbacks?"

She grins. "No more than usual." And then she returns to her book.

CHAPTER EIGHT

may, eleven years ago

Nia was the last of them to board the bus, on account of Chin placing her significantly closer to the stage than Pardo or Sarfati. Her neck was sore from craning to view all the speakers (none of whom were Jade, who'd intentionally gotten an A– last semester to avoid having to give a speech). *Bus three, bus three, bus three,* she repeated to herself. They'd gone over the plan so many times this morning, but she still felt nervous for being unable to send a confirmation text, what with her phone having been taken by her AP Psych teacher five minutes earlier.

Five years before, Parents Against Alcohol Poisoning had funded an all-night party at an undisclosed location immediately after the commencement ceremony. The idea being that if they got one night to run completely wild with absolutely no access to drugs and alcohol, they might not go as crazy later in the week. It was the first year their high school hadn't had a partying-related hospitalization the week after graduation. And, shockingly, the graduating seniors seemed to genuinely love it.

They got a grant for the next year, and it had been renewed ever since. The students lovingly called it the PAAP Smear.

Despite the general air of excitement, Nia had never been great with surprises, and jitters had been building in her stomach the entire evening. The jitters extended to her extremities, and she drummed her fingertips against her crossed arms as she waited on the first step, still unable to see into the row of seats. Praying that she had the right one, and that Michal and Jade had managed to save her a spot next to them.

She ascended the last step, her sightline finally bobbing above the seatbacks. Michal was standing next to a window in the back third of the bus, leaning over the seat in front of her so the purple dip-dyed ends of her wavy hair dusted Matt Stucker's forehead.

He whipped his head toward her, shoving her hair back to her side of the pleather divider. "The fuck, Michal?"

"Nia!" she shouted, as though they weren't already making direct eye contact, and Nia wasn't already walking toward her. As though even if they weren't, or she wasn't, Matt Stucker hadn't been voted Most Likely to Be Heard in the Hallway.

When Nia was a couple of yards away, Jade peeked her head out into the aisle next to her, laughter in her eyes. She nodded toward the seat behind them, her long, auburn braids sliding over her shoulder. Nia's eyes followed the gesture.

Jonah.

They were seniors. Not even seniors—they were high school graduates. They weren't going to sit three to a seat. Of course, the spot they'd saved her was next to Jonah.

Nia took a deep breath and marched on with all the solemnity of a walk to the gallows, inhaling again (even though she didn't really remember having ever breathed *out*) as Jonah scooted toward the window and she took her place next to him.

Their legs weren't touching, but they were *barely* not touching. She could feel the heat of his thigh warming her knees, of his eyes on the side of her face.

When the bus rumbled to a start, she still hadn't dared look up at him.

She'd confessed to Michal last week, locked in the single-stall bathroom on the second floor of their school, not sure if she was nearer to tears or a heart attack.

Before anything else, Michal had said, "OhmyGod, we're gonna see *Jonah* make the face."

"*What* face?" Nia had sputtered.

Michal had squeezed her hands. "You know! The *I've seen you naked* face." She barked out a laugh. "*Jonah* is going to make the *I've seen you naked* face. And it's gonna be at *you*. Ho. Ly. Shit."

"He is not."

"All guys have one, and Jonah Pardo is not going to be the exception." Even though they were alone, Michal had dropped her voice to a whisper. "Was it big?"

"Michal!" Nia had whined.

"You're right, don't tell me. Better if only one of us has to look Jade in the eyes while actually knowing the answer to that."

Nia had tipped her head back against the wall, staring up at the strips of fluorescent lights set into beige ceiling panels. "How am I going to tell her?" She hadn't said the other question on her mind, less important, but pressing harder: *This means it'll never happen with us, doesn't it?* A stupid thing to have been thinking about, but she couldn't stop. She'd come out to Jade that fall, before she'd told anyone else. Nia had tried not to hold any hope for how Jade might react. She'd failed, and then when Jade had responded with comfort and excitement and absolutely nothing else, she'd been proven right to try. Which was fine—good. It was good. She'd tapped her head against the wall, letting out a shaky breath. "Is she gonna hate me?"

Michal had swung their arms up then, bringing their interlocking fists to the space between their faces. "Are you gonna do it again?" Nia had shaken her head, and Michal kissed the tops of her knuckles. "Then you're not going to tell her."

Now, as Nia felt Jonah's unwavering gaze on her face, she thought about whatever face he might be making, and she tried to shoot the words "help me!" like a laser beam through the back of Michal's seat.

The seconds ticked by into minutes. Michal didn't turn around to save her. Nor did Jade, but she had no reason to believe she needed to.

Eventually, Nia broke. She forced a small smile that no doubt looked as pathetically nervous as she felt, and looked up at him.

The expression on his face mirrored her own. He seemed to realize this at the same time she did, because he relaxed into a real Jonah Pardo Grin as she felt her own cheeks soften with relief.

"Hi, Jonah," she said.

"Hey, Nia," he replied. Voice deeper than you'd expect for someone still so teenage-skinny, tone as sultry as the look in his deep-set, slightly upturned eyes.

Yes, losing her virginity to her best friend's twin brother—someone whom Jade had a lot of jealousy issues and competitiveness with, having been compared to one another for their entire lives—was not her best idea. But Michal and Jade had gone to a party that they had no interest in (on account of it being thrown at Jonah's ex's apartment, and on account of Nia never really liking their school's parties or watching Jade flirt with other girls), and they were left alone and a little stoned. And *God*, look at him. Could you really blame her?

"You good?" he asked.

Nia nodded. "Yep. I mean—well, yeah, I'm okay. You?"

Jonah's eyes roamed her face. "Did I"—he paused, leaned up to look over the seat in front of him, then lowered his voice—"do something wrong? Was everything, uh, okay for you?"

Nia's eyes went wide. "Oh no, Jonah, *that's* what you're . . ." she trailed off. "It was good—it was *great*," she whispered. She took a long inhale, hoping to quell the rising flush in her cheeks. There was a rush of memory then: her gasped-out *I don't know what I'm doing*, his short laugh, and *We'll figure it out together* pressed into her neck. Fuck, *Nia* was the one doing the face, wasn't she? "You were lovely."

"Lovely?" There was a hint of teasing in his voice.

She crossed her arms. "Yes, lovely."

He reclined against the seat, his smile turning sheepish. "You were, too," he said, so quickly she might've missed it. "Did you tell *Jade*?" He mouthed her name, not even willing to risk the whisper.

Nia shook her head. "Since we decided it was only once, I thought maybe we shouldn't start Civil War Two: Pardo versus Pardo over it."

Jonah held her gaze for a moment, then nodded. "Yeah, I mean, makes sense."

"I don't regret it, though," she rushed to add.

That real, grade-A-certified Jonah Pardo Grin crept back into his lips. "Me, neither," he said. "I'm glad it was you."

She didn't hear so much as see the last bit, because his voice was sucked into the cacophony of thirty-five teenagers chanting, "PAAP Smear, PAAP Smear, PAAP Smear!" as they rolled to a stop.

JADE GULPED DOWN the last of her shitty coffee and tossed the takeaway cup in a nearby trash can. Even in the high-ceilinged room where they'd stocked all the provisions—PowerBars, barely edible pizza, popcorn, coffee, Red Bulls—everything smelled of chlorine. It was the kind of place she'd spent handfuls of school days off and birthday parties at in elementary school. It was weird celebrating their embarkment into adulthood somewhere that made her feel so much like a child.

Weirder still that everyone seemed to like it. Even Nia, who had been so touchy around her for the past couple of weeks, ever since she and Michal had ditched her with Jonah to go to a party. Which was fair, she supposed. Michal had gone willingly, but Jade had definitely been the driver of that decision, as Ari Torres had *specifically* asked her in Calc BC that morning if she was going. It's not like they'd ever really tried to integrate their friend groups, and Jonah had been more annoying than usual recently, so they'd kind of inadvertently thrown Nia to the wolves.

But since the moment they'd stepped off the bus, Nia and Michal had been bursting with excitement. Even the "okay, meet us in the natatorium!" Nia'd offered when Jade announced she was dipping in search of caffeine had been delivered in an animated shout. Jade was incredibly relieved. The party had been fun, sure, but not worth the ensuing guilt. No matter how good of a kisser Ari had been. Or how hot she looked now, doing a finger wave at Jade that she returned with a nod and smile as she left the room.

It wasn't hard to find them when she got to the room

with the pool. Nia and Michal were deep in a game of chicken with two of Jonah's basketball teammates. Not on their shoulders—Michal was stacked on top of Nia, and they were playing *against* people who easily had a collective foot and a half on them, shrieking in delight. Michal tumbled into the water before Jade even finished stuffing her clothes into a cubby.

"J!" she called out when she surfaced, grabbing for the ladder. "Wanna hit the water slide?"

Jade used the extra-large, heavy-duty hairband that had been doubled on her wrist to secure her braids in a top knot. "Hell yeah!" she called back.

"Hell yeah!" Nia repeated, pushing herself out of the water using the tiled edge of the pool. Her hair was down, plastering to her shoulders and chest in long waves. Trails of water snaked from her clavicles and disappeared into her cleavage. It was a beat too long before Jade looked away (*it's just Nia* was an unfortunately common mantra of hers).

"*Fuck* yeah!" Michal said, never to be outdone. She rushed toward them, passing several No Running signs and ignoring the lifeguard's perturbed whistle.

Jade had barely registered Michal's fingers threading through hers when she was tugged toward the stairs leading up to the slide. Nia was in tow on the other side, laughing.

She was struck then by all the ways in which this was a goodbye of sorts. They still had the summer, and it wasn't like they were going very far after that—NYU, Columbia, and Sarah Lawrence could be accessed from one another by bus and subway, and Nia had probably already memorized the commutes. But they'd all been at the same public schools since eighth grade, and it had only taken two weeks for Jade to completely forget what it was like when they weren't. She didn't want to find out again. She hated that they would be her *best friends from high school* or maybe *childhood best friends* to whomever she met in the fall. It was a cruel joke that Jonah would be the only one she'd still have classes with.

It wasn't that she didn't have faith in their friendship. She did. These bitches were hers forever, as Michal liked to say. Part of her just wished they could be hers forever like *this*. Or that she could see into the future to know what their forever looked like when it inevitably diverged.

They reached the stairs then, taking them two at a time until they approached the logjam toward the top.

Another lifeguard sat on the platform, a white boy who looked a year or two older than them and *very* bored. He leaned back in his chair, obviously intentional in showing off the ripple of muscle above his low-riding sweatpants. Nia elbowed Jade, nodding toward Michal, who looked like her tongue was going to fall out of her mouth.

"You do like 'em a little douchey, huh?"

"Shut up, J," she said, bright-eyed.

Nia snorted, then stage-whispered, "She's not denying it!"

Michal rolled her eyes. "Oh, come on, Nia! You're gonna say he does nothing for you?"

Nia looked at him, long enough that Jade could watch her eyes peruse the length of his body. When she looked back toward Jade and Michal, her cheeks were tinged pink. "Maybe not *nothing*," she said, "but he's definitely more Michal's type than mine."

"What even is your type?" Jade asked.

Michal laughed, then pressed her hands to her cheeks.

"What?" Jade demanded. "I can talk about hot boys! Or I can listen to you talk about hot boys," she amended.

"She doesn't only like boys," Michal said.

Jade shrugged Michal off and crossed her arms. "Yeah,

I *know* that. But I feel like this is something you guys talk about with each other more than with me."

"I don't know if I really have a type," Nia said. "But I will make sure to tell you every time I think a boy is hot from now on."

"I think Matt Stucker is one of the hottest boys at school." Michal giggled.

"I didn't mean you needed to list them *now*," Jade said, but neither Michal nor Nia gave any indication that they'd heard her.

Nia frowned. "Ugh, he's so loud, though."

"Loud, but cute," Michal argued.

Nia nodded. "Fair. I think Camilo's really hot."

"Oh my God, and Dwayne!"

"Ji-min."

"Larry."

"Terrible name, though."

"Right? Can you imagine trying to moan *Larry*. Like, 'Yes, Larry! Right there, Larry!'"

Nia waggled her eyebrows. "I'd try, just for him."

Michal nudged Jade's shoulder, her smile a little wicked. "What if we told you that Jonah was one of the hottest boys at our school?"

"I'd need cotton balls to sop up the blood coming out of my ears, I think."

Michal's entire face scrunched. "Gross. You should take it as a compliment, Jade. You look alike."

Jade batted her eyelashes. "Are you saying I'm one of the hottest boys at our school?"

Nia shook her head. "No. But only because you just graduated."

"Awww." Jade pouted. "I think I get to wax poetic about Ari Torres's boobs for listening to this."

"What makes you think we *wouldn't* want to hear that?" Michal asked.

"Your turn," the lifeguard said, expression placid.

"Can we go together?" Nia asked.

"Two at a time, max."

"Here's the thing," Michal started, "it's our graduation, and we've been best friends since—"

"I really don't care," the lifeguard interrupted her. "And I'm not getting paid enough for this. Go, but if you get in trouble, I'm gonna say you ran past me."

That was enough for them. They climbed into the chute, Nia, then Michal, then Jade, fitting between each other's legs, wrapping their arms around the person in front of them. Nia's arms were trembling from the pressure of holding them all in place by the time the lifeguard gave his signal.

He counted down and dropped his arm, and then they were off, screaming into the orange plastic tunnel as they hurtled toward the deep end of the pool. The few seconds of the path down seemed to stretch indefinitely, and Jade watched the memory form in real time.

They touched down with a splash, limbs colliding against limbs until they all buoyed to the surface and swam away from the opening of the slide.

"Fuck yeah!" Michal declared once more, one arm anchored on the edge of the pool. She extended her pinkie, and Nia and Jade curled theirs around it. "I'm going to miss you guys so much next year. Don't forget, you bitches are mine *forever.*"

"*Forever,*" they agreed.

CHAPTER NINE

saturday morning, june 28

Jade's legs are threaded through Nia's, her right knee bracketed by the smooth, warm skin of Nia's thighs. Nia breathes long inhales and short puffing exhales that fan across Jade's cheeks. They've turned toward each other overnight, and Jade senses the heat of Nia's body all along hers, even where they aren't touching.

As she awakens, she slowly regains her proprioception. She's aware of her knee, then her foot, which is resting on Nia's ankle. Her left arm, tucked under her own pillow. Her right arm extended lazily forward, fingers gripping silk, knuckles pressing into something soft.

Finally, she opens her eyes. They focus first on Nia's lips, which part with each gentle huff out. Then her right hand, which is clutching onto the neckline of Nia's sleep tank, bunching it to reveal the ample curve of her breast. Jade can see the tiniest sliver of rosy brown, the rest obscured by her fingers.

It takes her a split second to react, during which she feels warmth spread through and tighten in her abdomen, before she jerks herself back so abruptly that she quite literally falls out of bed.

Her shin breaks her fall against one of her Docs, and she rolls over, pressing her palm flat across what she's sure will be a bruise. She sucks in a breath, squeezes her eyes shut, mouths *fuck* on her exhale.

"Jade?" Nia's hand pats across the bed, searching, before she sits up. Pillow lines crease her right cheek and chin.

Jade's eyes are watering in pain, but Nia's blinking at her like she might not be awake enough to register anything yet. "Gotta walk Luna," she says.

Nia flops back down, practically shoving her face into the pillow and mumbling something unintelligible. Jade dresses without turning on the light, nearly tripping again in her unlaced boots as she grapples for the leash.

She finds Luna asleep on the couch. Only then does it occur to her to check the time. Barely past six—almost an hour until her usual walk time. As much as Jade itches to get out, she's not willing to take her now for fear of Luna demanding an earlier wake-up for the rest of the trip.

Jade slips into the bathroom, pees, washes her hands and face, brushes her teeth, stares at her undereye circles (less prominent than yesterday, thankfully). Tries desperately not to think about the feel of Nia's pajamas in her hand, the feel of *Nia* around her leg, against her knuckles.

At the sleepover after Nia's fourteenth birthday, Jade had dreamed about her. It had been a perfect re-creation of the party, up until the cake was placed in front of Nia. When she'd blown out the candles, everyone else vanished, snuffed out with the flame. Jade stood, rooted in place, as Nia plucked a candle from the cake and sucked the frosting off the end.

Come here, she'd said, her words forming around that candle.

But Jade had felt like she couldn't move, couldn't do anything but stare at the bit of buttercream painted on her lower lip.

So, Nia had stood up, crossed the room toward Jade, grabbed her by the nape of her neck, and made her lick it off herself. Jade had only kissed one person at that point—the only other Black girl at Michal's sleepaway camp two summers prior—so the dream went fuzzy after that. She couldn't identify exactly what was happening, only that it was Nia and it was *good*.

She'd awoken in a cold sweat, Nia sandwiched between her and Michal amid a pile of blankets and pillows, and teetering on the edge of a panic attack, only calming once she'd convinced herself it was because they'd slept so close together. It would've happened with any girl. Not because it's Nia, and not because she's *her*.

But she'd had the same dream the next night. And the next. And the one after that.

Got jittery and weird and eye contact avoidant every time Nia was near her.

After a week of this, Michal grabbed onto Jade's hand and thrust their arms into the air, telling their AP Chem teacher that they both needed to use the restroom. Because it was Michal, it worked, and she dragged Jade into the only single-stall bathroom in the building and poked and prodded until Jade spilled everything. After a lot (a *lot*) of laughter, Michal snapped her out of it. Not the attraction, necessarily—Nia always was . . . Nia—but the weirdness.

Now, though, Jade doesn't have a week to get over it. She has two hours, if that.

Her phone reads 6:43. Close enough.

* * *

THEY ARRIVE AT Callie's Hot Little Biscuit at exactly 9:29 and loiter to the left of the out-the-door line as Sarah had instructed. Luna promptly lies down to nap. Nia can't imagine what it must've taken to tire her out like this; yesterday she'd thrown a stick and tennis ball until her arm was sore, and the dog was still excitedly trotting on the way home. Jade fidgets with the leash, not looking at Nia.

She hasn't looked at Nia much this morning. *Hunger and lack of caffeine,* Nia tells herself once again. They went to bed on good terms—on *better* terms than they've been. When Nia woke up, Jade was off walking Luna. Nothing happened. She can't possibly have messed this trip up already.

A man about their age and roughly Jade's height wedges himself out the door, carrying an enormous brown paper bag and drink tray, and makes a beeline for them. He's swarthy in the way white people mean the word, wearing denim cutoffs and a Callie's T-shirt, both of which are cuffed. Line work of what looks to be a rutabaga decorates his right biceps, a similarly inked bunch of kale peeks out from his shorts on his left thigh. His loose curls are shaped into the general suggestion of a mullet. When he spots Luna, his face splits with an almost blindingly wide smile. But by far the most notable things about him are his eyes: dark brown, deeply set, and slightly upturned.

"Hey, y'all," he says. "I'm Benji."

And Nia can't help but laugh. Both Jade and Jonah snap their attention toward her, heads tilting. She gestures between them. "The mystery has been solved."

"Of whether Sarah's friend Benji exists?" Jade asks.

Benji scratches at the back of his head. "Yeah, sorry about that. I have to be here at four o'clock on Saturdays, so I didn't want to go and risk having Sharon try to set me up with her nephew again at Kiddush."

"No worries, man," Jonah says.

Nia looks between him and Jade, waiting. They stare back. Benji chuckles. "Seriously?" she asks, squinting.

"What?"

"Do you not realize why Sarah wanted us to meet Benji so badly?"

The twins do their head tilt at Benji this time, brows in matching furrows. Still nothing. For a brief moment, Nia wonders if she's misread everything, but then Benji shakes his head and says, "My bad. Hey, y'all, I'm Benji *Pardo*. Great-great-grandson of Bechor Pardo. Want some biscuits?"

"Holy shit," Jonah says. Jade stands in stunned silence, eyes widening.

"Sarah didn't say anything?" He looks at Jonah for a beat. "I guess that's not surprising. Come on, the biscuits are better hot."

They walk to Marion Square and crowd themselves onto a single bench. Benji doles out paper cups of coffee and little white takeout boxes, about two per person, and Luna promptly falls asleep. The biscuits are small in footprint but almost obscenely tall, sliced and stuffed with all manner of breakfast accoutrements.

The food is good—more than good, really—and they spend a solid fifteen minutes listening to the birds as they chew, only speaking to ask to trade bites.

Missing Michal is something Nia lives with daily, but certain moments intensify it. Like now, when she's enjoying good food on a nice day, early enough for it to only be *approaching* horrifically humid, the pleasure is undercut by an intense guilt, a deep ache. The three (and later four) of them always enjoyed meals out as a group, every entrée treated as a family-style shareable dish. It's not a particularly unique thing to do, she knows. And Michal had a tendency to talk with her mouth full, which never stopped being disgusting, no matter how long they'd been friends.

The banality of it might be what hurts most. It's a stupid, normal thing. Nia doesn't always feel deserving of stupid, normal things. Not when Michal doesn't get to have any of them.

She swallows a bite of an avocado, kale, and egg biscuit, chasing it with a swig of coffee. One day, she hopes she'll feel appreciative in these moments. Maybe she even does already sometimes. It's hard to remember when she's busy feeling sick over the basic joys, or even neutralities, of life.

"I ate too much," Jade says. "I think I'm in actual pain."

Nia swallows the last bite of her sandwich. "Yeah, me, too."

"The best compliment a baker could ask for." Benji grins, then checks his phone. "The teen service is over. Y'all ready to get Sarah and head to Folly?"

Jonah offers to drive, which is a good thing, judging by the sigh of relief Sarah breathes when she finds herself climbing into the back with Nia and Jade. She tells them about how two of the kids disappeared two prayers into Shacharit, returning at the end of the haftara decorated with hickeys. She had to pull them aside afterward to give a "time and place" lecture, and the whole thing made her feel ancient.

Really, she's quite funny, even more so when she's not stumbling over herself trying not to stare at Jonah. Nia knows that a promise to keep in touch after this trip likely wouldn't be kept, so she doesn't plan to make one. But if she'd met her at a bar in the Bay Area, or the twins had stumbled upon her in Brooklyn, she can't help but feel like they could really be friends.

Benji is nodding, laughing, frequently half-turning to look

at whoever in the backseat is speaking, but he doesn't add much himself. It's the same tactic she uses in an unfamiliar group, a way to promise that her quietude isn't due to a lack of desire to be sociable. A way to observe and participate all at once.

They get to Folly Beach without event from Luna, who seems suddenly revived by the smell of salt in the air and the feel of sand under her paws, bounding and jumping and digging in with joy. They walk a little before making camp, setting out their beach towels, portable doggy bowls, and Sarah's comically large cooler. As promised, the stretch of beach Sarah and Benji chose isn't overly crowded, and everyone they see seems to be within a decade of their age.

Nia rubs sunscreen onto her arms and legs, watching as a handful of surfers in bikinis and swim trunks paddle out into waves that sparkle in the sun. The sand is pale and hot under her feet, the water clear, and it reminds Nia of the spot a half-hour drive from her dad's midlife crisis apartment in Kingston. Not as picturesque as the Caribbean, but not far off, either. She bets that the water will be bath-warm, and she plans to lie out long enough for it to feel cool against her sun-baked skin when she finally wades in.

When she turns back around, Jade has already peeled off her shirt and is in the process of working sweatshorts nearly identical to the ones Jonah wore the other day down her thighs. She's wearing a deep brown string bikini and inches upon inches of freckled, tattooed skin stretch below the triangle top, beckoning Nia's eyes to roam. Jade straightens, and Nia looks downward, noticing that the ties of the bottoms bisect a tattoo of a moon on her left hip and a sun on her right. Except, as she studies them further, she realizes that the delicate lines camouflage abstracted nudes.

"New?" she asks.

Jade does a half shake of her head and shrugs simultaneously. "About a year and a half?"

Right. She's had them longer than she's had a license. She used to put a picture in the group chat of every new piece, second skin still on and wrinkly. "They're nice," Nia says, swallowing. "Could you get my back?"

"Sure," Jade answers, reaching for the bottle. Nia turns away from her the moment it's handed off.

She expects the lotion to be cool against her skin, but it's warm, as though Jade rubbed it between her palms before pressing them on either side of Nia's spine. When her hands trail up her shoulders, gliding firmly along the muscles that support her neck, Nia sucks in a breath.

"Knot?"

Her voice is soft and low, and Nia worries that if she tries to say anything, it'll just come out as a gasp for air. So, she nods instead.

Jade presses her thumb right into that tender spot, gently gripping above it with her other hand. When she starts to circle it, the sound Nia makes is barely human.

Jade chuckles, and Nia feels her cheeks redden. "Jesus Christ, your fingers are strong now."

"Potter's hands," Jade says, and after she feels the knot give, she smooths over the skin with her palms. Her touch disappears for a moment, and Nia is about to turn around, but it returns against her midback, dipping just barely under the seam of her high-waisted bottoms. Nia holds her breath. She might be melting into the sand. Struck by lightning, turned to glass.

Was it like this three years ago? Nia honestly can't remember. Does her touch feel this intense because of the time that's passed, or was it always this bad, and Nia was just better at handling it? Because she's not handling it well now.

She feels like a furnace with a broken thermostat, throwing heat in the middle of summer.

"My turn," Jade says.

Nia closes her eyes and gives herself one inhale before she turns around.

Jade is already facing away, her arm extended behind her to offer the bottle of Hawaiian Tropic. Nia takes it, rubbing a dollop between her hands just as Jade had done for her. "It has tiny sparkles; I hope that's okay. I got it because it's supposed to be reef safe and I didn't realize until I was directly in the sun."

Jade laughs, her head tucking toward her chest as if to give Nia access. "Are you saying I'm not femme enough to pull it off?" She hears the tease in Jade's tone and presses her hands against her shoulder blades before she's finished her question. "I'll take that as a no."

When Nia's done, Jade sits down on her towel and unscrews her water bottle, rinsing each of her hands over the sand. As soon as she's done drying them, she withdraws the baggie she got from Andy, laying out her supplies between her knees.

"Can you get my back?" Jonah asks her.

"I *just* cleaned my hands. Do you want the j to taste like sunscreen?"

He shrugs. "I'll roll it."

"You suck at rolling."

"I'll get you," Nia offers. Jonah starts to stand, and she laughs. "Maybe kneel?"

"I forget that you're tiny," he says.

"I'll have you know that five-four is the national average for women. You, at six-foot-one-million, are the statistical freak." The smile he gives her is almost bashful.

Jade turns toward their new friends. "We won't get in trouble for this, right?"

Sarah looks up from where she's carefully applying sunscreen to the tops of her toes. The brim of her woven straw hat shades down to her décolletage. "Nobody'll care."

Benji opens one eye. "It's encouraged, actually. At least by me."

Nia focuses all her energy on applying the lotion to Jonah's back. And not watching Jade's nimble fingers or the drag of her tongue against the paper. He yelps when she first makes contact—she forgot to warm it up first. She mutters an apology, and looks *very intently* at the mole on his left shoulder. Many years down the line, if he ever wonders if it's changed and he needs to get it looked at, he should call her. She's committed its exact shade and size to memory.

She probably should avoid touching Jade as much as possible. Since it's been minutes now, and she still can't be fucking normal about it.

Nia finishes rubbing the sunscreen in and tosses the capped bottle back into her tote bag, nodding in response to Jonah's thanks. She lies down on her towel, wiggling her butt and shoulders to mold the sand below her to her body, just as Sarah insists she shouldn't take the first hit and Benji accepts it instead. He passes it to Nia next, and she lazily props herself on one elbow to take a drag.

"Really putting in the effort, there," Jade says, the corner of her mouth twitching.

Nia exhales a thick cloud of smoke, handing the joint off to Jade and nestling back into the sand. "It's a vacation. Trying to get in that R and R."

Jade tokes, then passes it to Jonah. "I personally find confronting my ancestors' complicity in the transatlantic slave trade to be quite restful."

"Can't imagine anything more relaxing," Jonah agrees.

The way Jade smiles at him makes petals of peace unfurl in Nia's chest. Even more so, the way Jonah nods back. She was right yesterday. He just needed time.

"I'm sorry," Benji says.

They look at him for a moment. Jade tilts her head. "For . . . slavery?"

He lets out a breath through his nose. "Uh, yes, I guess. But also, our branch of the family's involvement, and for not reaching out to y'all's. The Pardos here are deeply proud of KKBE. Our foundation in the Jewish community, the recent allyship with the Black community. And also, very, very few Jewish families in the US were in the position to own slaves, and ours was one of them. And they—we—have a tendency to want to grip onto the pride and shy away from the other stuff. From what I know, my great-grandfather wanted to pretend you didn't exist. But my avuelo kept tabs. He knew there were still Pardos in New York, even did one of those DNA tests and got matched with one—your avuelo, probably. He didn't reach out, and he told me that there were grandchildren, and I didn't try to reach out, either."

Sarah nods encouragingly as she accepts the joint from him, patting him on the thigh. They exchange a look, and Benji just barely shakes his head.

"Did you know we were Black?" Jonah asks.

Benji shakes his head, shrugs. "I never looked you up."

"Would you have said all that if we weren't?" Jade says, and Nia itches to pat her thigh, too.

"I really hope so."

Jade nods, looking ahead at the water. Nia looks up at her, trying to telepathically shoot an *are you okay?* at the side of her face. She looks down, meeting Nia's gaze, and nods. *Water?* Nia mouths. Jade nods again.

"I'm going in," she announces.

Jade stands, casting a shadow over Nia. She dusts the inescapable grains of sand off her butt, then extends her hand, pulling Nia up after her.

CHAPTER TEN

saturday afternoon, june 28

Maybe going to the beach with your best friend after waking up in intimate contact with said best friend's tits is not the best idea in the world. It's one of the fundamental laws of the universe that people look sexy when they emerge from water, flipping their hair out of their eyes and smoothing it back with their hands: the perfume ad effect. Particularly people who look like Nia.

Her hair sticks to her neck, curling at her clavicles. Her skin glows. In that 1950s-esque buffalo-check bikini top her breasts are practically presented on a platter, and Jade has to force her gaze skyward.

"It feels *amazing*," Nia says, lying back to float. "The Perfect Beach Day, you know?"

Jade nods and clenches her jaw. Nia takes a deep breath, the expansion of her rib cage drawing Jade's eyes toward her tattoo. *Their* tattoo, really. Fat water droplets bead over the thin black lines, distorting the image. Without thinking, Jade presses her right hand to her side.

"Still the only one I've got," Nia says, looking at Jade's fingers.

Jade purses her lips, meeting her gaze. "You're a better Jew than I am."

Nia barks out a laugh. She takes another deep breath, her eyes fluttering shut. Jade lets herself drift back, extending her arms and legs, pushing her torso up to float. The water is warm, the waves gently rocking her, dulling their sound in her ears. Even after closing her eyes, she can feel Nia floating next to her. She'll keep them shut. If she opens them, she knows she'll instinctively turn to look for Michal.

They stay there floating for longer than Jade can keep track. When the sun on her skin begins to prickle, she hears the splash of Nia submerging herself, probably to cool off. Jade holds still, even though she's starting to feel like she's being baked alive.

"See you on the sand?" Nia murmurs.

Jade nods, and floats a few minutes longer.

Finally, she drops her legs down to stand. The whole front side of her body is flushed a faint purple-y red from the heat. She dives under, cooling herself, then turns her attention back to shore.

Benji and Nia are engrossed in conversation, three empty towels scattered around them. Jade scans the beach, eventually spotting Jonah and Sarah walking along the edge of the water a few hundred yards away. Sarah bends down, plucking something from the sand and dusting it off against her sarong before showing it to Jonah. He takes it carefully, putting it in the pocket of his swim trunks.

Wishing Michal were here is an actual, physical ache.

Jade walks lazily toward Nia and Benji, cataloging how her heels sink into the sand. Nia is lying on her stomach and using her hand as a visor as she laughs up at him.

When Jade reaches them, Nia flips over, propping herself up on her elbows. "D'you have a good time out there?"

"Excellent," Jade replies. Nia slowly lowers herself down, and an intense, unwanted image of what she might look like doing that from the vantage point of someone straddling her hips flashes across Jade's mind. She flops down on her towel unceremoniously, folding her arms and tucking her face into the nook of her elbow.

"You're quiet today," Nia says, nudging Jade's leg.

Jade rolls her head just enough to make eye contact with Nia over her arm. She grins. "I'm high."

Nia smiles, poking her toe into Jade's calf once again. "Okay, Stoney, I'll leave you be."

And she does. Jade lies there for who knows how long, listening to the wash of the waves against the shore, the call of seagulls cutting through the low hum of conversation. She's on the edge of sleep for the remainder of the time they spend at the beach, but she never lets it overtake her. She spends the minute-hours focusing on the tickle of a soft breeze and the heat of the sun that occasionally forces her to flip over.

Jonah and Sarah come back, roping her into conversation, and she participates sparingly, without ever opening her eyes. She doesn't feel that anybody expects anything else of her, and that's a really, really good feeling. Maybe the best feeling, and one she hasn't had around other people in about three years. It keeps her from floating entirely outside of herself, grounded just enough not to be carried away by the quick-moving ocean air.

Even as her high fades away, she still feels that heavy, relaxed warmth stretched all through her limbs. Her pinkie twitches, ever so slightly, like maybe it's longing to be looped through Michal's.

Jade's on her stomach again, and Nia lies down next to her, hooking her foot over Jade's ankle. She's definitely in her body now, most of her sensory awareness focused on that little slide of Nia's skin against hers.

"Jade?"

"Hmm?"

"Benji invited us to a party at his place tonight," Jonah says.

"There'll be karaoke," Benji adds.

"If you can handle Jonah's terrible Kendrick impression"—sand pelts Jade's back before she even finishes her sentence—"I'm down."

NIA WASHES HER hands, becoming aware for the first time tonight that she is, in fact, drunk. She surveys herself in the mirror, her reflection vignetted by the subtle blur at the edge of her vision. Her cheeks and neck are flushed, red splotches peeking out from the low neckline of her tie-front cream shirt.

She hasn't been drunk in a long time. It's been even longer since she's had a drunk-in-the-bathroom moment at a house party, muffled music and her thumping heart the sound track to her realization that the cloud shielding her from her social anxiety is entirely artificial.

Nia takes her time drying her hands, wanting to linger. In undergrad, she found herself in the bathroom of Phebe's, Double Down Saloon, or a dorm party around 1:00 a.m. most Fridays, whether she actually had to pee or not, decompressing from the chaos outside and contemplating whether what she was experiencing constituted "drunk" or "tipsy." Also, whether the cute person she'd been brushing elbows with during pong or at the bar was doing it on purpose. She could hide in there for precious minutes as she talked herself out of leaving and into making a move. Sometimes vice versa.

But those places usually had several other working toilets, and Benji's and Sarah's early twentieth-century bungalow has this lone bathroom. She's probably already been there longer than is socially acceptable. And, unfortunately, the only person she's able to think about is Jade. Who wasn't, and never has been, doing whatever is eliciting Nia's goose bumps on purpose.

She takes one last deep breath, eyes not so precisely focusing in the mirror, before she emerges from her enclave. Someone with both a nostril and septum piercing leans against the wall of the narrow hallway, and Nia tries not to look thoroughly ashamed as they smile, nod, and duck past her.

This is stupid. This is bad and stupid. Maybe *she* is stupid, because why is she here, drunk, rounding the corner to the living room where Jade and Jonah are duetting "All the Stars," knowing full well that she's wearing every thought she has on her face.

It's Jade's turn, and she's scream-belting her favorite incorrect lyrics, easily misheard in SZA's melodic slur: *It's maybe tonight and my dreams might let me know/All the stars are kosher/All the stars are kosher/All the stars are kosher!*

On the last line, Jade spots Nia in the thin crowd. She points at her, wiggling her hips sort of nonsensically, a smile creeping into her lips and stretching out the last of her words.

Heat coils through Nia's chest and lower belly simultaneously, quickly followed by her cheeks. This is bad, and stupid, and embarrassing. It feels like high school. Like discovering her queerness almost entirely because she was discovering *Jade* (she probably should've known based on her reaction to Lindsay Lohan in *Herbie: Fully Loaded,* but still).

Nia perches on the arm of the overfilled couch, averting her eyes from Jade and toward Jonah. He's in a wide stance, one foot in front of the other, knees slightly bent, arms crossed, his posture a shockingly accurate imitation of Kendrick Lamar. She looks then to her fingernails and starts picking at an already shredded cuticle, inhaling deeply.

Maybe it's because she's drunk. Though if she's being honest, she's not *that* drunk. And she was completely sober earlier when she was nearly panicking at the beach at the simple press of Jade's thumb into the back of her neck.

She could blame it on the three long years that have passed since she last saw her. Perhaps that's it—she's forgotten how to deal with it. That feeling of *maybe* . . .

Maybe the way she pressed up against Nia on Michal's bed was on purpose. *Maybe* Jade zoning out across the table from Nia was actually a lingering look. *Maybe* when she glanced at Nia's lips and smiled, she was thinking about how they'd feel. *Maybe* she was never meant to be with Toni. *Maybe* Nia could be brave.

Realistically, it might just be being here, without Michal. She was fooling herself into thinking they'd already adapted their relationship to her absence. They'd adapted it *over text*. Their very last interaction, just the two of them, after Michal's death caused a three-year-wide chasm.

Or maybe it's none of that. It's just her, and her pathetic, years-long crush on her best friend.

Bad, stupid, and embarrassing.

And maybe she *is* that drunk, because she can't even reprimand herself for the negative self-talk. She lets it loop through her head, dimly aware that it'll be a conversation with her therapist next week.

MAYBE SHE'S JUST drunk, but Jade feels like Nia is mad at her. On the walk home, they were next to each other for a few beats, and then their shoulders brushed. And sure, maybe it wasn't totally unintentional, and Jade could have avoided it. But the moment it happened, Nia gave her a wide berth, a few steps later falling into stride on the other side of Jonah.

They're back at the inn now, and Nia is in the bathroom going through her ten-step routine. She gathered her pajamas and her toiletry bag, wordlessly slipping past Jade the moment she'd returned. Like she'd done something wrong, offended her in some way. Except she doesn't know what the fuck it was.

She climbs under the covers, but doesn't lie down. Instead, she leans against the headboard and folds her arms across her chest, waiting. Staring at the door in anticipation.

It's probably too intense, because Nia looks almost startled when she shadows the doorway, pausing and swallowing before she makes her way into the room.

And yes, maybe she's just drunk, but she's also annoyed. Too annoyed even to demand an explanation.

She looks away as Nia gets in bed, still not saying anything. Jade sinks down, curling to her side as Nia flips off the light.

Jade stews, and her annoyance thickens into frustration. There's no place on the floor of their friendship free of eggshells for her to tread.

Nia exhales loudly, and Jade barely restrains the *what?!* clawing at her vocal cords. She turns her back to her and adjusts her head on the pillow, striving for comfort and failing.

And then the mattress moves a little, and Jade turns over again. Nia full-body shivers.

"Are you cold?" Jade asks, unable to withhold the frustration from her tone.

Nia *hmm*s, nodding her head.

"Well, come here then," Jade says.

It's a demand; she hears it in her voice before she thinks better of it. But *also* before she has time to think better of it, Nia tucks herself into Jade, pulling her arm across her rib cage.

Jade tightens her grip, her hand slipping under Nia's silk tank top. Nia arches into Jade; Jade presses back. She lets out a breath, and Nia gasps, the skin of her neck pinching into goose bumps against Jade's cheek.

"Better?" Jade asks. Her heart is beating loud enough for them both to feel it. Maybe for both to hear it.

Nia nods. "Warm," she says, and it's more like an exhale. "Comfy," she says, and it's more like an excuse.

CHAPTER ELEVEN

december, eight years ago

"I have something I need to tell you guys," Michal said, wiping her greasy fingers on her thigh.

"Oh no," Nia said on a laugh.

"Please don't tell us you're talking to Brendan again," Jade said. "He's your TA. It's a terrible idea."

"His name is Brandon, and the semester's over anyway!" Michal protested.

"Still don't think you should be texting him," Nia said. She did her best to clean her hands, then crumpled her napkin onto her tray, looking out toward the water.

It was the last afternoon of their ten-day stay in Nia's dad's guest bed. All three of them—he'd bought an air mattress for the occasion, and Nia had tried to explain to him that it was going to go unused, to no avail. Nia had felt it was her duty to take Michal and Jade to Hellshire before they left, so there they were, just barely on the right side of sun exhaustion and overfull on fried fish and festival she and Jade had bought by the pound. They'd left Michal behind to guard the towels and also to avoid getting overcharged (or at least avoid getting *egregiously* overcharged, as she was pretty sure it was a couple of bucks cheaper last time she was here with her dad).

The trip had been perfect. Once they got back to New York, they'd still have time before any of their classes started up again, but this was their last winter break of college, and maybe the last time it'd be this easy planning such a long trip together. Michal had applied to MFAs all over the country, Jade was all but definitely going to be staying at Columbia for her PhD, and Nia was planning to use her double major in social work for a year or two as a caseworker before she went for her clinical psychology doctorate. Who knows how well their breaks would line up, and even if they did, time would have to be shared with family that was no longer always nearby.

Michal and Jade had needed to remind Nia daily that she couldn't plan every spare second. That they should have time to just fuck around, too, and rest, and that it not being perfect didn't mean it wouldn't be amazing. She relinquished as much control as she could, and they spent so much time fucking around (literally, in the case of Michal and not one but three different men on their nights out, which was a PR for her but not totally out of the ordinary) and resting. And it *was* perfect.

"That's not what I want to tell you guys," Michal continued. "It's—I need you to promise we'll have a good night tonight, no matter what."

Jade looked at Nia, with the *what the fuck is she talking about?* that Nia felt written across her own face. "I think the plan for tonight was just to get very drunk at my dad's and talk our way through a movie. Our flight is at ten tomorrow, so . . ." Nia said.

"Right, then promise we'll do that," Michal insisted.

"Jesus. Okay, I promise," Nia said.

"Me, too," Jade said. "Can you just tell us?"

"You know how I thought I needed reading glasses? Because I'd get headaches when I read for too long and stuff." Michal swallowed, then pressed her hands into her cheeks before dropping them with an audible slap onto her thighs.

She was dragging this out, and even if Nia didn't know why yet, it made her chest tighten. "Yes," she said.

Jade's eyebrows scrunched together. "That's not it, though, right?"

Michal shook her head, letting out a distinctly anxious laugh. "No. I, um, have anaplastic astrocytoma."

Nia blinked, instinctively looking at Jade in confusion. Hoping uselessly, for a split second, that what Michal had said wasn't as bad as it sounded. But Jade's eyes had gone glassy.

"You have a grade-three *brain tumor*?" Jade asked, her voice catching.

And then the tears sprang to Nia's eyes, as well. Her vision blurred with surprising quickness. Her mouth opened, and all that escaped was a whispered "what?"

"Ah, oh fuck," Michal said, her voice quavering. She pressed the heels of her palms into her eyes. "Fuck. Looking at you guys is like finding out again. I don't know why I thought . . ."

"What?" Nia repeated.

"You have brain cancer," Jade said.

"Yes," Michal said. "I have brain cancer."

"Wha—" Nia started, but she clamped her mouth closed before she could say it a third time.

"I know, it doesn't feel real," Michal said. "It still doesn't feel real to me, and I knew already." She gulped, then rubbed at her chest, like she was trying to massage the words out. "I don't know if I'm lucky because I only had headaches and not the seizures or personality changes, or unlucky because if I'd had those, I would've gone to the doctor sooner." Michal looked at her hands, playing with the frayed edge of her denim shorts. "I mean, I guess I'm unlucky. For having it at all."

Jade shut down. Nia could see it happening, the way her cheeks went slack, even as tears started rolling. Jade lost her words; Nia forced herself to find hers. "When did you find out?" she asked.

"I got the biopsy results the day before we left. But we did a bunch of scans, so I knew there was a growth for like a week, maybe? Um," she said, and then she burst into tears.

She was sitting between them, and immediately, Jade and Nia crowded in. Michal dropped her head to Jade's shoulder, threading her fingers into Nia's.

Nia used her free hand to wipe at her cheeks. It was a little bit of a relief to sit like this, able to grip onto Michal tightly while looking at the gentle crush of the waves against the shore. The sand was hot under her feet, and she wiggled her toes into it, like she wanted to find some way to ground herself. "What's the treatment plan?" she asked.

"Surgery first. The day after we get back. And then radiation, and then chemo." She hiccupped. "I think the chemo is going to overlap with the radiation at some point? They told me I could delay further if I wanted to freeze my eggs. But I—" She broke off her sentence, and Nia could feel the sob rack through her. "But I'm not sure whether I want kids. And it's not guaranteed to make me infertile. It could, but I just—I don't think it's worth the delay."

Nia nodded, wiping her face again. She could smell the fried food, the heartiness of the sea air, the occasional whiff of unpleasant ocean fishiness. The sun would set soon, disappearing behind the outcrop of land to their right, and the sky was painted purple and pink and orange, all the colors reflected back up from the water. She'd seen this sunset so many times before, and loved it a different way each time. It felt almost cruel now. Disrespectful. How dare it be this beautiful, the breeze on her skin this perfect? Storm clouds should brew. The earth should feel this cataclysmic shift, too.

Michal's hand was warm in hers, soft, and she ran her thumb over the back of it. "You could have told us, you know," Nia said. "I'm not mad, but you could have."

"Yeah," Jade said. "We would've been there."

"I didn't want to ruin the trip," Michal said.

"Mich," Nia said, "that's not—"

"It would've been different, and you know it. I just wanted this one last thing."

She was right, and neither Jade nor Nia said anything for a long moment.

"I'm so sorry," Jade said.

Nia took a shaky inhale. "*So* sorry."

"Yeah." She let a sad breath out, almost like a laugh. "Me, too," Michal said, and they all got quiet again. Seagulls were squawking, the faint baseline of dancehall was coming from somewhere far behind them.

"Is that why you were so determined to get laid this trip?" Nia asked eventually. She turned to Michal, whose teeth were sunk into her bottom lip.

"Mayyyyybe," she said, and a smile started to spread.

"Here I was, blaming the dearth of eligible men who like women at Sarah Lawrence," Nia said.

Michal threw her head back in laughter. "Ms. Lawrence still shares plenty of the blame."

"What do we do now?" Jade asked.

Michal shrugged. "I don't know. Nothing, I think. Other than just being there."

"We will," Nia said.

"We will," Jade agreed.

"And," Michal pressed on, "we drink the finest liquor your dad's kitchen cabinet has to offer, and cry our way through a movie."

THEY WERE ALL appreciably drunk an hour after getting back to Kevin's apartment. They'd showered off the sand and salt, changed into pajamas, put on Michal's party playlist (exclusively popular rap and reggaetón), and emptied an entire bottle of Wray & Nephew white overproof rum into a pitcher for mojitos.

Jade and Nia were sitting cross-legged on the floor, looking up at Michal as she gave a dramatic reading of a sexy text from TA Brandon, and laughing so hard that Jade was genuinely concerned she might pee. Laughing so hard that Nia was wiping tears from her eyes, and Michal had completely lost her breath, unable to continue reading through the message.

But then Michal's laughter turned to hiccups, and her face crumpled. "My hair," she said, and she started to cry. "I love my hair. It's my best feature! And they're going to have to shave some of it for the surgery. But they might as well shave all of it because of the chemo anyway."

Jade watched Nia's expression sober, felt hers, as well.

"That fucking sucks, Mich," Nia said, resting her hand on Michal's knee. "But, babe, your hair is *not* your best feature."

Michal shook her head. "It is," she said.

Jade forced a laugh. "Have you seen yourself? You have

great hair, but your face is objectively beautiful. You'll be just as hot bald."

Michal sucked in a breath. "Really?"

"Yes, really," Jade said.

"And you can trust us because we're gay," Nia added.

"You're not *technically* gay," Michal said.

Nia waved her off. "You know what I mean."

Jade propped her chin on Michal's other thigh. "Would it help if we did it, too?"

"Did what?"

"Shaved our heads."

"My dad has clippers by his sink," Nia said.

"You'd do that?" Michal asked, wiping her snot on the sleeve of her T-shirt.

"Yes," Jade said at the same time as Nia's "absolutely."

That is how, at nine p.m. on a Wednesday night, Kevin Chin walked in on his incredibly drunk daughter and her equally drunk friends, surrounded by tufts of auburn, brown, and black hair, somewhere between laughing and crying.

"Dad," Nia said, immediately straightening, in a voice that to Jade sounded impressively sober.

"My crazy daughter," he said, his accent thickening in disapproval. "What have you done?"

"We borrowed your clippers," she said.

"I can see that."

"And your rum."

His eyes slid to the pitcher on the bathroom counter, now only a third full. "I hope not the overproof." Jade watched him take in Nia's expression—she was going for ashamed or bashful, maybe, but was far too gone to pull it off. "Nia, princess, that stuff is not for the faint of heart."

"I have brain cancer, Mr. Chin," Michal blurted. "I just told them today."

He laughed at first, a deeper, more booming version of Nia's, his face scrunching in just the same way, smile lines deepening in his brown skin. But the three of them just stood there, looking back at him, until he dropped his hand from his stomach. "You're—you're serious."

"Unfortunately. I have surgery in two days and they were trying to make me feel better about losing my hair. We'll clean up, I promise."

He looked around the room, nodding slowly. Jade watched his expression crack when his eyes lingered on Nia's face, and there was something there that made her crack, too. She wanted her mom, and her dad. She wanted to tell Jonah. She wanted to talk to Nia about it, just the two of them, so they could figure out what to do. She felt a little unsteady on her feet, and she was trying so hard to keep it together, because she knew she'd fully fall apart eventually. She only hoped she could get to the point where it wouldn't be in front of Michal.

"Well," Kevin said. "Pour me some of that and I'll help before you hurt yourselves."

Over the next hour, he cleaned up their shoddy work, explaining in great detail how to trim around the ears. The mojitos dwindled and then disappeared.

It started to blur—Kevin bringing them water, shooing them into the living room so he could clean. Talking and laughing and crying and laughing again while something played on the TV. Rubbing each other's freshly bald heads, arguing over who had the nicest scalp. Falling asleep in a pile in the queen-sized bed.

Getting out of bed to pee, Michal still completely knocked out. Rounding the corner toward the bathroom and hearing Nia crying through the cracked door to Kevin's bedroom.

"It'll be okay, my big daughter," she heard him say.

She couldn't hear what Nia said back. It was too garbled, and Jade's brain felt too fuzzy.

But whatever it was, Kevin replied, "You are strong. And you have Jade."

CHAPTER TWELVE

sunday morning, june 29

There is a creature inside Nia's skull and it is pounding on the bone in an unsuccessful attempt to escape. One of its siblings probably died in her mouth last night, if the taste left behind is any indication. Everything feels clammy, and she seems to have thrown half the covers off her. Luna has taken the opportunity to lick her exposed leg. This hangover is a freight train, and she is tied to the tracks.

She rarely has more than one drink in a night, and this is why. Perhaps her little undergrad flashback in the bathroom last night should have warned her it was coming.

"Fuck," Jade groans.

The sheets stir, and Nia supposes it's the movement of Jade sitting upright. She isn't yet willing to risk opening her eyes for fear the room will spin. She grunts her agreement.

"I think I'm dying," Jade says.

Nia grunts again. "I want to scrape off my skin."

"Too gross, don't say that."

Nia shrugs limply. "'S true."

"Fuck, Luna," Jade says. Nia opens one of her eyes to Jade swinging her legs over the side of the bed and clutching her stomach. "I'm so sorry, baby girl. I didn't mean to make you wait. Oh God, if she pooped somewhere I think I'm actually gonna die."

"I'll clean it if she did," Nia mumbles.

The mattress depresses as Jade pushes herself to standing. "You don't have to do that."

"I will, though." She closes her eyes again, burrowing her face into the pillow.

She hears Jade's retreating footsteps, then some muffled talking as she runs into Jonah in the living area. His tone sounds equally sore and grumbling. Nia finds no solace in the fact that she isn't alone.

Her pulse throbs through the vein in her forehead. Water. She needs water.

She peels herself upright, smacking her lips as she unsticks her tongue from the roof of her cottony mouth. Nia genuinely, truly, feels like garbage. Or maybe compost. The stuff at the bottom of the bin on your countertop that's already warm with decomposition.

The walk to the edge of the room feels more like a crawl. As she reaches the doorway, she can clearly make out Jonah's grumbling: "Jade, I wanted to talk to you—"

"Whatever it is, Jonah, I promise I'll listen later. I gotta take Luna before she pees herself. You should pack."

The door to the suite clicks behind her, and Jonah spots Nia propping herself up against the doorframe. "Hey, Nia."

"You look bad," she says.

"So do you," he says.

"I feel bad. I feel worse than bad. What time is it?"

"Nine fifteen."

"Fuck, Jonah. Checkout is ten." He looks utterly crestfallen at this information. "Go pack."

He leaves, and she does a quick (or as quickly as she

can manage at the moment) sweep of the living room. Luna did, indeed, leave them a gift. At least it's on the wood and not the carpet. Nia retrieves a doggy bag and the enzymatic cleaner that Jonah and Jade had stored in Luna's diaper bag of supplies and proceeds to clean the mess while trying her best not to breathe.

It's 9:25 when she makes it into the shower. She scrubs viciously at herself, wishing desperately that she could linger but knowing two people need it after her. She runs the washcloth over the back of her neck, and despite the stream of near-scalding water pelting her, she shivers with a memory.

Jade's lips were there last night. Not kissing her, not really. But just barely open, and gently pressing, her breath hot against Nia's skin.

What was she thinking? And *how* did she not remember it until now?

Does Jade remember?

She takes a few deep breaths, then turns the water cold and flips her head forward to rinse out the conditioner. There's no time for this kind of crisis.

Out of the shower, she rushes to towel off, apply face sunscreen, swipe on deodorant, and repack her toiletry bag.

At 9:38, Jonah slides past her into the bathroom. It was a *very* quick shower by Nia's standards, and she hopes he can appreciate it.

In the room, she clothes herself, and even though the shorts and cotton shirt she chooses are loose-fitting, she still has the sensation that she's stuffing herself into them. The shower and water she gulped down before it made her feel moderately better. Emphasis on the word "moderately." Her clothes are all folded and easily tucked into her luggage, so she goes about gathering loose items through the rest of the suite as Jade returns and replaces Jonah in the bathroom.

At 10:05, they drop the key in the designated jar in the lobby. Nobody behind the concierge desk says anything, and Nia takes that to mean they've made it out within the unwritten grace period.

None of them speak as they make their way around the corner to the car. The pea-soup green shimmers in the light, and the color is somehow exactly what it feels like inside Nia's head. She reaches for her sunglasses.

They load up the car and climb in: Nia behind the wheel with Jonah in the passenger seat, Jade and Luna in the back. Nia pulls up Google Maps and types in the address of their Savannah Airbnb, passing off the phone to Jonah.

After a moment, the opening notes of Kendrick's "Rich Spirit" start blaring through the speakers.

"No," Jade and Nia say in unison.

Jonah reaches for the volume dial and spins it all the way down. "Accident, sorry."

"Oh, thank God," Nia says on a sigh.

"Okay, it wasn't *that* loud," Jonah says.

"I mean, it was. But I was talking about that." She signals and pulls into the drive-through lane of a little coffee stand.

"I know you can't tell," Jade says, her voice still very much the texture of a groan, "but I think that makes me the happiest person in the world."

They get their coffees and egg sandwiches and eat in silence as they head toward the highway, Jonah obliging each time Nia asks him to hand her something. A few exits later, Nia says, "Okay, I think I can handle music now. *Quietly.*"

She gets a Jonah Pardo Grin and he presses play.

Every now and then she looks up in the rearview mirror, and sees Jade pressing her face against the windowpane as though the cool glass will save her. The coffee and food brought color back into her cheeks, but she still looks a little worse for wear. Occasionally, she mumbles something like *this is why I don't fuck with alcohol.* And it's good for Nia to know, she supposes, that that's the only thing Jade is thinking about. A little nauseating, but good.

She drains the last of her vanilla oat milk latte, passing it off to Jonah.

"Oh no, oh no, oh no no no," Jade cries, her words swallowed by the whistle of air through her cracked window.

"What?"

"Take the next exit, Nia!"

She hits her turn signal. "Are you okay?" she tosses over her shoulder as she checks her blind spot.

"Luna is about to vomit, and if she does it in here, *I'm* going to vomit."

How did we forget the Dramamine? Jade thinks as she strokes Luna's heaving back, once again sitting in gravel on the side of some Carolina road.

Jade knows how, she guesses. They barely made it out of the Lodge Alley Inn in time to avoid a fine. She hasn't even had a chance to talk to Nia about what happened last night— not that she knows what she would say if she did. It just seems like something she should address, especially in light of her resolution to be less avoidant.

But maybe Nia doesn't remember it. If she does, she hasn't given any indication that she wants to talk about it. So, it meant nothing. To her. Probably.

They weren't *that* drunk, though, were they? She's pretty sure her hangover is a combination of her nearing thirty, the sugary margarita mix, and lack of sleep more than anything else. Maybe Nia was further gone than she seemed.

God, that makes her feel worse. She should apologize to her, if she can get a moment away from Jonah.

Or maybe Nia doesn't want to talk about it at all.

Fuck. *Come here then.* What was she thinking?

"How's our girl doing?" Nia asks.

"I think we're getting to the last of it."

"I got food and water when she's ready," Jonah says.

Jade rests her cheek on her knee, still rubbing Luna's back.

"You good, J?"

"Yeah. Do you think those margaritas were made with Everclear?"

Nia sighs, kicking some gravel. "Today's going well, huh?"

"Absolutely smashing it," Jonah says in a British accent, the kind he's prone to randomly burst into whenever he's bingeing *Love Island.*

Jade snorts, rolling her head up to look at him. He's smiling, but there's this kind of pain around his eyes that tells her he's just as hungover as she is.

Luna perks up, trying to lick Jade's face (unsuccessfully, otherwise Jade herself would probably be heaving), and Jonah deposits collapsible bowls of food and water at her feet. She laps away, and Nia tosses a bit of cheesy egg reserved from her breakfast sandwich atop the kibble, which the dog accepts happily.

"Very generous," Jade says.

"The Dramamine was stuffed in it. Thought it was worth a shot."

Jade nods slowly. "Ahh, smart. How are you smart right now?" Nia chuckles in response, shrugging. "I feel like half my brain still hasn't woken up."

Nia looks at her then, and the moment dilates. Jade

doesn't know what the look means, can't tell what Nia's feeling. But she knows then, deep in her bones, without any doubt, that Nia remembers Jade's face nuzzled into the crook of her neck last night.

"I'mma try to get her to pee," Jonah says, and Jade passes the leash off to him.

"I'm gonna have to pee soon, too," Nia announces.

"Same. I chugged three glasses of water before we left and the coffee hasn't helped," Jade says.

"We need to get gas soon, anyway."

"Are you gonna pee for me, sweetie?" Jonah coos at Luna.

Jade groans, throwing her head back. "Please never say that sentence again."

He makes a disgusted noise. "Get your mind out of the gutter."

"Can't. The gutter is my home now. It's where I belong."

Jonah ignores her, but when she turns toward Nia, she knows exactly how to read *this* look: mild amusement, genuine happiness. She thinks about that moment over coffee on Friday morning, when she was annoyed at Jonah for something she can't even remember now. Nia had said, "I missed *y'all*," and Jade didn't think much of it then. It was a throwaway comment, a continuation of a running joke. But now, looking at the warmth in Nia's face and the light in her dark eyes, Jade knows that she meant it.

They find a gas station just across the nearest highway overpass and she takes her time to stock up on snacks and Gatorade on her way back from the restroom while Nia fills the tank. Jade finds herself feeling better by the minute as she meanders back to the car. The sun is glorious down here and though the air is sticky, it doesn't smell of urine, which even she can admit is a marked improvement over June in New York.

"I got you Glacier Freeze," she says when she reaches the car, passing the bottle to Nia.

"Ah, thank you," Nia says, uncapping it and taking a swig. The column of her throat bobs as she swallows, and she makes this tiny sound of pleasure. And, God, maybe *Jade* is the one who doesn't remember what happened last night very well, because she immediately knows she's heard it before. Yet somehow, she hasn't been replaying it in her mind all morning. A bead of liquid is left behind on Nia's bottom lip, and this becomes one of the many, many moments when Jade can't seem to force her gaze away. "The best flavor."

And, oh, you can *count* the seconds before Jade manages to respond. "Is orange?" she offers, and Nia scrunches her nose in disgust.

Luna is asleep in the backseat, and Jonah is presumably off in the men's room. She inhales deeply, steadying herself, because she's going to say something. What, she's not sure, but it's definitely the right thing to do. She takes a sip from her own bottle and swallows thickly. "Nia," she starts.

"Ready to go?" Jonah asks, coming up behind her.

She closes her eyes slowly and nods. There's still tonight. Or even today, when they're settling into their room, before they leave for the architecture tour.

They've only been on the highway for ten minutes when the car is shaken by a loud *thunk*. They hear it again, but more muffled, two seconds later, as the car behind them passes over the same strip of asphalt. And again, just after that. Then a persistent beep, and the low tire pressure light flips on.

"Oh shit," Nia says, hitting the hazards and merging toward the shoulder as quickly as she can. Jade cranes her neck around to look through the rear window, and sees several other cars doing the same.

Nia puts the car in park, folds her arms across the top of the steering wheel, and drops her forehead to her wrist.

Jade reaches out to pinch her shoulder. "Hey, it's okay. We've got Triple A."

"Me, too," she says, but doesn't move. "But I can change a tire. Just give me a sec."

Jade and Jonah climb out of the car to survey the damage. The back left tire is completely shredded.

Someone calls out from behind them, and they both turn.

"What?" Jade shouts, and though he repeats whatever he was saying, they still can't hear over the cars whipping past.

They walk toward the person, and once they're within earshot, he says, "Did y'all see what it was?"

They both shake their heads.

"There's fuckin' potholes on the highway now! What're my taxes for, then? They sure as shit ain't fundin' schools." The guy puts his hands on his hips, looking at the punctured wheel of his pickup truck. Their poor, dinky Kia Soul never stood a chance.

"I know that's right," Jonah says, and the guy takes a couple of steps his way, opening his mouth again.

"I'll check on Nia," Jade says, low enough for only Jonah to hear. "You can entertain."

When she gets back, Nia is hunched into the open hatch, her back tense.

"No spare tire?" she guesses.

"They have a 'tire mobility kit,'" Nia answers, "which seems to be for, like, nail punctures. It'll do absolutely fucking nothing for that," she says and gestures at the strips of rubber.

"Fuck, okay," Jade says. "I'm calling."

Fifteen minutes and several *yes, a whole line of cars on the shoulder* later, and Jade has assurances that help is on the way.

They climb into the car for the wait. It's supposedly the safest thing to do in this situation, but it hardly feels like it when the entire vehicle rocks each time someone speeds past. Whatever distance they'd gained from the collective bad mood this morning has been lost, and they sit there, drinking and eating through more of their provisions than they probably should in total silence, until the tow truck arrives.

CHAPTER THIRTEEN

sunday afternoon, june 29

Their tow truck driver raps the window with the back of his hand. In his several-sizes-too-big unbuttoned coveralls with *Deion* embroidered on the breast and a cigarette hanging out of his mouth, he is a sight for sore eyes. He motions for Nia to roll down her window.

"Three a y'all?" he says, and Nia isn't sure how the cigarette stays in place. Or how she hears him over the traffic—his voice is raspy, low, and aged in a way that doesn't match his baby-smooth brown skin and peach fuzz–adjacent scruff. She nods. "Only one passenger in the tow truck."

"Could two of us stay in the car?"

He sniffs. "Illegal."

"Jonah," Jade says, "why don't you go? We can call an Uber—"

"Won't come," Deion says, shaking his head. "Cab."

"Right. We'll call a cab and we can take Luna—"

"Service animal?" Deion asks.

"No . . ."

"Ain't gone happen. Dog can ride with me."

"Thank you, Deion," Nia says. "That's really kind of you." He nods in response. Nia looks to Jonah, who's frowning. She remembers what she overheard this morning, how he was trying to tell Jade something, clearly without her there. Maybe now's his chance. "I'll take Luna in the tow truck," she says.

Jonah's expression is one of relief and gratitude, and Nia knows it was the right thing to do. Jade, however, furrows her brow. "Are you sure?"

Nia nods. "Yeah, it's no problem." She looks back to Deion. "Where should they meet us?"

He gives the name of the nearest auto shop—thirty miles off course, apparently—and Nia retrieves Luna and her bag of supplies and follows Deion to his truck.

Deion doesn't seem to be the most enthusiastic conversationalist, which right now is fine by Nia. Her nausea is gone but a headache is creeping, and it's certainly not helped by the secondhand smoke. At least Luna has gone to sleep on her lap.

After fifteen minutes of silence, Deion says, "Pit mix?"

"Oh, um, I think? I don't know for sure. She's the twins' dog." Nia realizes it's sort of a dumb thing to say, when Deion can obviously tell just by looking at Luna.

He flicks some ash out the window and glances down at Luna. "Pit mix," he says. Then, without taking his eyes off the road, he removes his phone from its mount on the dash and swipes to the photo app, handing it to Nia. She looks at the screen, and a gray-and-white dog with a similar head shape to Luna stares back at her, mouth wide and tongue hanging out. She's wearing an enormous yellow petal-adorned collar around her neck that makes her head look like the seeded center of a sunflower. "Named her Fran," he says.

"She's adorable," Nia says.

Deion nods, and Nia returns his phone to the mount. He doesn't say another word.

However badly Jade thought last night had impacted the trip, she now knows it's worse. Cigarette smoke gives Nia a headache even when she's not hungover. And she *chose* to ride with Deion, even in the face of Jade volunteering Jonah. Who probably would have felt better being the one with Luna, anyway.

She presses her forehead against the window of the cab, deeply aware that it's probably filthy. But it feels incredible. The driver is practically shouting into a Bluetooth headset. If they ever make it to the Airbnb, she's going to go digging for Advil.

"Are you awake?" Jonah asks.

Jade grunts her affirmation.

"Sarah told me it was okay to tell you this if I wanted, but she didn't say anything about Nia, so I wanted to wait until it was just us."

At that, Jade's eyes flutter open. She lifts her head, turning toward him. Jonah's expression is deeply serious, a ghost of their father's most notable wrinkle bisecting his brow. "What'd she tell you?"

He exhales slowly, and Jade straightens in her seat. "You know what Benji told us yesterday?"

Jade pushes a soft, sardonic laugh through her nose. "The 'sorry about slavery' speech."

Jonah's brow lowers. "It wasn't only that."

"Yeah, I know," she mumbles. "I just . . ." She trails off, mostly because she didn't have a plan for the rest of that sentence.

His eyes narrow, assessing her—he's deciding whether it's worth continuing at all. *That* piques her curiosity.

"I'm sorry," she says. "I'm listening."

Jonah takes a deep breath. "Well, he—his family—there was money. Avuelo said that when his avuelo came to Brooklyn, he had nothing, and had to build a life from scratch." Jade nods. She's heard the story, as have most people who've spoken to her avuelo for more than a handful of minutes at a time. "But he grew up with money."

"Right." Jade hadn't given it an especially high amount of thought before going to KKBE, when what Vidal Pardo had been running from was shoved in her face. But he hadn't really been starting from scratch; he'd been starting *over*.

"Benji had a trust. By now, most of the money isn't from plantations, or directly tied to the slave trade at all—"

Jade's frustration flares, flames fanned by her throbbing skull. "The generational wealth they built was on a foundation of owning people, Jonah," she says. "Even if now it's from being doctors or bankers or whatever the fuck, the descendants of—"

"I know, Jade," he hisses, his voice low enough that she momentarily picks up a piece of the cabdriver's shouted conversation (that she would rather die than eat leftovers for dinner again) and has to blink and shake her head to refocus. "I'm not— *Fuck*. We don't have to do this again. That's what I'm trying to say. Benji learned about their history, and then when he turned twenty-one and got access to the trust, he dissolved it completely. Donated every cent—to the Equal Justice Initiative, smaller abolitionist organizations, local stuff, too. He's waiting to go to culinary school until he can save up from the bakery."

"Oh," Jade says. *Wow*. "That's . . . I mean, that's the right thing to do, I guess."

"He meant what he said," Jonah says.

She shrugs, considering. "I don't know that I ever really thought he didn't. I guess it's good to know that he's meant it for a long time, though." Jonah nods. "Sarah told you this when you were walking along the beach yesterday?"

"Yeah," he says. "She said Benji never would say it himself."

"I wonder why she only told you," Jade mutters, resting the side of her head on the glass this time.

"I asked her that."

"And?"

"She said that Benji probably wouldn't want her talking about it, and it was only worth the risk on me because she thought it would make me feel better," he replies.

Her cheeks flush with guilt and a touch of shame. Sarah was nothing but nice to her, and Jade was so quick to assume she was motivated solely by her attraction to Jonah. She can't even blame it entirely on her hangover. "Did it work? Do you feel better?"

He nods. "Do you?"

She shakes her head. "Not really. I like Benji more, but that's not really what was so upsetting."

"Yeah," Jonah says. He bounces his leg, drums his fingers on his knee.

"Is there something else?" Jade asks.

"You never really fixed things with Nia, did you?" he blurts.

Jade's cheeks go hot. She told Jonah when it happened—not in excruciating detail, she couldn't bring herself to. But about how Nia had tried to talk to her about Toni, and how badly she messed up. She told him about the apology, too. And the length of time it took for it to be accepted.

When she still hasn't responded, he says, "It just feels like there's a lot going on there that maybe hasn't been sorted through but probably should've been before we got here."

She closes her eyes slowly. He's right, she knows he's right. But she's hungover and exhausted and she can't quite find the words.

"Jade," he says. "I know how . . . important she is to you. I just think that you need to think carefully about that, and then talk things through."

"I will," she says and swallows. "It just might have to be after the trip. This whole thing is hard enough."

"I think you're making it harder."

Jade narrows her eyes. "Wow, thanks."

He sucks his teeth, expression souring. "I'm not going to tell you what to do. It's not like you'd listen," he mutters.

She draws in a breath, pressing her head again to the window. "I heard you," she says softly. The look on his face doesn't budge.

The cabbie pulls into the lot of the auto shop, jerking the car into park without breaking her conversation. Even as Jade taps her card on the reader and Jonah hands over a tip in cash, all they get is a parting nod.

They traverse the gravel lot toward the waiting area, and Jade prays that nothing sharp enough to puncture a tire is hidden between the rocks. The sun beats on their backs, and sweat gathers under Jade's armpits and at the nape of her neck. It took over forty-five minutes for the cab to even get to them. This shop was completely out of their way, so it's probably another hour and a half to get to Savannah. She doesn't want to check her phone for the time, but if she had to guess, she'd say they were supposed to be on the architecture tour right about now.

The blast of cool air she anticipates when Jonah swings open the shop door doesn't come. Shaded from the sun, inside is a few degrees cooler but twice as stifling. The relief Jade feels when her eyes land on Nia and she realizes that she's already signing something at the register is immeasurable.

Luna notices Jade and Jonah before Nia does, and she dashes toward them, tangling her leash around Nia's legs.

"Luna," Jonah says, rushing to unhook her so that Nia can extract herself. He scoops her up, hugging her toward his chest, and then proceeds to hold her at arm's length to avoid getting licked.

Nia looks drained, her cheeks flushed in a way that suggests she's overheating. Jade has no idea what to say to her. Not a first on this trip, and yet the feeling is still paralytically foreign. She stares blankly, swallows, then essentially vomits out: "Let us know how much to Venmo you."

At the exact same time, Nia says, "We missed the architecture tour."

"Oh," Jade says.

"Did Luna get a chance to pee?"

Nia nods. "Yeah, I walked her while they changed the tire. They said we were lucky there wasn't worse damage with how badly it was shredded. And that they had the right one on hand."

Jade nods along, even though she feels the furthest thing from lucky right now. Jonah puts Luna back on solid ground, and Nia leashes her.

"Wanna roll out?" Jonah asks.

Nia nods, then closes her eyes slowly. Her lips part with an exhale, and her forehead scrunches just barely, like she's in pain and doesn't want to show it. Jade itches to grab her hand, or better yet, to wrap her arms around her waist and press her close.

Jade stays rooted in place. "Are you okay?" she asks.

"I'm just so fucking *tired.*"

"Jonah will drive. You take Luna in the back and you can sleep." Jade waits for Nia to say something, maybe rib her about her shiny new driver's license being just for show (which, in fairness, it is). But she doesn't. She nods, and mumbles her thanks, and follows them outside.

CHAPTER FOURTEEN

sunday evening, june 29

Nia doesn't wake until they arrive in Savannah. The place she picked is a carriage house in the South Historic District with brick variations that make it seem as though repairs have been made at random, decades-wide intervals. They unload the car and approach the wide, wooden door, which is painted a sage green that almost shimmers in the late afternoon sun, and she learns that its ornate brass knob is hot to the touch.

Inside is blessedly cool, if rather dim. She beelines for the main window in the living room and thrusts opens the curtains. The sunlight that streams in is paltry due to the close proximity of the building next door, but Nia hopes it's enough to keep her pineal gland at bay.

As if to punctuate the thought, she yawns.

"I'm taking a nap," Jonah announces. He ducks his head into one bedroom, then the other, before returning to the first. "I guess the twin is mine?"

Nia sighs. She'd hardly blinked when the listing said one twin and one queen—as an American woman of *perfectly average* height, a twin bed may not be her first choice, but poses no real problem, especially considering this place's cost-to-location ratio. Jonah, on the other hand . . . "Oh, uh, you don't have to," she says.

He grimaces. "You and Jade aren't seriously gonna sleep in a twin together? I curl up, anyway."

She glances at Jade, whose face is impassive. Nia doesn't want to assume that they'll be sharing a bed tonight, and she doesn't want to assume that they won't. But with Jade standing there, saying nothing, Nia settles under the weight of knowing it probably should be the latter. And that now is when she's supposed to say something.

But as she opens her mouth, Jonah closes the bedroom door behind him.

It takes her too long to look at Jade again. She isn't nauseated, and the backseat nap cured her of her hybrid hangover-tobacco headache, but her brain feels like soup that's been thawed and refrozen too many times.

Jade offers her a small smile. Her undereyes are bruised purple again. "I'm gonna nap, too," she says.

"Okay," Nia replies, and Jade disappears into the other room.

The door clicks shut, and Nia digs out her toiletry case and slips into the bathroom. There's a sheen of sweat on her forehead, unsurprisingly, but her reflection seems considerably less haggard than it was this morning. She washes her face, then applies a bit of makeup, mostly to pass the time.

She returns to the living room and takes her seat on the couch. Luna trots over, hopping onto the cushion beside her and dropping her head to Nia's lap. She scratches behind her ear, and she swears the dog lets out a happy sigh.

There's rustling beyond the door to her and Jade's room. And maybe Jade's just settling in, but maybe she's unpacking. Something she never particularly cares to do, and would have no reason to do behind a closed door. Unless she's avoiding Nia.

Nia takes a deep breath, holds it for four counts, then exhales for seven. She repeats this process, conscious to breathe into her belly, and rests her neck on the back of the couch.

They've been on a road trip for four days now; it's normal for Jade to want time to herself, even if nothing is wrong.

Her next exhale is shaky. It's hard, to feel like this, when she can hear clearly what she'd tell a client in this situation. She was never naïve enough to wholeheartedly believe that becoming a therapist would cure all that ails her. But she'd be lying if she said some small part of her hadn't hoped that doing the work would start to feel less like, well, *work*. That's not to say that the skills she practices don't get easier. They do. Just at the same glacial pace as always.

Nia knows she would tell her client to reach for a distraction, so she does. On her phone, she toggles between the website for the tour she'd booked and Google Maps, sketching out a route in the notebook a previous guest must have forgotten, left on the side table.

If they don't go, they don't go. But it's a part of the trip Michal had been excited for when they were first planning, and it's something for Nia to do.

Jonah emerges from his room first, nodding at Nia before ducking into the bathroom. He joins her on the couch in fresh clothes and a squeaky-clean face. He tugs on the edge of the notebook, pulling it into a better angle for him to view. "Bank heist?" he asks.

"Architecture tour," she says.

"Ah. I'm down."

"Your lips are chapped," Nia remarks. He sucks his teeth

at her. "Jonah! We drank too much, and it's hot out. You need more water," she says, and shoves her bottle at him.

"I can get my own," he grumbles, pushing himself to standing.

"She's right," Jade says, and Nia tries not to snap her neck whipping toward her. She's got her Ziploc bag full of toiletries in hand and is making her way to the bathroom. She's changed, too, discarding her sweats for baggy midrise jeans and (shocker) a cropped tank top. Jade is wearing jewelry, too: small gold hoops in her ears, a chain, and a חי pendant around her neck. "You forget to drink water when you're hungover."

Jonah pouts, holding a cup under the kitchen faucet and flipping on the water. "I don't forget, it just tastes weird."

"You're letting the tequila win," Nia says.

"I maintain that it was Everclear," Jade calls as she splashes her face with water.

"I feel like I should change, too," Nia says.

"Nah, you're the only one who didn't dress like shit today," Jonah says.

"It's because Nia never wears comfy clothes outside," Jade answers, pressing moisturizer into her skin. "She's gonna say these *are* comfy clothes."

"I'm just not a sweatpants person!" Nia protests.

Jade shoots her a playful side eye. Nia's shoulders relax, and despite her breathing exercises, she feels like she exhales deeply for the first time all day. "That's not a real type of person," Jade says.

"Nia planned a new architecture tour," Jonah says. "Wanna go?"

"It'll be highly abridged and very uninformed."

Jade leans against the bathroom doorframe, pulling a few

rings out of her front pocket and slipping them on her fingers. "Perfect."

NIA'S PLAN HAS them starting by the river and looping back toward the house they're staying in, which she informs them is roughly the opposite of what the original tour was going to be. It's after 5:00, so going inside any of the museum stops is off the table, but they start at the Ships of the Sea Maritime Museum.

It's worth it, Jade thinks, when Nia tells them that the walking tour website she looked at said the architecture of the mansion itself overshadows the museum, because Jonah replies in his Senator Clay Davis voice, "Shiiiiit, good thing we're too late for the museum."

They weave their way, making progress in a general southeastern direction, though not particularly efficient in doing so. Jonah leaves Luna's leash slack, and they indulge every stop to sniff or pee.

Second on the tour is the Telfair Academy, and even if they're too late to tour the works from local and native artists, at least it has the added visual interest of sculptures decorating the lawn in front of the visibly historic but otherwise bland façade.

The buildings they view vary superficially, some candy-colored, some white-washed, some brick. Beautiful, almost exclusively built by the trafficked for their traffickers. She supposes this is what it is to experience anything still standing from this era: beauty entwined with horror.

It's fitting, then, that one of their last stops is Flannery O'Connor's childhood home. It's the same Greek Revival style as Kahal Kadosh Beth Elohim, but tall and narrow. They pore over pictures of the interior on Nia's phone, and

Jade finds herself surprised at how relatively bright and mild it all is.

"I thought it would be more . . ."

"Southern Gothic?" Nia asks.

Jade laughs. "Yeah."

They zig and zag another few blocks in the vague direction of their Airbnb, ending up in front of a two-story red-brick Italianate building. With its arched windows, wrought-iron balconies, and off-white pillars interrupted by shocks of green from palm trees and shrubbery, it might be Jade's favorite of the whole tour.

"The Mercer House," Nia reads from her notes app, "is most notorious for being the location of the events of the bestselling book *Midnight in the Garden of Good and Evil.* Preservationist Jim Williams purchased the main building and carriage house to live in, renovate, and run his antiques business. He had a secret lover: Danny Hansford, his twenty-one-year-old assistant. Allegedly, Danny pulled a gun on Jim and Jim shot him in self-defense. Williams was acquitted, but he died of pneumonia not long after his last trial, in the same spot where he'd shot Hansford, so some people believe that Danny had been haunting him to exact his revenge." She looks up, raising her eyebrows. "Spooky," she whispers, and Jade and Jonah laugh.

It's a little kitschy and a lot morbid, two of Michal's absolute favorite things. Jade's throat feels tight, her eyes prickling. It's the tail end of golden hour now, but even without the sun directly overhead, the heat clings to the humidity in the air, and the sensation is almost overwhelming. She focuses on that solely, not really listening to whatever Nia and Jonah are saying as they stroll their way toward Forsyth Park. Not saying what she's thinking, like maybe if she says the words aloud the pain will be sharper.

It's as beautiful as the pictures Jade's seen, maybe even more so at this time of day. The Spanish moss is illuminated more gold than green, dripping from the branches of sprawling live oaks like honey from a dipper.

They stop in front of the fountain, and Jade takes a deep breath and releases, "Michal would've loved this tour." The sharpness she expected is missing; it has more of a balm-on-burn effect. Not a fix, but relieving all the same. "Especially the last house."

There's a beat, and then Jonah transfers Luna's leash to his other hand so he can sling his arm across her shoulder. Nia follows suit, snaking hers around Jade's waist. Her hand finds bare skin. It's not damp but not dry, just barely-there perspiration that makes Nia's thumb stutter briefly as she runs it back and forth.

Jonah lets his head drop to the side, resting it on top of Jade's. "She would've yelled at Nia for implying there was any doubt about the haunting."

"MY BAD!" Nia announces. She lays her head on Jade's shoulder. "Just in case she can hear me somewhere, you know?"

Jade inhales, nodding. And she can feel her cheeks wetting, but when she exhales, there's a laugh with it.

"I AM REMAINING NEUTRAL ON THE EXISTENCE OF GHOSTS," Nia says, near-shouting once again. There aren't a ton of people around, but they certainly aren't alone.

Even so, Jade joins her. "I AM WILLING TO SAY THAT THERE IS A POSSIBILITY."

"SORRY, MICH. NEUTRAL IS THE BEST I CAN DO."

Jonah slides his arm off Jade's shoulder, putting a few paces between them. "I DON'T KNOW THESE WOMEN."

"I SHARED A WOMB WITH HIM," Jade says.

"I'VE NEVER SEEN THEM BEFORE IN MY LIFE," Jonah insists, even though the person feeding pigeons from the bench closest to them has yet to look up.

"JONAH WILLIAMS PARDO IS A LIAR," Nia says. "HE IS HERE OF HIS OWN VOLITION AND WE ARE HIS FAVORITE PEOPLE ON EARTH."

"DON'T LISTEN TO HER. SHE IS AS DELUDED AS SHE IS SMALL."

"THEN I AM ONLY AS DELUDED AS THE AVERAGE AMERICAN WOMAN!"

Jade shakes her head, laughing as she wipes under her eyes. "I'm still not sure I buy it."

Nia throws her hands up. "Why must it always come back to this? *You* guys"—she points—"are tall. I am a normal size."

Jonah lopes back toward them, Luna in tow, everyone laughing. "Sure," he says, and then, no joke, loops his arm around her and tries to give her a noogie.

She ducks out of his embrace, crouching behind Jade, her hands on Jade's shoulders. "I'm gonna lock you out of the fucking Airbnb, Jonah."

"Hey, hey!" He raises his hands. "I surrender."

"Good," Nia says, straightening.

The weight of her hands disappears, but a moment later, she slides her arms through Jade's and links them around her middle, giving her a brief squeeze. Jade leans back into her, feeling the side of Nia's face press against her shoulder, and thinks about turning around to pull her into a real hug. But before she can act on it, Nia's hands are gone.

"C'mon," Nia says. "We should probably find something to eat."

CHAPTER FIFTEEN

january, three years ago

Jade washed her hands in a Disneyland bathroom, feeling an intense wave of embarrassment when faced with the reality of her reflection. The outfits were a stretch for her already, and now, for the first time that day, she was without Michal and Nia. Any onlooker would have no reason to believe that the words ONE LAST RIDE screen-printed in burnt orange above a winking pin-up cowgirl weren't an earnest fashion choice.

The back said SAVE A HORSE, RIDE SPLASH MOUNTAIN, which made absolutely no sense. But Michal found it hysterical (and maybe Jade and Nia did, too, for the sheer nonsense of it) and it was *her* bucket list.

She adjusted her Minnie Mouse ears, which had been sliding around her head all morning. The ears had seemed a better idea than the shirts when Nia made a beeline for a stand maybe fifty feet into the park's entrance that morning, but Jade hadn't considered that they weren't really designed for someone with next to no hair. But even in high-waisted, quite short denim cutoffs and sparkly cowboy boots, her reflection still managed to look capital-Q Queer, so she couldn't complain about her (lack of) hair too much. That, and the thigh tattoos.

Jade exited the bathroom, blinking as her eyes adjusted to the light. She withdrew her phone from her back pocket (the front ones on these shorts could fit *maybe* a single Chap-Stick, and she had no clue how Nia and Michal put up with clothing like this in their daily lives). Nothing from Toni, still. She hadn't texted or called since she liked the message Jade sent saying they'd landed at LAX. Maybe she had just been trying to give Jade space for this, which she supposed she should appreciate. But she'd rather Toni actually asked her whether she wanted the space, because she didn't. Maybe they didn't need to have an hours-long FaceTime every night, but radio silence made her feel . . . forgotten, maybe.

She knew she could text Toni and just tell her this, but she felt nervous even thinking about it. Besides, she could picture the response: *Babe, I'm trying to let you have this time with Michal. You don't know how much you have left, and it would be unfair of me to demand that much of you.* They didn't see each other almost every weekday the way they used to—trading off between movies on Jade and Jonah's couch and fucking on every available surface of Toni's one-bedroom. Jade had been busy with starting the bucket list and pulling longer days in lab with the revision deadline for her second paper coming up next month. It was good to have a girlfriend who let her prioritize her most important friendships—not that she always prioritized them over Toni. And not that Toni never had her qualms; she'd said something pretty fucked up to Jade in a fight a couple of months ago that had been hard to forget. But Jade didn't feel like she was made to count the times per week she saw Toni against the number of times she'd seen Nia and Michal, and forced to make up the difference the next week (not that she was speaking from experience [it took her three whole months of that to break up with Anabelle. Embarrassing]). It's just that she had begun to feel like Toni was pulling away.

It was probably all in her head.

She pocketed her phone, spying Michal and Nia near the Matterhorn line entrance.

"What's wrong?" Nia asked as Jade approached. She was clearly between licks of her chocolate-vanilla swirl soft serve; white cream decorated the seam of her lips.

"Nothing," Jade replied.

Michal wrapped one of her arms around Jade's waist. "Why the long face?" She pouted. "Is someone dying?"

Jade snorted. Nia groaned. They both rolled their eyes.

"I'm allowed to say that!" Michal insisted, all but stamping her foot.

"Mich." Nia paused to lick a dribble of ice cream melt that had trickled all the way down to her wrist, and Jade shifted her weight. "You're *allowed* to make that joke. But you make it, like, once every two hours."

Michal flicked her hair over her shoulder. It just barely reached her clavicles, and it was much curlier than before. Jade felt a little swell of joy at the gesture—she remembered so clearly how the first time Michal went through chemo, she'd insisted she had made peace with the hair loss, even though it had been her favorite feature. Then one day, she instinctively went to put her hair in a ponytail, and had a full breakdown in Brooklyn's Central Library. Jade and Nia skipped the rest of their classes to go retrieve her from the bathroom stall she'd locked herself in. "Okay, fine," she said. "I will work on a new bit. Or at least adapting the bit in a different way, so as not to lose the interest of my most valued audience members."

Jade shook her head, laughing. "You are the most."

She nuzzled into Jade's neck. "Aww, love you, too, J. You're good, though? Did Toni say something that upset you?"

"Why—no, she didn't. And seriously, I'm good. Or as good as I can be, given that *someone* is dying," she said and looked pointedly at Michal.

"Who?" Nia asked, her face the perfect picture of shocked.

Jade and Michal's laughter started slowly, but a beat passed and Nia let herself laugh, too, and then they found themselves in hysterics, doubling over (Michal and Nia), clutching at the others for support (Michal and Jade), and wiping tears from their eyes (all three of them).

Nia tossed the waffle cone wrapper into a nearby trash can, switching to her water bottle. It had four new stickers since Jade saw it last, all from Madison establishments.

"I guess we should actually get in line now?" Michal said, still half-gasping. She'd been able to laugh herself out of breath her entire life, but it happened more readily now with the metastases (*plural*) in her lungs.

Jade cleared her throat. "Our forty-five-minute wait awaits."

"How is it always a forty-five-minute wait?" Nia scowled. "I researched it, and we're here on the least busy days of the least busy week of the season."

"I think it's probably usually worse," Jade said.

The corners of Nia's lips stayed downturned. Michal and Jade exchanged a look; they both could hear Nia's thoughts as easily as if they were spoken into a bullhorn: *I wanted this to be perfect.*

"I am having a *fabulous* time," Michal declared. "And I would love it if we got in line under those fans and misters. How is it this hot in January?" she asked, already rounding the wooden rails, Jade and Nia at her heels.

"California," Jade said.

"I love the sun, though," Nia said. "And at least the heat is dry. We actually get that evaporative cooling." She leaned toward the fan, closing her eyes as the sprayer below it coated her in tiny water droplets. It made her skin, which was already browner than it'd been yesterday, seem to sparkle in the light.

"Evaporative cooling, in casual conversation?" Jade teased.

Michal clapped her hands, then gripped onto Jade's upper arm, leaning toward her ear. "I love it when Dr. Chin talks dirty to us," she stage-whispered.

Nia side-eyed her, still fully facing the fan. "On the East Coast, these things would just make us wet, not cool. Don't say it, Michal"—Jade could hear Michal's mouth clamp shut beside her—"and besides, Jade's doing her PhD, too."

"Yeah, but she's not as much of a nerd."

"She's doing neurobiology!" Nia protested, fully turning toward them this time.

"I'm not sure I even like it anymore," Jade said.

Michal rubbed her arm, and Nia tilted her head sympathetically. "I think that's probably just the paper revisions."

"Or the diversity committee," Nia said.

"Both," Jade said. *Neither,* she thought. *I don't like any of it anymore.* "At least the paper will be done in a couple months."

"In time for our most glorious trip." Michal waggled her eyebrows.

"I can't tell if you're talking about shrooms or the road trip," Jade said.

Michal pressed her hands into her cheeks, grinning. "Both."

"I think I might have to pee," Nia said.

"Oh my *God,* why didn't you just go with Jade?"

"I didn't have to pee then?" Nia said.

"Is that a question?" Jade asked.

"I thought Mich would be less mad if it was?"

"Is *that* a question?" Michal asked. Nia pouted, looking up at her with her very best puppy dog eyes. "Go, obviously. But you gotta hurry because if the line gets too much longer, you're gonna get shivved by a Disney adult."

Nia made prayer hands in front of her face, bowing her head before running off.

"I think *we* count as Disney adults," Jade said.

Michal clutched her chest, the word Last disappearing under her hand. "Us? *Moi?* What makes you say such a thing? Is it the matching-themed crop tops and animal ears?"

Jade laughed. "It's the sparkly cowboy boots."

"That just makes us sexy, not Disney adults."

"I don't think I've dressed this femme since middle school."

Michal dropped her hand, biting her bottom lip. "Are you uncomfortable?" she asked softly.

Jade nudged her with her hip. "Surprisingly, no."

"Good." Michal's grin split across her face, and Jade tried to memorize it: Michal in this silly baby tee, with her dark curls swallowing the band of her Minnie Mouse ears, rocking back and forth on those heeled boots, smiling. "Because your ass looks *fantastic* in those shorts. And, don't worry, you still look very gay."

Jade grinned right back. "I wasn't worried."

"Do you want me to snap a picture for Toni?"

Jade shook her head. "No, I'll send her one of the three of us later. Or maybe show her when we get back."

Michal gave her a long look. "You're happy? With Toni?"

"Yeah," Jade said. "I am. And . . ."

"And what?"

"And I'm happy that you know her."

"I don't know if that on its own is a good enough reason to be with someone," Michal said, her words careful.

Jade nodded, and they both shuffled forward with the motion of the line. "I know that. It's just . . . I don't know. It brings me peace to know that you know who I end up with. Doesn't it bring you a little bit of peace?"

Michal linked her arm through Jade's, letting her head drop to her shoulder. "Yeah, I guess it does," she said.

NIA DIDN'T GET shivved on her way back from the bathroom. Nor did Michal when she left and returned to the line at the Haunted Mansion for the very same reason, much to Nia and Jade's delight. They were still laughing about it when they got into the parlor room that doubled as an elevator down to the ride, and they were shushed by an elementary schooler.

"Can I tell this kid that I have cancer and I got it from shushing?" Michal whispered.

"Absolutely not," Nia and Jade whispered back.

"I wasn't *going* to," she said, although they all knew she would have at the slightest encouragement.

They went to Splash Mountain next, strategically timed at the heat of the day so that they'd dry off the quickest. Michal and Jade could make fun of her all they wanted, but at the end of the day, they appreciated her attention to detail.

The line crept forward, and the returning logs came into view for the first time.

"Holy shit, those people are soaked," Jade said. "I don't remember getting that wet the last time I was here. Don't say it, Michal."

"First, it's no 'I'm dying' jokes, then it's no clever riffing on accidental innuendo?" Michal huffed. "Tough crowd."

"Clever riffing?" Nia laughed. "You were just going to say 'that's what she said!'"

"You don't know what I was going to say. And now you never will."

"The people getting off that length of wood look much less wet," Jade said.

Michal groaned, throwing her hands up. "Okay, you *have* to be doing that on purpose."

"I don't hear it," Jade said, but the twitch of her lips as she tried to keep from smiling gave her away.

"I have a secret," Michal said.

"Please don't say you're dying," Nia replied.

Michal glared. "I've stopped. For today. Anyway, there are children around, so lean in." Nia and Jade did as told, and Michal wrapped her arms around both their waists. "I snuck some gummies in," she whispered.

Nia furrowed her brow, confused. "I'm the only one who brought a bag."

"They're in my bra."

"They better be the individually wrapped kind," Jade said.

"Why, you don't want to taste my boob sweat?" She pouted.

Nia laughed. "Let's leave that to Jonah."

"I am truly *so* okay with him being your boyfriend, but please don't say stuff like this in front of me."

"Nia's the one who said it!" Michal complained, and Nia laughed again.

"I don't care who said it, I need the line to be drawn somewhere, preferably on the other side of me picturing my *twin brother's* mouth on your tits."

"Nobody said you had to picture it," Michal said.

"I hate you guys," Jade said.

"We'll stop," Nia said. "Promise." She elbowed Michal in her side.

"What?" she asked, and Nia shot her a flat look. "Okay, yes, I promise to keep the sex-with-Jonah jokes to a minimum. Even if this one was *Nia's* fault."

"Thank you," Jade said.

"I thought you were abolitionists, but you won't stop policing my jokes!" They both groaned. "*See?* Anyway, they're individually wrapped, but don't act like you wouldn't take them if they weren't. Both of you have had much worse in your mouths, and if we take them now, we'll probably be peaking around the fireworks show."

Nia and Jade formed a shield around Michal so that she could dig them out, and then they did their best to eat them discreetly (which proved difficult given that they'd melted entirely into their packaging, but Nia told herself that as far as anybody else knew, they could be eating any candy, and probably nobody cared anyway) before they climbed into one of the log floats.

Because there were three of them, Jade ended up in the very front seat on her own. And their length of wood ended up getting them as wet as possible, Jade bearing the brunt of it.

They scurried off down the exit hallway, the edibles just starting to hit. Michal skidded to a stop in front of the screens displaying the pictures snapped during the largest drop of the ride, and Nia and Jade practically slammed into her.

"A little warning would be nice," Nia said.

"Look at us!" Michal pointed, and they did. All their eyes were squeezed shut, mouths hanging open in identical squeals of delight. Michal's arms were in the air above her head, Jade's hands were on either side of her headband, carefully holding it in place, and (unsurprisingly) Nia was white-knuckling the safety bar in front of her.

"Should we buy it?" Jade asked.

Michal shook her head. "Let's just get a picture with it."

They crouched around the screen, and Michal handed her phone off to Jade, whose lanky arms long ago designated her the group selfie taker. It was dim enough in this little enclave to trigger the automatic flash, and the picture they ended up with featured the three of them in various stages of blinking, glare reflecting off the sweat and water on the high points of their faces and columns of their necks.

And, perhaps most notably, Jade's nipples: highly visible, dark brown, and standing at attention on either side of the pinup girl's enormous cowboy hat.

"Oh my *God*," Michal said, and Nia clamped her hand over her mouth, unsuccessfully trying to keep from laughing.

Jade groaned. "White shirts were a *terrible* idea."

"Some of us wear bras," Michal said.

"*Some* of us have A cups and don't see the point of putting them in a metal cage. It's not like they need any support."

"Well . . ." Michal sighed wistfully, staring almost longingly at Jade's chest, "they do sit so pretty."

Nia looked, too. The wet cotton clung to Jade's skin, stretching over the swells of her breasts, the creases between them disappearing and reappearing with every breath in and out. She swallowed thickly. "Yeah," she said, looking away. "I think other people want to look at their pictures, we should get out of here."

"Is it better in the sun?" Jade asked once outside.

"I think it's worse, actually," Michal said, and Nia grimaced sympathetically.

Jade crossed her arms, obscuring her chest. "Fuck, okay. I'm gonna go try to dry this off in the bathroom," she said and slipped away, leaving them under a tree for shade.

"Nia." Michal paused, then inhaled, and Nia felt her stomach drop. "Babe—"

"I feel like I should be scared," Nia said. "Should I be?"

"Maybe? But I'm going to say it anyway." She grabbed Nia's hand, threading their fingers together. Michal was taller than her—not as much as Jade, but enough that she usually noticed. But she sat back against the short wall around the tree so that she had to tilt her head to look up at her. Probably to seem less threatening. With her free hand, she tucked a loose curl that had fallen in front of her face behind her ear, and took another deep breath. "You need to tell her."

Nia shifted on her heels, holding Michal's gaze. "Tell her what, exactly?"

"You need to tell Jade that you're in love with her, Nia."

"I'm not in love with her," Nia said quietly. She tried to drop Michal's hand, but Michal only tightened her grip.

"Let's not do that." Michal's voice was gentle, but it stung.

"She's in a relationship, Mich."

Michal pushed a laugh through her nose. "Toni? You can see the cartoon storm cloud forming above Jade every time she texts her. Or *doesn't* text her. You think that relationship is gonna survive my death?"

"You're not a part of their relationship, and you can't fully know what goes on between them. If Toni is who she wants, that's who she should be with," Nia argued.

"I don't think she'd want Toni if she knew you were an option."

"You don't *know* that! What if I said something to her, and it ruined everything?"

"What if it didn't ruin everything?" Michal asked, insistent.

Nia wrenched her hand away. "This"—she pointed toward the bathroom, then back at herself—"is the relationship that has to survive your death. Me and Jade. You'll be gone, and if I don't have her anymore, *I* won't survive it. You can't . . ."

She glanced upward, blinking away the tears that threatened to fall. "You can't encourage me to risk losing that."

Michal reached forward, hooking her thumb through one of Nia's belt loops. "I'm not trying to meddle." She took in Nia's sharp look, then amended: "Okay, I am trying to meddle. But it's because I want you guys to be happy! Desperately. I've been sick for a while now, and I've sat with Dr. Sandoval suggesting we stop treatment long enough to have accepted this as much as I can. I'm soaking up what's left of my time here, and I'm worrying about the two of you."

Nia nodded, looking back at Michal, still blinking. "Not Jonah?" She laughed.

"Him, too, I guess." Michal shrugged. "It's different."

They went silent for a moment, and Michal moved her hand to the small of Nia's back, drawing her close and resting the side of her face against her stomach.

"I can't force you to do anything," Michal spoke again. "And I get it if you feel like you can't right now. But you're going to have to tell her eventually. Whether it's in six months or a year or five years from now, you're going to have to tell her."

"Maybe I'll have gotten over her by then," Nia said.

"Maybe," Michal said, like not even an ounce of her thought it was possible.

Nia linked her arms around Michal's shoulders, and they stayed like that until Jade got back.

"I did the best I could," Jade said, and they both swiveled their heads toward her.

Nia squinted. "Did you make pasties out of paper towels?"

"It was still kind of see-through when damp! I thought it would be better than getting banned for life for public indecency."

"I like the way you think, J," Michal said.

Jade looked between them, her eyes lingering at all the places they were joined. "Are you guys okay?" she asked, her expression sobering.

"I'm not sure if you've heard," Michal said, interrupting herself with a sad laugh, "but somebody is dying."

Jade wrapped herself around Nia and Michal, her spicy-earthy scent enveloping them.

They went on one more ride—the railroad roller coaster—before making it back to Main Street, U.S.A., for the fireworks. Michal was right about the weed gummies, and Nia felt the booming swell of the finale through every nerve in every limb of her body. In every nerve in every limb of Jade and Michal's bodies, too, it seemed to Nia, the way they were all pressed up against one another. She didn't know where her body ended, or *if* it ended. When a sob racked through her, she couldn't be sure it was hers, or whose hand it was wiping at the wetness on her cheeks.

"I'm so, so happy," she said, hearing the quaver in her voice, and meaning every single word.

CHAPTER SIXTEEN

monday morning, june 30

They leave Luna in a peaceful slumber on the couch. Jonah, knowing that they couldn't expect the same level of accommodation at Congregation Mickve Israel as at KKBE, took his turn as the early riser, and spent an hour doing whatever was required to keep her horizontal for the duration of the tour. Nia thought it might give her a little bit of time to talk to Jade while neither drunk nor hungover, but Jade had gotten out of bed maybe fifteen minutes after the door had swung shut behind Jonah, mumbling about finding them food and coffee.

Very clearly, she needed time. Whether it was to cool off or to collect herself for the day ahead, Nia wasn't sure, but she wasn't going to deny her.

Mickve Israel turns out to be directly opposite the Mercer House, only separated by the trees of Monterey Square. Yesterday, it looked to Nia more like a cathedral than anything else, and she hadn't registered the possibility that it'd be part of her trip. The tawny building is adorned with ogival arched windows, and the street in front of it is lined with palm trees. Gothic tropic, she supposes. They push into the foyer, and find another handful of people waiting around, presumably for the tour.

Instinctively, Nia reaches for Jade's hand. It remains still in her grip, long enough for her body to flush with embarrassment, but just as she moves to snatch it back, Jade shifts and threads her fingers through Nia's. Warm fingers. *Long* fingers.

And maybe it's just the vestigial Catholicism, but it has to be sinful to feel like this in a house of worship.

"I think everyone's here," the older man leaning on the opposite wall says. "I'm Gil, I'll be guiding you today."

FOR MOST OF the tour, Jade is waiting for the other shoe to drop, for the guide to say something that makes her mind stutter and snag, and she's grateful for Nia's hand fitted in hers.

That moment doesn't come. Maybe it's because Gil, even with his *I smoked so much weed in the 1970s* soothingly soft voice, is no Shirley. Maybe it's because it's not a private tour. Maybe it's an accident of history—the founders arrived just before slavery was legalized in colonial Georgia, and this building they stand in was built thirty-five years after Kahal Kadosh Beth Elohim, on the other side of the Civil War.

She listens for the name Sarfati carefully, but never hears it. Which figures, she supposes, since Michal's family immigrated to Savannah in the late 1700s, a solid fifty years after the congregation was first founded.

The story of its inception sounds much like KKBE's: primarily Sephardim, descendants of or former Spanish and Portuguese crypto-Jews themselves, living in London, embarked for the American colonies and formed a congregation upon settling. The year was 1733, making Mickve Israel the third-oldest synagogue in the United States and the oldest in the American South.

Jade and Jonah make eye contact at that, and Jonah raises his eyebrows. "I'm texting Avuelo," she whispers, and Nia drops her hand.

Jonah shakes his head. "He's going to call us in an hour to tell us why that's wrong on a technicality," he whispers back.

When Jade pockets her phone again, she reaches back out for Nia.

She doesn't know why she does it. It hasn't felt like she's needed it. A quiet voice in her head tells her she shouldn't be doing it when they still haven't talked about Saturday night. A quieter voice says she shouldn't be doing it when they still haven't talked about their fight three years ago.

But Nia folds her hand around Jade's.

Gil tells them that after the Spanish invasion of St. Simons Island, most of the Jews fled, and the resultant tiny, remaining community held informal services in one of the few Ashkenazi founding families' homes. It didn't become formalized again until 1774, moving from Benjamin Sheftall's home to a chapel in his son Mordecai's house, when the Jewish population reached a critical mass once again. This fact, she guesses, will be Avuelo's technicality.

She absorbs other facts, too: Mordecai Sheftall was the highest-ranking Jewish officer in the Revolutionary war, and when captured, the British tormented him by rubbing lard on his silverware so he'd refuse to eat. Over the nineteenth century, the wave of German-Jewish immigration shifted the population to be more Ashkenazic than Sephardic, as with everywhere else. They took a bit longer to adopt Reform Judaism than other similar congregations, because despite shifting populations, they remained committed to Portuguese Sephardic traditions.

Jade is deeply aware of what it meant to be a landowner

over large swaths of this synagogue's history, and yet none
of it hollows her out quite like KKBE had. Perhaps it's self-
centeredness that protects her, then; this place is only her
history in the abstract.

After the end of the official tour, they stand in the museum,
staring at a framed letter from Thomas Jefferson, largely il-
legible due to age and quill-scribed cursive. The placard below gives them the gist: he waxed poetic about the necessity
of self-governance and religious diversity, proclaims his happiness that Jews will have their social rights in this country.
Jade laughs.

"You're familiar with his writings about Judaism?" Gil
asks.

It's a moment before Jade realizes he's talking to her. "Oh,
um, not specifically, no. I did read parts of *Notes on the State
of Virginia* in college, though, so I wouldn't expect it to be
particularly good."

Gil nods, smiling softly. "He called the Cohanim 'blood-
thirsty' and promoted the dual allegiance conspiracy, among
other things."

"Ah," Jade says, and Nia squeezes her hand.

"He was very good at beautiful prose regarding rights
he only believed in under very specific conditions," Gil says,
and then he moves on to peer over the shoulders of the other
people on the tour.

"That guy is you in forty years," Jonah says.

Nia clamps a hand over her mouth, barely stifling her
laugh.

"What is that supposed to mean?" Jade demands in a
whisper. Jonah just shrugs. "Are you saying I speak that
slowly?"

"I think he's calling you a stoner, actually," Nia says.

"I'm calling you a stoner who . . ." Jonah trails off, looking at another display case. Jade and Nia follow his gaze to a framed photograph a few spots away on the wall. On the mat board inside, the words Dedication of the Mordecai Sheftall Memorial Hall, 1902 are embossed.

The hall looks to be a much smaller version of the current add-on to the neo-Gothic building that they stared at from the sidewalk this morning. Outside it, standing in front of a small crowd, is a young pregnant woman. Her hair is done up in a Gibson Girl pompadour, wavy locks framing her face from beneath her hat. She's close enough to the camera to make out some features: big, dark eyes with outer corners that tip gently downward, a strong nose with a smooth bridge, and a barely-there smile, emphasized by her pouty lower lip.

Jade darts her gaze to the placard below the frame, scanning the list of names until it snags: Sarfati. Her breath hitches, and she hears Nia's gasp. She looks back a few words: Albert and Lillian Sarfati.

The bottom of her vision starts to blur.

She looks to Nia, and Nia bursts into tears.

She looks to Jonah, and he's already blinking and looking away, his face impassive. Heat creeps up the back of Jade's neck, like she's nearing her flashpoint and is about to flame. *Do you seriously have no response to this* claws at her vocal cords, and she has to physically swallow to force it away.

Instead, she tightens her grip on Nia's hand, fixating on Lillian's round belly. Michal decided not to freeze her eggs when she was first diagnosed—even though her doctors offered it, just in case, she hadn't wanted to compromise their trip to Jamaica or wait to start treatment. But long before that, she'd joked about how, if she ever had kids, she'd be the highest-maintenance pregnant person in the world. Earth goddess aesthetic, princess attitude.

They'll never get to find out if she was right.

NIA CURLS THE index finger of her free hand and uses the knuckle to wipe at her tears. She's not just teary, like Jade yesterday, mostly still, with fat, cinematic tears trailing down her cheeks. Nia is sobbing, only semi-quiet gasps that sound garbled as she tries to choke them back. She knows it's not pretty, and she is sure that the other stragglers who are still hanging around the museum hall must hear and see what a mess she is.

At twelve, Nia got her period for the first time in the middle of Block class. Jade hadn't gone to school with them yet, so Michal alone had followed her to the bathroom. She was embarrassed, and hormonal, and generally in terrible spirits. Michal took off her sweatshirt, rolled it into a ball, and shoved it up the front of her T-shirt. Then she stood on her tiptoes, arms stretched overhead, and in a monster voice, said, "I AM YOUR FUTURE!" Nia laughed so hard, she cried.

Imagine telling that girl that the closest she'd ever come to seeing Michal pregnant for real would be like this.

She presses the back of her hand to her mouth as another sob rips through her.

God, she can't be in here, in public right now.

"I have to, um," she says, shaking her head. "I need to go."

Jade hasn't even replied when Nia wrenches away from her, all but running toward the nearest exit. The air outside is crushingly hot and humid, and she has to blink a few times to adjust to the brightness. There's a bench in the square across from the synagogue, and she glances either way down the street before running toward it.

It's under a live oak, and though the shade doesn't provide quite the relief from the heat she's grown accustomed to on the West Coast, it provides the benefit of partial concealment. She sits down, folds her legs under herself, and drops her head to her hands. Of course, this had to be the first outing where she's forgotten her water bottle.

A few minutes (she thinks) pass while she is blessedly alone, and she manages to catch her breath, her inhales strengthening even as her exhales shake.

Jade sits down next to her on the bench. She feels, rather than sees or hears, her approach. And that's probably not strictly true; after all this time, she's unconsciously memorized the exact heft of Jade's footsteps, and just didn't register having heard them. But to Nia, it *feels* truer that she is feeling Jade's presence, rather than experiencing it any other way.

She doesn't say anything to Nia until the exhales strengthen, too.

When they do, all she says is, "This is a good bench."

Nia nods, pushing an almost-laugh through her nose. "I'm partial to the tree."

"I see them as kind of a package deal."

She looks up then, expecting to meet Jade's gaze. But she's looking ahead, focused on one of the identical trees across the way, and Nia cannot express how glad she is that she doesn't have to be the one to avoid eye contact. Jade must feel Nia's eyes on her, but she doesn't turn her head. Like maybe she can also feel her gratitude. Nia looks back down, picking at her fingernail.

"Is it okay that I'm here?"

"What?" she asks, snapping her attention back to Jade in

time to catch the column of her throat bobbing as she swallows. The freckles on her neck almost twinkle with the movement, like constellations.

"You said you needed to leave, and I couldn't really tell if you meant the building, or me"—she swallows again—"and Jonah. Or maybe this whole thing."

Nia shakes her head. "I just—I didn't want to be crying so much, in public. I felt like I was going to panic."

Jade nods, glances at her feet. "Yeah, I get that." She laughs softly. "Believe me, I get that."

"Thank you for letting me go," Nia says.

Jade turns her head to look at her, body still facing forward. Her eyes scan down Nia's face, then back up, more slowly. Nia can feel that, too.

"And thank you for coming to find me."

Jade sucks in a breath. "If you're doing it for you, that's fine. I know there's still—we should probably talk about, you know, the three years at some point. But I feel like I just need to tell you that I don't want you to run away from me *for me*. If you need to not be in public, and I'm public, I'll stay back. But if that's not it, I'll leave with you. Always."

"You're not public, Jade."

Jade's teeth sink into her cotton candy bottom lip, like she's trying to stop her smile, but it's a losing game. The corners of her eyes crinkle, and she tucks her chin toward her chest, nearly bumping her short, silver chain. "You're not public for me, either," she says, kicking at a fractured stick on the ground. "I don't think you ever could be."

CHAPTER SEVENTEEN

monday afternoon, june 30

Jonah meets them at Savannah College of Art and Design's art museum, having gone back to walk Luna while Jade took off in search of Nia. He looks fine—chipper, even—as he weaves through various modern sculptures to reach them. And though Jade and Nia have put themselves back together enough to fool any casual onlooker, they're certainly not *chipper*.

"What's up?" he says as he approaches, and Jade bristles.

Neither Nia nor Jade answer directly. "Luna okay?" Nia asks.

"Yeah. PTFO. We met another puppy at the park. Left her a chew stick to keep her occupied for a while after she wakes up."

Jade nods at him, reminding herself what Nia said on Friday—*he's just processing, J.* "Thanks for taking her."

He nods back, and Jade can tell he doesn't even realize that she's been feeling any type of way about his reaction to the picture. Which, of course, makes her feel like a petulant child for caring. "Yeah," he says. "They got food here?"

They get sandwiches, iced matcha (Nia and Jonah), and

iced coffee (Jade) at the TAD Café before heading first to the temporary exhibitions. It's always been one of Jade's things—even if realistically she doesn't plan to return, she always wants to see the limited-edition pieces first, because the permanent halls will always be there. Nia and Jonah know this, and let her lead the way without argument. Not surprising on Nia's part, but Jonah has been known to put up a fight, particularly on vacation. She's thankful he doesn't today, because in the fragile mood she's in, she's not sure she could handle it maturely.

They're standing in front of a photograph of a colorfully dressed hijab-wearing woman, a Chanel storefront in the background, when Jade's phone buzzes. She'd taken it off silent after texting her grandfather, and when she checks the screen, it's his contact picture: a truly terrible, low-angled selfie he'd taken with her and Jonah when he got his first smartphone.

"Avuelo?" she answers.

"It doesn't count if it was just in some schmuck's living room," he shouts through the receiver. "That's not a real congregation!"

"Avuelo, slow down, Jonah and Nia are here, let me put you on speaker."

Jade presses the button and holds the phone out in the space between them.

"Can they hear me now?"

"Hi, Avuelo," Jonah says.

"Hi, Mr. Pardo," Nia echoes.

"Nia! Now that's someone I haven't heard from in a while. Are you still in school? And, please, it's Ted"—Jade and Jonah mouth his next words along with him—"none of that tea-with-the-queen shit."

Nia muffles her laugh in her hand. "Just about done now. A couple months left in my intern year and then it's official."

"Well, that's something!" he says.

"Thanks, Ted."

"Anyway, so I was just telling Jade. I went on their web-site, and they're trying to claim 1733, when they say *in plain language* that there wasn't a real synagogue from 1742 to 1774. On their own website!"

"Avuelo," Jade cuts in. "I think maybe they're trying to count it as a congregation, not only as a physical building."

"It was in some guy's basement!"

"You just said it was the living room."

"Forget about it," he says, and Jade can practically see the swatting motion of his hand.

"Do you know why they fled, Avuelo?" Jonah asks, and Avuelo doesn't cut in during the pause he offers, which means no. "They were afraid the Spanish were going to invade. It was still the Inquisition."

Avuelo sighs loudly. "Well, that's terrible. But even if it's for a terrible reason, I'm telling you, KKBE is the oldest syn-agogue in the South. The year 1749 came before 1774, last I checked. I have my poker buddies over here for scotch and cigars every Friday, all Jewish, and you don't see me claiming a twenty-year congregation, okay?"

The three of them are shaking with silent laughter by this point, and it takes every ounce of Jade's available effort to say, "Okay, Avuelo," in an even tone.

"So, why are you in Savannah again?"

"Oh, um . . ." Jonah says.

"Michal's family," Jade answers. "They were part of the 1774 crowd, from our understanding."

There's a long beat of silence, followed by an uncharac-teristically soft exhale. "Oh, that must be so difficult. I'm so sorry, Jonah," he says, and then he falls silent.

It's a minute before Jade feels her throat tighten, the backs of her eyes prickling yet again. Like maybe she can't quite believe that she heard right, or if she did, he'll backtrack and correct himself. But he doesn't.

And all Jonah says is, "Yeah, thank you."

Forget crying, Jade could *scream*.

She can feel Nia's eyes on her as they exchange goodbyes. Avuelo offers an "I love you," this time to them both, and Jade manages to mumble hers in return.

When she hangs up, and not even a moment later, she grits out, "Oh my *fucking* God."

Nia's hand finds Jade's shoulder, her thumb rubbing gently along her clavicle. Jade sways toward her touch.

"Are you upset?" Jonah asks.

Nia pulls a face. "*Jonah*," she warns.

"I'm sorry." Jade laughs humorlessly. "Am I *upset*? 'Yeah, thank you,'" she mimics, her tone as cruel as his felt.

He does a half shrug, turning his face away from her. "I was her boyfriend, and Avuelo's a different generation, Jade. It's not out-of-bounds that he'd say something to me first."

"First?" She seethes, her hands trembling. "You're the only one he said anything to. And you heard that, and in front of me and Nia, you still said 'yeah, thank you.'" He's still not looking at her, his gaze traveling from the photograph to his shoes. "Avuelo knew Michal for twenty years. The Sarfatis did Seder with us because of me, Jonah. She was over all the time because of me. When she stayed with us when Avuela was sick, that was because of me! You dated her for *nine months*, at the very end of her life."

Jonah's eyes cut to Jade, his brow lowering. "I knew her before that."

"Yeah," she says and laughs again. The sound is sharp, low. "Because of *me*. And he can't spare me an 'and Jade'? Can't say something to Nia? And you listen to that, and thank him, and say nothing else." She sucks in rapid breaths. Her chest heaves. Jonah stares at her, his face as blank as it was this morning. Whatever rope she was holding herself back with snaps. "Lillian was the spitting fucking image of Michal," she says, her voice cracking. "And it had absolutely no effect on you. You saw what it did to Nia and me. And you think *you're* the one deserving of condolences?"

Nia's hand falls away from her shoulder; with it, her jaw falls open. Dimly, Jade's aware that this means she should be burning with shame at what she just said, and she probably will later. But right now, every fiber of her being pulses with anger, and her heartbeat thunders in her ears, and she can't bring herself to feel anything else.

"I'm gonna go walk Luna," she says, and turns on her heels to leave.

Nia watches Jade push through the doors of the museum, not ready to look at Jonah. If he says one wrong thing, she thinks she might scream at him, and she doesn't want to salt his wounds. Or rather, she knows she *shouldn't* salt them.

"Can you believe—"

"*Jonah,*" she says through her teeth, blinking slowly. "I am trying not to lose it right now."

"Et tu, Brutus?"

Nia turns to face him, narrowing her eyes. "Oh, you thought I'd be on your side in this?"

His exhale is quick and loud, like she's knocked the wind out of him. "But, she—"

"Yes, I heard you *and* Jade—" She takes a deep breath. "You know what? We do not need to be doing this here," she says, and strides toward the exit without checking to see whether Jonah follows.

He catches up to her at the door, reaching out to stop it from swinging back into him.

"Come on, Nia," he says, falling in step beside her. "What she said was so fucked."

"Yeah, it was," Nia agrees. "So was what your grandfather said, and how you handled it, and your utter failure to recognize how much all of it was hurting Jade." She can feel him looking at her, but he stays quiet. "What? Nothing to say now?"

She looks up at him in time to catch his thick swallow, the way his gaze tilts skyward. "I know the three of you were, like, a unit," he says, looking back at Nia. "I was there. But I—I loved her, too."

They round the corner then, far enough away from the flow of museumgoers for Nia to stop walking and spin toward him. "I know that, Jonah," she says, her voice going tender. "But—"

"Does Jade?" Jonah interrupts.

Nia shifts away from him, stunned. Her first instinct is a pang of sympathy, but it sharpens into annoyance just as quickly. "You guys aren't *children*. You need to talk to Jade about this, not me."

Jonah sniffs, looking away. Nia folds her arms under her chest. "Yeah, that's . . . yeah," he says.

Nia tilts her head, regarding him carefully. "Are you really going to act like you don't know how your family is about you two? The 'are you upset?' . . . were you being serious?"

He scrubs his hand over his face. "I . . . no? I don't know."

"Jonah, you're not as oblivious as you pretend to be," Nia says, and it's a little biting, but not as much as it would've been a couple of minutes earlier. Before he'd hit her with *"does Jade?"* "She knows that, and I know that. If you want to keep pretending, do it in front of someone else."

"You're mad at me, too," he says.

Nia raises her eyebrows. "Are you holding for applause?"

He laughs, and it's genuine. A full Jonah Pardo Grin follows. "Fuck. Nia, I'm sorry. I am. Jade's been pissed at me all day and I wasn't . . . it doesn't matter. Avuelo was being a dick to you, too. You knew her longest of anyone."

She tightens her arms around herself, letting out her breath slowly as she releases them to her sides. "Thank you," she says. A quick glance at her phone tells her they've still got time—she'd budgeted three hours for the museum, and they'd only been there for twenty minutes when Ted called. Jade probably needs as much of it as she can get to cool off. "Want to walk to the waterfront?"

"Sure," he says, and they start moving again. Jonah laughs to himself.

"What?" Nia says, trying her best not to sound snappish.

"Holding for applause? Funny as shit. I missed you," he says, and slings his arm across Nia's shoulders.

It's entirely too hot, but she leans into him a little, her heart squeezing. "Missed you, too, Two."

"Whatever it was with Jade—" Nia opens her mouth to speak, but he shakes his head. "I don't need an explanation. Not my business. But whatever it was, can you try not to let it go three years again?"

Nia flushes from her navel to her nose with guilt. "I mean, she and I texted a bit—I know. I know." She looks down, and Jonah drops his arm away from her. "I won't let it go three years," she says. "I don't think I could take it."

A moment passes, and Jonah says, "You could text me, too, you know."

Her attention snaps up to him, and he's looking at her with this bashful, almost sheepish smile. She's seen it on him only once before, a lifetime ago. Nia's stomach churns: déjà vu folding into more guilt. Because, yeah, of course she could have. It's not like she didn't have his number. And though it's different than with Michal, and certainly different than with Jade, she loves Jonah deeply. Even if she hadn't before Michal died, she would now. And though he's not going to volunteer it, because she's not dying in the immediate future and he's, well, Jonah, she knows he loves her deeply, too. "Yeah?" she asks, because she can't think of anything else to say.

"Yeah, Nia. Hit me whenever."

"Okay," she says firmly. "I will."

They reach River Street, crossing over cobblestones and streetcar tracks to get to the sidewalk closest to the water. The angle of the sun makes it almost blinding to look at, so they spend most of their time staring at the shops and restaurants designed to draw tourists like them in. It's charming and exceptionally On Theme, down to the monstrous, mostly white riverboat with red capital letters declaring it *Georgia Queen*. A small part of her regrets booking only one night in Savannah—they could've explored more of the Historic District, or gone to a Savannah Bananas game (she strongly considered pushing for this based on their TikTok account alone, but considering she'd be the only one interested in baseball butts and none of them give a shit about the actual sport, she nixed it early on).

A bigger part of her looks back on the events of the day and counts her lucky stars. Savannah was always going to be the most Michal's. Better not to torture themselves longer than they needed to.

"Are you in therapy?" Nia blurts.

Jonah laughs. "Today was that bad?"

"No—well, yes. But I mean, more generally. I asked Jade how you were a few times, and usually the answer was vague and noncommittal. Though once, she said, and I quote, 'It sounds like he and whoever is in his room are fantastic right now.'"

He hums. "Jade was slut-shaming me?"

"Slut-*congratulating,* definitely." She pauses. "Seriously, Jonah. Are you talking to someone? A professional, I mean."

"I did a few sessions a couple of years ago," he answers quietly.

"None since?" He shakes his head. "I know it can be really hard to find someone you like. It's a lot of trial and error. But, Jonah, you *really* should."

Jonah shrugs. "I can talk to Jade. She actually knew her."

"You can." Nia pins him with a severe look. "But you don't. The last couple of hours have made that blatantly obvious. And even if you did, you still should go to therapy. You need to do some of this without one another."

He regards her for a long moment. "Okay."

"You'll start looking when you get back to Brooklyn?"

"Yeah, okay."

"And," she says, "you could text me, too, you know."

He chuckles softly, shaking his head. "Fair enough."

Yeah, Jonah, Nia thinks, *I love you, too.*

CHAPTER EIGHTEEN

monday evening, june 30

Jade is sitting on the couch, not reading her Ashe Cayne novel, when she hears the beeping of the keypad and the sound of the lock sliding open. Without thinking, she jumps to her feet, dropping the paperback onto the cushion behind her. It bounces into Luna's paw, and she only stirs enough to tuck it under herself. She hadn't needed another walk, which Jade knew. But after a while, she got restless enough to try for one, and Luna happily trotted along, sniffing to her heart's content. Which, according to Toni, has always been what tires dogs out the most—that mental stimulation. So she's been sleeping like a rock for the last half hour, while Jade sits on pins and needles.

Nia comes through the door first. She's looking back at Jonah, who's still out of eyesight, the corners of her eyes crinkled, her mouth open in laughter. Jade takes a deep breath, ready to deliver the speech she'd practiced in her head: apologize for her behavior, for putting her on the spot like that, and asking for a moment alone with Jonah. But Nia silences her with a small smile and a shake of her head. "I need to pack up my things. With headphones in," she says, holding eye contact with Jade.

Thank you, Jade mouths, and then Jonah comes into view. "Hey," she says. He nods in reply. Nia slips past her, the door to the bedroom clicking shut. Another deep breath. "I didn't—that wasn't . . ." She trails off. "What I said wasn't fair to you. I was mad at Avuelo, not you. Or I should have been mad at Avuelo, not you. And I'm sorry."

Jonah toes the door shut, and Jade startles at the noise. "Thanks," he says.

They stand there, just looking at one another, for several seconds. Jade prepares herself for the possibility that this will be the entire extent of the conversation. Which is always a risk when you're apologizing—that no matter how much you want one, *deserve* one in return, it might not come. Most of the time, with Jonah, that risk feels greater than the potential payoff. But she needs this trip, because Michal wanted it to happen this year. Because Nia's here, and it can't be over before she's sure they'll see each other again, and soon. Maybe she and Jonah can't have it out the way they need to right now, and maybe he's not capable of doing it or willing to do it at all. If that's the case, she'll lick her wounds and tape herself together, at least until they're on a flight back to New York in two days.

But he sits down on the couch, reaches down to scratch behind Luna's ears, and says, "No, you should've been mad at me, too," still looking at the dog.

"Oh?"

He looks up at Jade, his brows drawing toward one another, his eyes focused on her, cheeks slack. *Earnest.* Her heart cracks when she realizes how long it's been since she's seen this look on him. "Yeah. I should've said something, but I didn't. And when the moment passed, I could've said something to you, or, I don't know . . ." He shakes his head, looking away. "I didn't have to act like I *agreed* with him, that I was the only person worth saying that to."

Jade nods. "Thank you."

"You didn't have to say nine months, though."

She nods again, more vigorously. "I know. I'm sorry."

"I could've said something," he reiterates.

"I know," she says again.

"I'm sorry," he says.

He's still looking at her like that, and she feels overwhelmed with it, this space between them. That's what it is. They've been in the same nine-hundred-square-foot apartment for the past three years, and if you'd asked her on Wednesday what their issue was, she'd have said that they were always on top of each other. Too much time together, their whole lives. But it's clear to her in this moment that despite seeing more of each other since she quit graduate school, they've never been less close than they are now.

"I want to talk more," she says. "When we get back."

Jonah nods, looking back to Luna. "Okay, yeah. We good?"

"Yeah, we're good. Let's go to Atlanta."

THEY DO NOT forget the Dramamine this time, not that Nia's sure she ever could again. She might keep it on her forever, just in case, even if she never adopts a dog as long as she lives. Jade and Jonah seem genuinely okay, if not jumping at the chance to chat with one another.

They stop at a drive-through for dinner, the same chain they'd seen advertising its over forty milkshake flavors across the Carolinas. None of them had ever even heard of it before this trip. Upon reading the menu, and discovering that two quesadillas count as a main, while one constitutes a side,

WHENEVER YOU'RE READY ❧ 185

Jade orders a tray with four chicken quesadillas. The person on the other end of the semi-broken speaker seems baffled by this choice, and there's a back-and-forth of "just quesadillas, ma'am?" and "yes, please" and "no other sides? Just the quesadillas?" and "yes, please" and "so, four quesadillas?" and "yes, please" while Jonah tries not to pee himself laughing in the backseat.

Jade rubs her hands excitedly when the person at the window hands over their plastic bag of goodies, diving in before Nia makes it back onto the highway. Jonah half stands to pull the two trays he ordered out of her hands.

"I can't see out the rearview when you do that!" Nia complains.

"It's for one second, and I'm hungry."

"Yeah, clearly," Jade says around a mouthful of quesadilla, eyeing the feast he's opening on his lap.

"You ordered four quesadillas for dinner. You can't make fun of me ever again."

Nia keeps her eyes perfectly on the road as she merges, but she can sense Jade's mouth gaping. "It was a side! A quesadilla as a side! I've never *seen* that before. I love it here," she says.

Nia's cheeks warm. "Not so eager to get back above the Mason-Dixon anymore?"

"It's a side!" she says again, laughing. "I will drawl and y'all forever for this."

"I had no idea your affections were so easily bought."

"Well," she says, then pauses to swallow her bite, "I didn't really eat lunch."

"My bad," Jonah says.

In her periphery, Nia sees Jade turning to look at him. She risks a quick glance when Jade turns back, and sees that she's smiling. Nia loosens her grip on the steering wheel. "I'm ready," she says.

"For what?"

"For you to feed me my Cajun chicken sandwich. And hush puppies. And *singular* quesadilla."

"Those things don't go together. How is that less weird than four quesadillas?" Jade demands.

"Just is," Nia and Jonah reply in unison.

"Come on," Nia says, patting Jade's thigh. "I'm hungry."

"Yes, my queen," Jade replies, and gingerly places an entire hush puppy on Nia's outstretched tongue.

Nia closes her lips around it too quickly, catching the tips of Jade's index finger and thumb as they withdraw. She freezes when they make contact, doesn't press her mouth shut, nor does she shy away. And Jade does too. *Maybe* she doesn't mean to. *Maybe* it's a total accident, but when Jade does move her hand again, she pulls downward a little bit, Nia's bottom lip curling open. It reverberates back, like it might if her lover had taken it between their teeth and then let go.

She tries not to choke on the hush puppy, consciously reminding herself to chew first, then swallow.

It's almost dark now, and she should keep her eyes on the road. That, she tells herself, is why she doesn't look at Jade.

Jonah polishes off his food and falls asleep not five minutes later, his hand still resting on (also sleeping) Luna's back every time Nia glances up in the rearview to check. It takes Jade a lot longer to eat, and longer still to feed Nia. Her fingers don't make contact with Nia's lips again, but when a bit of sauce dribbles down her chin, Jade catches it with her thumb first, then follows it with a napkin.

Nia hears a suction sound, like Jade is licking the spicy mayo that had recently been in Nia's mouth off her own skin. Nia *intently* keeps her eyes on the road this time.

Eventually, Jade falls asleep, too.

Nia hits play on the sound system, wanting to stave off the impending highway hypnosis. Jade's phone must still be connected, because eight of the eleven songs that come on before they reach Midtown are by Pop Smoke.

When she parks in front of their "cozy, pet-friendly guesthouse!" near Piedmont Park, Nia wakes Jade with a hand on her shoulder.

Jade, in turn, wakes Jonah by throwing a balled-up straw wrapper at him. Or, rather, she *tries* to wake him. But she misses, and ends up waking him with "fuck, why'd I do that!" instead.

"Nice, Jade," he says, still blinking. An impression of his seat belt streaks his left cheek. "Okay, Luna, time to pee," he coos, lifting them both out of the Kia and walking off as Nia and Jade unload.

"It's wild how paternal he is," Nia says as they walk up the driveway toward where the listing said the entrance would be. "Didn't know he had it in him."

"Luna was his idea entirely. It was actually a big fight at first. Can you believe it?"

"Uh," Nia says, and Jade laughs.

"Not the fight! That *he* was the one who wanted the dog. Code?" she asks, grabbing the lockbox.

"Fifteen twenty-one," Nia replies.

"Thanks," she says, withdrawing a key and passing it off to Nia. "And, I'm sorry. For today."

"You don't need to apologize to me. I knew what I was getting into, remember?" Nia unlocks the door, pushing inside. Cozy, as she suspected, means *small*. But their party is three people and a dog, and Jonah really wanted to be in this neighborhood because it's near some of the places where his business-school buddies like to go out, so beggars couldn't be choosers. It's nice enough, and has two bedrooms with queens, even if, by the looks of it, not much else can fit inside them.

"You're too good to me," Jade says. "I'll wash up first?"

That's not true, Nia thinks. She nods her assent and Jade disappears into the bathroom with her bag.

That's not true, she thinks again as she unpacks. And when she switches with Jade in the bathroom, going through her nighttime routine. And when she gets back to the room, the overhead light off but both nightstand lamps on, Jade in a durag reading her detective novel. And when she climbs in next to her.

"I'm not," she says.

She hears a bookmark slide into place for the second time this trip, and her stomach does a Pavlovian dip. "You're not what?" Jade asks.

"Too good to you," Nia says, looking at her. "Or even good enough. We hadn't seen each other in *years,* J. Hadn't even spoken over the phone."

Jade shakes her head. "That's on me, too, Nia."

"But," Nia says. But *what? I started the fight?* That's not really true, not the way Nia sees it. She needed to say what she did. Maybe she hadn't gone about it well, but Jade was the one who took her heart when she hadn't even known she'd been offering it and trampled it.

It was my *responsibility,* she wants to say.

Even in her head, she can hear how bad that sounds. Centering herself, infantilizing Jade.

"I think," Jade says, "that you've been worried that you couldn't reach out for real. Like maybe too much time had passed and too much had changed." She sighs. "At least, that's what it was for me. But you're—*I'm*—that's wrong. You can *always* talk to me."

"Even if it's about academia?" Nia says, sort of laughing, trying to make fun of herself.

"Especially if it's about academia," Jade replies earnestly. "I told you that the other day."

"You can talk to me, too. About whatever."

"Even if it's about Toni?" Jade asks, her voice impossibly soft, with that hint of gravel. The feel of velvet stroked against the grain.

Nia closes her eyes, sucks in a breath, and nods. It still makes her nauseous, hearing Toni's name in Jade's mouth.

"That wasn't particularly convincing," Jade says.

"You *can*," Nia insists. "I want you to. It just made me think about—"

"I know," Jade interrupts. "I don't really think about her anymore. I mean I do, but about her in the abstract, not about *her* her." She inhales, looking at the ceiling. "Like, I thought I had it figured out. Because I was with this woman for so long, who I thought I loved. I *did* love, at one point. And Michal saw me with her, saw us together. It made me feel better, to think that she knew who I'd end up with. So I tried to stay, even when I started feeling lonely in the relationship." She laughs. "Even when, well, *Cheyenne.*"

Nia places her hand, palm up, between them on the duvet. Just in case. Jade takes it without hesitation. "Sometimes," Nia says, "I feel so lonely that it hurts. Not just these last few years—these last few years especially—but before that. The first year of grad school was really bad for me. Adjusting to being away from home. You, Michal. Even Jonah." Jade lets out a quiet snort. "I didn't handle it well."

"I didn't know," Jade says.

"I didn't want you to," Nia replies. "Fuck, I didn't want anyone to. I'm just saying, I get it. Being lonely. Not that I get experiencing the Toni situation, specifically. Just that you aren't alone in your loneliness."

Jade runs her thumb along the back of Nia's hand, and Nia holds her breath, keeping as still as possible, so she can focus on that singular sensation. "Are you saying we can be lonely together?"

"I've never been lonely with you."

"Me, either," Jade says, looking down at where their hands are joined. She brings her other hand in, too, folding it so that Nia's hand disappears entirely. "Michal told me that she was happy to have known I was with Toni. At Disney. That's part of it, I think. That knowing helped her, too."

"What?" Nia sputters. She was there that trip. She was there for all of Jade and Toni's relationship. She was there to listen to Michal talk about Jade and Toni's relationship. And there is no fucking way that Michal told Jade she was *happy* that she was with Toni.

Jade's gaze meets hers. "I asked her if knowing who I was going to end up with brought her peace, and she said it did."

All Nia can bring herself to do is nod, maybe breathe out an "oh." Two things become abundantly clear.

The first: Nia is angry at Michal. Maybe furious, and she withdraws her hand before Jade can feel her vibrating with it. Because anger at the dead has nowhere to go.

The second: Nia can't pretend she isn't in love with Jade forever. She might not even last through the end of this trip.

CHAPTER NINETEEN

april, three years ago

The night began the same way every biweekly Shabbat dinner at the Williams-Pardo household had for the past six months: Michal and Jade lighting the candles and leading the blessing with their hands over their eyes, Jade and Jonah's dad insisting on the long form of Kiddush even though nobody really wanted to sit through it, and Jonah saying hamotzi and cutting into their mother's wonky but delicious challah while she and Nia sat and watched.

Michal had attended plenty of times before, but her presence hadn't been a guarantee until Michal and Jonah started dating and their parents started insisting. Jade was used to it, mostly, though she still did the occasional double take when Michal put her hand over Jonah's at dinner or he pulled her onto his lap during whatever game they played afterward.

Nia came whenever she was in town. She'd explained the situation to her advisor, and she'd only had to miss one of these dinners since January.

Toni came, too, sometimes, but a small part of Jade was relieved that she wasn't there tonight. She'd been working late a lot, trying to set up an after-hours emergency clinic at her office. And Jade had happily used those free evenings to soak up all the time with Michal and Nia (in person or over FaceTime) that she could.

They were all dispersed around the coffee table tearing up slips of paper to play Fishbowl, with the exception of Jade's mom, who got too competitive for it to be fun, and had retreated into her home office with an Octavia Butler novel she'd probably read five times already.

"Shit, I don't think we have any pens," Jonah said.

"Watch your fucking mouth," Michal said. "There are ladies present."

Jonah made a show of looking around the room, leaning over Michal's legs, which were draped across his lap. "Where?"

"You're *fudging* hilarious," Jade said dryly as she stood up from her seat. "I'll get some."

Her mom was curled on a chaise in the corner of her office, reading glasses perched perilously low on her nose. It was somewhat difficult to believe that this had ever been Jade's bedroom—now it was a veritable shrine to architecture and science fiction (business *and* pleasure).

"Yes, baby?" her mom said as she entered.

"Hey, Mom. Thought you might have some pencils in here for the game."

"Pens okay?" Jade nodded. "Top right drawer of my desk."

"Thanks," Jade said, but as soon as she opened the drawer, her mom slid her bookmark into place, clearing her throat.

"She's not doing too well, is she? The coughing seems worse."

Jade swallowed, folding her arms around herself. "Not doing too well" is generous. When the last-resort clinical trial got shut down in December, Michal's doctor had said she had ten months or so. At her checkups through March,

Dr. Sandoval had said she should be able to make it to Rosh Hashanah (Jade suspected that she'd actually said late September, but Michal had relayed the information that way to lean into the Jewish mysticism of it all). But last week, Dr. Sandoval delivered the news that the mets were growing faster than predicted, and she'd be lucky to see the end of June.

Michal insisted, despite Jade's begging, that Nia couldn't know until after her prelim next week. Jade understood the sentiment—Michal said she didn't want to pull her focus before the exam, and she'd be dead either way, so what was the difference?

The difference, Jade thought, was that Nia wouldn't have talked about the Southern Jewish history trip they'd already booked most of with such excitement. That Michal and Jade wouldn't have had to play along to the excitement knowing how soon it would be crushed.

That *Jonah* knew. If Jade were the one kept in the dark, and Jonah knew, it would've killed her when she found out.

That Jade had to know, and deal with it, without Nia.

But it was what Michal wanted.

Jade could feel her eyes prickling. She tightened her arms around herself, pressing her fingers into her ribs. "No, she's not." Jade shook her head. "She's really not, Mom," she said, her voice breaking.

Her mother's face crumpled. "I'm so sorry." She unfolded her legs and swung them over the side of the chaise, pushing herself to standing. Jade met her in the middle of the room, dipping her head onto her mom's shoulder when she wrapped her in a hug, even though she was a few inches too tall to really do that anymore. "Does Jonah know?"

Jade *um-hmm*ed, holding back her tears with everything she had.

"Are you taking care of him?"

Jade lifted her head, waiting for her to say more. When she didn't, Jade pulled back entirely. "What?"

"He's losing his partner, Jade," she said. "He needs you now more than ever."

She tried not to let it gut her. Her mom could've been asking because she didn't trust Jonah to care for himself. She could've meant that they needed each other, and it was just a poor choice of words. Still, Jade felt her throat tightening, her eyes stinging. "Have you asked him if he's taking care of me?"

Her eyebrows pulled together and her lips parted, but before she could say anything, Nia's voice came, moving toward them from the hall: "J, did you find something to write with?"

"Yeah, just getting them from the desk," Jade said, turning back to the open drawer.

Nia appeared in the doorway then. She looked from Jade to her mother, her brows raising almost imperceptibly when she looked back to Jade. "Oh! Hi, Diane." Her voice was careful, even cheery. "You sure you don't want to join us?"

Her mom laughed, settling back in with her book. "Very sure."

In the hallway, Jade and Nia made eye contact.

She could tell Nia was asking, *Are you okay?*

Jade shook her head, widening her eyes and looking back toward the room like, *I'll tell you later.*

Jonah? Nia mouthed.

Jade nodded. Then shook her head. Then shrugged.

Tell me later, Nia mouthed, and they made their way back to the living room.

* * *

MICHAL HAD A coughing fit during the third round of Fishbowl after acting out the word "circumcision" (a submission from Manny Pardo, of all people). Nia was in the seat closest to the spot they'd cleared for optimal charades, so she reached out to take her hand. She got a squeeze, but then it was dropped. She knew there wasn't much more she could do that would be accepted.

Out of the corner of her eye, she saw Jade shake her head at Jonah, who looked about ready to leap out of his seat.

"Sorry," Michal said, and the rest of the group murmured their disapproval at her apology. She dropped onto the cushion next to Jonah, resting her hand on his thigh. He tucked a curl that had fallen forward behind her ear, pressing a kiss to her temple. He wrapped his arm around her shoulders, and she nestled into him, while Manny stood up to do his turn. It was so tender, Nia almost wanted to look away. But she couldn't. She never really wanted to stop looking at Michal now. And she'd gotten better at using moments like this, when Michal's focus was elsewhere, so she wouldn't get scolded for doing the "moony-eyed you're dying" thing.

Manny started to do something that looked very much like a blow job, and left Jonah and Jade gaping at him for a full minute before figuring out that he was trying to act out "recorder."

They dissolved into laughter at his exasperation until Michal started coughing again, this time running off to the bathroom, holding up a finger to stop any of them from following her.

Nia looked at Jade first, then Jonah. Near identical devastation.

God, he *really* was in love with her.

Jonah is a better person than me, Nia thought. He'd known Michal since they were kids, so it would've been painful regardless. But they'd only started sleeping together last June, and dating in September.

Nia and Jade had *loved* her since they were kids. They didn't have a choice.

And maybe it wouldn't be quite as bad for him as it would be for them—how could it, really? He'd never been promised forever the way they had.

But it didn't have to even be *this* bad for him, and yet he marched right in, knowing how it would end.

So, yeah, he was better than her. Because she didn't think that she would have been able to do the same.

CHAPTER TWENTY

tuesday morning, july 1

Just like she had on Friday, Nia takes Luna for her walk, Jade sleeps a little longer before going off to find them food and coffee, and Jonah sleeps in entirely. They eat their breakfast sandwiches over the tiny kitchen table, then take their coffees to go. There's something comfortable about it; even though they've only done this once before, it feels like a kind of routine.

Also becoming routine: the nugget of unease in Jade's stomach. Like something could go wrong at any moment, and she knows she needs to talk to Nia, but she doesn't know how, or when. Things seem okay right now, and somehow, that's only more cause for concern.

The four of them pile into the Kia Soul and make their way downtown. They find parking between the first and last stops of the walking tour, hook Luna up to her leash, and walk the rest of the way back to Forsyth Street.

Nia squints at a free-standing sign that reads SAM NUNN ATLANTA FEDERAL CENTER. "This can't be right," she says, looking down at the address in her notes app.

Almost as soon as the sentence is out of her mouth, a tiny

woman about their age with a halo of dark ringlets calls out to them. She's standing beside the building that bookends the sparse cement courtyard of the federal building, and on their way toward her, they pass a barbershop and a Western Union before coming to a stop in front of what looks to be an abandoned fast-food restaurant. Up close, Jade can see that she's got a piercing in each nostril, blue gems the same shade as her Breman Museum T-shirt.

"Talia," she says, pointing at herself. "Nia Chin?"

"That's me," Nia says. "This is Jade and Jonah."

"And who's this?" she asks, bending down to offer her hand to Luna. She sniffs readily and nuzzles into it. Talia scratches behind her ears.

"This is Luna," Jade answers. "We figured since it's outside, we wouldn't leave her in the Airbnb."

"Oh, I'm happy to have her! Ready to get started, or do you need a minute?"

Jade looks at Jonah, and he gives her a brief head shake. Nia, standing on his other side, smiles. "Ready," she says.

"All right," Talia says. "I'm sure you read the tour description on the website, but I'll warn you, we're starting off with a tough one."

Jonah laughs, nodding. "Of course."

"We're doing a Southern Jewish history road trip. It's been . . . a lot of tough ones," Jade says.

"Where were y'all before?" Talia asks.

"Kahal Kadosh Beth Elohim in Charleston, and then Mickve Israel in Savannah," Nia says. "Atlanta's our last stop."

"Oh, are you Sephardi?" Talia asks, and something about the way she draws it out makes her sound more Southern to Jade than she had on first blush.

"They are," Nia says.

"Cool, me, too. Well, half. My dad's family is from Savannah. Anyway," she says and clears her throat, then gestures to the building behind her. "In the late-nineteenth and early twentieth centuries, this former McDonald's was the National Pencil Company, where Leo Frank worked as a factory superintendent."

Talia starts to set the scene of 1913 Atlanta, the murder of Mary Phagan and its surrounding political climate. She was a recently laid-off white Christian child laborer at the factory, and her body was discovered by Newt Lee, a Black security guard, the night after she came to collect her last payment. He immediately notified the police, who found notes left around the body that seemed a naked attempt to implicate him. They entertained him as a suspect, but as more evidence emerged, quickly doubted his involvement.

Their sights turned toward Leo Frank, who'd been perceived to behave weirdly when questioned by police. The lead detective, under immense political pressure due to poor solve rates, became convinced of Frank's guilt from the outset, and colluded with the private detective Frank had hired to prove his innocence. He pushed the theory that Frank enlisted Lee as an accomplice and then tried to frame him by planting the notes at the crime scene and a bloodied shirt in his home. The perception of Frank as a rich Jew who'd easily be able to get away with the crime created a rift between the previously mostly-assimilated Jewish community and broader white Atlanta, and news coverage fanned the growing flames of antisemitism around the case.

Jade digests this, staring at the holes and streaked grime on the wall where the McDonald's sign was once mounted. She tightens her grip on Luna's leash, wishing Nia were beside her instead.

"The case hinged on the testimony of Jim Conley, a janitor

at the pencil factory, who admitted to writing the notes and claimed Leo Frank had enlisted him to frame Newt Lee," Talia continues. "The prosecution and defense essentially tried to out-racist one another, with the prosecution adopting the 'happy darky' framing, asserting that Conley was too stupid to fabricate a story, and the defense painting him as essentially what would become the 1990s 'super predator.'"

She tells them that ultimately, despite many inconsistencies in Conley's testimony and the prosecution's case, their framing won out—or maybe the jury was prejudiced by antisemitic news coverage, or succumbed to the pressure of the "Hang the Jew" chants from the mob at the courthouse. Frank was sentenced to death, and his appeals were unsuccessful. During the appeals process, the defense uncovered more and more evidence that seemed to implicate Conley as the murderer. Conley's own lawyer, who had originally accepted his case believing his innocence, came to believe his guilt, as is now the historical consensus.

While Frank's defense team had exhausted legal remedies, Governor John Slaton read the facts of the case, and knowing that he was near the end of his term in 1915, took the political risk of commuting Frank's sentence from death to life imprisonment. *The Atlanta Constitution* began advocating for his lynching. His throat was slashed by his cellmate, who claimed to fear that a lynch mob would harm the other imprisoned men, and that his actions would buy him favor with his sentencing. While recovering, Frank was kidnapped from his cell by former and current police officers, a former governor, and well-respected white community members alike. He was driven to Marietta, where he was publicly hanged. The crowd was allowed to cut souvenirs from his clothing; like many lynchings of Black Americans, the event was photographed and sold as postcards.

"It's the only Jewish lynching on record, and while the volume of news coverage nationally temporarily slowed lynchings in the area, it led to the revival of the Ku Klux Klan at Stone Mountain," Talia says. Jade can feel Talia's gaze on the side of her face, and so she peels her own eyes away from the spot of wall that once held a McDonald's sign, which is the only thing she's managed to look at as she listens. Talia's eyes shift between the three of them, assessing. "Let's sit down. There're some benches in front of the federal center."

Jonah falls in step behind Talia first, and Jade takes a moment to move, but she does, giving a gentle tug on Luna's leash. Nia waits, watching her, and then she crosses the sidewalk so she's walking parallel to Jade. As they make their way toward the courtyard, the knuckles of her left hand brush the back of Jade's right. It's slow, how Jade reaches for her. She extends her pinkie, and it trails along the outer line of Nia's hand before their pinkies link. Secure, but not too much contact. Maybe that's all Nia's up for right now—she didn't grab her hand outright, like she did yesterday. But Nia starts to twist her palm open, keeping her pressure against Jade's pinkie constant. Jade does the same, and their hands fold into one another. Jade squeezes. Nia strokes gently with her thumb.

Then, without giving it a second thought, Jade pulls their clasped hands up to face level and presses a kiss to Nia's knuckles.

She can't regret it. Not with Talia and Jonah facing away. Not with Nia's exhale, sheer relief in a sound.

The four of them wedge onto a bench, and Talia waits for a few deep breaths before she continues. "I know it's a lot to start off with, and maybe some people would prefer to push it to the end of the tour. But you can't understand Atlanta Jewish history, or really Southern Jewry writ large, without understanding the lynching of Leo Frank." Talia sighs, rubbing her hand at the back of her neck. "It laid the pervasiveness of antisemitism in Georgia bare. Many Jews left the state. The governor who commuted Frank's sentence left the state. The Temple's rabbi at the time, David Marx, led the remaining Jewish community with the idea that assimilation to whiteness was the most important strategy. Stay quiet, conform, keep your head down, survive. He urged the community not to take a stand against segregation, urged newly immigrated Russian Jews to assimilate the way the German Jews had. It took thirty years, and the end of Marx's tenure, for the broad Atlanta Jewish community to begin organizing for racial justice."

Cars go by, pigeons pick at crumbs. Nia's hand remains folded into Jade's. On her other side, Jonah sits forward, his head hanging down, his elbows resting on his knees. Jade lifts her arm, the loop of Luna's slack leash sliding toward her elbow, and she rests her hand on Jonah's shoulder. They sit in the quiet. Maybe this is what they should've been doing the whole trip—what *she* should have been doing for Jonah.

Giving him time and grace. Giving it to herself, too.

TALIA ASSURES THEM that she's in no rush, and they take their time. Nia had her hackles up at the outset of this tour; neither of the last two history stops had gone well for the twins. For her either, she supposes, but especially for them. But Jonah doesn't argue any points, no matter how hard to hear, and Jade lets him be.

It's maybe fifteen minutes before they get up, and only then does Jade drop Nia's hand.

Or maybe Nia drops Jade's. She's not really sure. She was

worried that Jade would've been put off after she ripped her hand away so quickly last night—she'd tried to play it off by reaching for her water bottle several beats later, and a crease formed between Jade's brows. But she didn't say anything, and this morning, when Nia was off with Luna, she kept wondering if Jade would. Or if *she* should. But maybe they don't need to. Maybe there can be bumpy moments, and they can just move on, like they used to.

They meander their way toward Whitehall Street, the original home of many historic Jewish retail businesses. Like Rich's, a swanky department store that at one point was known for being kinder than other stores to African Americans, allowing them to shop in-store but barring them from trying on clothing or dining in their café. It eventually became the target of a sit-in, at which Martin Luther King Jr. was arrested. A year and a successful boycott later, Rich's desegregated, and activists reached an agreement to desegregate all downtown Atlanta lunch counters.

As Talia told them, it gets easier. And as Talia told them, they needed to understand what was done to Leo Frank to understand the rest of it. In 1947, Jacob Rothschild, the rabbi who replaced David Marx, used his pulpit to condemn segregation. He'd grown up in Philadelphia listening to the midrashim of a pro-union rabbi, and he hadn't had the survival-first ideology of his predecessor instilled in him. Many community members supported him; many feared retribution.

It did come, eventually, when the temple was bombed overnight in 1958. But unlike in 1915, there was a public condemnation of the bombing and an outpouring of support. This emboldened those who wanted to fight for racial justice, as they were no longer as fearful of losing their tenuous safety in the community.

The rest of the tour features the Southern Jewish history that Nia—and to her understanding, the twins—had grown up knowing: political allyship during the civil rights movement of the 1960s. Rabbi Rothschild hosting the celebration for Martin Luther King Jr.'s Nobel Prize, later delivering the eulogy at his memorial service in Atlanta. Images of rabbis marching in full religious garb.

Talia is kind and patient with Jonah's questions, and Jade is, too. Nia feels like they've cracked it somehow—like they've figured out how to do this trip, how to be around each other for the difficult stuff, how to give one another the space that each of them needs.

Of course, they're going home tomorrow. To opposite ends of the country.

Nia is *going* to make sure they have concrete plans to see each other again. Even if there's never a good time on this trip to talk about their fight, even if she can never bring herself to say the rest of it, she can manage this.

After the tour, they end up at Ponce City Market, eating around a hard-won table. The AC feels incredible, and everyone else in the city seemed to have the same idea. Nia takes two bites of her paneer kathi roll and blurts, "My mom is getting married in August."

"Helen's getting married?" Jade says, eyes wide.

Nia laughs. "You can say the 'again' out loud if you want," she says.

"I wasn't going to."

"Well, you probably should," Nia replies, taking another bite.

"So she fully divorced Matt?" Jade asks, and Nia nods her assent. "Wow. I really believed her when she said the separation was only temporary."

"So did Matt," Nia says.

"I thought it was Mike?" Jonah asks.

"Mike was before Matt," Nia says. "And after, actually. But they were only ever engaged. Now it's Gene."

"So Gene will be . . ."

"Fiancé number five, husband number three," Nia answers.

Jade takes another bite of noodles, quite literally chewing this over. "Are you okay?"

"Yeah. I mean, I like Gene well enough, and if I didn't, it's not like I live with Mom anymore. Or even on the same side of the Mississippi." A short laugh escapes her. "Definitely got a taste of my own medicine when my therapist reminded me to practice radical acceptance, though. Anyway, that's not why I brought it up. The wedding's August second, so I'll be in town then." She takes a deep breath, willing her nerves not to reveal themselves in her voice. What a strange thing, to feel like this when talking to Jade. "I thought that maybe I could come up early, or stay late, and we could all do something? If you're in town, and free, that—"

"I would love that," Jade says, while Jonah opens his calendar app.

"You haven't even checked," Nia points out.

"I don't leave New York very often. And I make pottery, I don't talk people through mental health crises. My schedule's pretty flexible," Jade says.

Nia doesn't love the way she says that, the sharpness of her self-deprecation, but she also doesn't want to call her on it in front of Jonah.

"Even if it wasn't," Jade continues, "I'd make the time."

The way she says *that* makes Nia's heart skip.

"August second is a Wednesday," Jonah says.

"Well, when you decide that you absolutely *must* get married within three months of your engagement, your options are limited."

Jonah whistles out a low note. "You sure you're good?"

Nia nods. "I am. Really. I know it'll be a lot the day of, but I'll get to see *y'all*, so I'm okay."

Jade smiles at her then. She's just taken a bite, so her left cheek bulges outward, and there's a bit of chili oil along her bottom lip. Her eyes are bright, the skin at the outer corners crinkled. And then she scrunches up her nose, squeezing her eyelids shut for a moment, like the thought of seeing Nia again so soon positively delights her.

Her heart doesn't just skip, it gallops.

"Leo and Sebastian found a club for tonight," Jonah says.

"Oh my God." Jade groans, swallowing her food. "It's my birthday, do I really have to spend it at a club that a bunch of frat-boy MBAs like?"

"Seb's gay," Jonah says.

"I didn't say he was straight, I said he went to business school."

Jonah pouts. "It's my birthday, too, and it's not my problem that you don't know anybody in Atlanta."

"It's neither of your birthdays," Nia says.

"But it *will* be after midnight, and I'd like to at least be enjoying myself," Jade says.

Jonah smirks. "It's a throwback to 2000s music theme night."

"You should've led with that!" Jade says, laughing.

"Should I not send the 'Jade would rather eat glass than spend a single moment in the company of the likes of you' I just typed out?"

Nia snorts.

"Have I mentioned that Seb and Leo are in the top three

least appalling of your business-school buddies? And that I love them and have never once questioned their taste?"

"I'm going to hold this over your head until one of us dies," Jonah says.

"Yeah," Jade replies. "Sounds about right."

CHAPTER TWENTY-ONE

tuesday evening, july 1

"Jonah, there is only one bathroom, you need to hurry the fuck up," Jade says through the closed door, leaning against the frame.

"What do you need so much time for? Never seen you step out in a full beat," Jonah calls back.

"Jonah knows the phrase 'full beat'?" Nia says.

"He may know the phrase, but he doesn't know one when he sees it. Otherwise, he wouldn't have stumbled home with foundation and highlighter that isn't his shade smeared across his nose and cheek a month ago."

Jonah opens the door, poking his head out and sending Jade stumbling forward. "That was one time."

"Yeah. One time *this year*," Jade says, laughing.

Jonah looks over her shoulder to Nia, and they exchange a look that Jade can't read. "Always slut-shaming me."

Jade places her right hand over her heart. "*Never.* You have my full support. I'm just not passing up a chance to make fun of your stupidity."

"How was I supposed to know she was wearing that much makeup?" he protests.

WHENEVER YOU'RE READY   209

"Did you think her cheekbones were naturally sparkly?"
Jade says, earning Nia's snorting laughter.

"No, I just wasn't examining her *cheekbones* when she
approached me. Besides, point stands. You're not doing
makeup, why would you need the bathroom?"

"You're not either! I'd still like to check how I look. And
I've been known to use brow gel and mascara, on occasion."

Jonah rolls his eyes. "That'll take thirty seconds. It's not
like you're doing eyeliner."

Jade folds her arms across her chest. "What if I am?"

"Like you know how," he says, and he closes the door
between them.

Jade has lifted her fist to knock again when Nia says,
"Want me to do it?"

She drops her hand, turning toward Nia, who's filing the
bitten edges of her nails smooth over the tiny trash can in
their room. Nia's makeup is done—her usual eyeliner layered over a soft, shimmery eyeshadow, a smudge of coral
blush, some highlighter brushed along her nose and cupid's
bow. Jade got dressed while Nia was in the bathroom and
then, unwisely, offered it up to Jonah, assuming he'd be in
and out, and then Nia could change while Jade was in there.
That was half an hour ago, so Nia is still standing there in that
silk pajama set of hers. The shorts have slits on the sides that
widen every time Nia shifts her weight. Jade is trying very
hard to pretend she doesn't know exactly what that fabric
feels like underneath her fingers.

She is not succeeding.

"Do what?" she asks, probably several beats too late.

"Your eyeliner, J," Nia says. "I know you were just fucking with Jonah, but I could if you wanted."

Jade bites her lip. "Like in high school?"

Nia laughs, her head tilting back. Her wavy hair slides

over her shoulder, and now Jade notices that it's been sun-browned since the start of the trip. She bets there're sunspots scattered across the highest point. "And college."

A little embarrassing, but true. "Still, it's a long time ago now."

Nia holds her gaze with an intensity that makes Jade's breath hitch. "I remember how," she says.

Jade swallows. "Okay, yeah. Make me pretty, Nia," she says, batting her eyelashes.

Nia nods, her eyes scanning Jade's face. "Come here then."

Fuck, Jade thinks, swallowing again as she steps into the room, *is she doing that on purpose?*

"Sit," she says, gesturing toward the bed, and Jade obliges. Nia opens her toiletry case, extracting a thin, black tube. Jade watches her as she moves. The room's tiny, she's barely three feet away, but it feels like it takes forever for her to make the few steps it takes to close the gap.

Nia taps the outside of Jade's left thigh, signaling for her to slide her legs closed so that Nia can plant her feet on either side of Jade's. The air conditioning must be too strong in here; the heat of Nia's legs and torso radiate through Jade, even from inches away. Jade's face is level with her chest, and she keeps her gaze carefully directed upward.

"Close your eyes," Nia says before she gently grips Jade's chin between her forefinger and thumb, tilting her face one way, then the other. Jade doesn't breathe. "Okay, open."

Jade blinks, and Nia's even closer than before, the eyeliner pen uncapped and at the ready. She rests the side of her hand against Jade's cheek for balance and softly touches the tip of the eyeliner to her eyelid three times, moving from the inner corner outward. She does the other side, then instructs Jade to close her eyes. It's impossible to ignore how close Nia is. Every breath curls across the bridge of Jade's nose. When Jade inhales, all she can smell is Nia—her coconut-vanilla deodorant that gives way to just *her*—and Jade can think of nothing but how much she'd like to bottle that scent and take it home with her. Diffuse it through her room alongside her morning incense every day. She misses Nia already, even though she's right here.

"You need to be still," Nia says, laughing softly.

Jade plants one hand on the mattress and, without thinking, wraps her other around Nia's leg to steady herself. The hem of her sleep shorts brushes along Jade's index finger.

They both freeze. Jade doesn't breathe, and as far as she can hear and feel, neither does Nia.

She should remove her hand.

But seconds tick by, and it feels more and more like she *can't*. If she'd drawn back immediately, it's an accident. If she draws back now, it's an admission of guilt. One she doesn't want to make. If she stays, then it's on purpose, but it's okay. It's nothing. It's just for stability.

Her thumb twitches. *Pull back,* she thinks.

She splays her fingers. *God, Nia is soft.*

Fuck, what are you doing? Pull back.

And she's about to, but she feels Nia's exhale on her cheek and the brush tip of the eyeliner touches back down near her lashes.

Jade clears her throat. "This better?" she asks, trying to keep her voice steady. Maybe she manages it, but she has no way of knowing. She can hardly hear herself over her thudding pulse.

"A little," Nia says, her voice quiet. "You still kind of sway back every time I make a stroke."

Jade blinks her eyes open, barely remembering to divert her gaze upward in time. At least Nia's wearing a bra. If she could glimpse the outline of anything right now, she wouldn't be able to look away. "There's nothing for me to lean back against," she says.

Nia sucks her bottom lip into her mouth, her teeth raking pale strips into the rosy brown as she releases it. "Lie down then," she says. "And *try* to keep your eyes closed, please."

"Bossy," Jade murmurs.

"Just trying not to mess this up."

Jade follows directions, her hand sliding down Nia's thigh as she lays herself back on the bed. Nia lifts her leg then, the bend of her knee stopping Jade's hand from falling away farther. Jade feels the mattress depress next to her right hip, then her left.

Nia hovers, and Jade squeezes her eyes more tightly shut, struggling not to register the heat of her. It's even worse like this. She leans over her, and Jade thinks she can hear the sound of her hair falling across her shoulder. Knows she'd be able to see the sunspots from here.

And then, *fuck,* Nia sinks down. Flush against her. Straddling her.

Both of Jade's hands find her thighs this time. She glides them up over soft, soft skin until she can feel the hem of those silk shorts again. Nia rests her elbow on Jade's sternum, then goes back to drawing on the eyeliner.

Nia's hips are so full in her hands. Jade aches to grip them, to pull her closer. To drag her up to her face, her mouth. Her heartbeat would register on the Richter scale. Nia must know.

But she just keeps doing Jade's eyeliner, tilting her face as needed.

They *have* done this before. Years ago, but maybe that's enough for it to feel comfortable, even routine, to Nia. Jade takes slow, careful breaths.

She sighs, shifting backward as if to admire her work.

WHENEVER YOU'RE READY   213

This makes her thighs clamp tightly around Jade's waist, and Jade's nipples pinch in response. "Open," Nia says.

Jade does, blinking against the harshness of the overhead light, her eyes taking a moment to properly focus. But when they do, she catches Nia's expression. Wide eyes, barely parted lips, a flush up her neck and in her cheeks that only intensifies with Jade's perusal.

"Nia," she whispers.

"It looks good," she says. The words sound like they're scraping out of her. "The wings are even, I mean. You have your own mascara?"

Jade nods. "In the bathroom."

"Okay," she says. Neither of them moves. Jade moves her thumb in a half circle; Nia shivers.

"*Nia,*" she whispers again. It feels like begging.

"I'm walking Luna. Bathroom's yours, Jade!" Jonah calls, and whatever the moment was, it fractures around them.

NIA'S HANDS SHAKE as she clothes herself. Her dress fastens shut with a series of tiny mother-of-pearl buttons, and she struggles to fit them through the loops as she trembles. Even when she succeeds, she often finds that she's skipped a loop, and has to struggle to redo it.

It feels like Jade's fingerprints are burned into her thighs. Jade's hand splayed on the back of her leg, millimeters below the curve of her ass.

Nia counts to slow her breath, imagines she's putting herself together, button by button. It's one more night. Just one more night, one more day where she has to be okay. If she wants to fall apart on her stupidly comfortable couch in her studio in Palo Alto, she can. She can let her heart break, and then she can tape it up, figure out how to tell Jade and how to keep the adhesive in place once she does. Because Michal was right, she has to. This isn't infinitely sustainable. She just needs to make sure their friendship can survive it.

One more night. She can do one more night.

One more night in a bed with Jade, knowing what Jade's long fingers feel like pressing into her skin, just barely slipping under her pajama bottoms. Knowing what Jade's breath feels like against her neck. Knowing that her touch *sears*.

She closes her eyes. *In for six, hold for four, out for seven.*

A knock startles her. "You ready?" Jonah's voice rolls through the oak wood, muffled. "The boys are outside."

"Yeah, I'm ready," she calls, hastily shoving her feet into her platform sandals and swinging the door open. Jonah's on the other side looking down at his phone. His hair is styled in finger curls—probably why he was in the bathroom so long—and he's wearing a green shadow-striped short-sleeved button-up with a single, tiny peach embroidered on the pocket. "Is this your 'I'm in Georgia' shirt?"

Jonah grins. "I look pretty, huh?"

"The prettiest."

"Leggo," he says nodding his head toward the door. Jade is, presumably, already outside with the Boys.

The driveway proves a little too steep for her sandals, and she ends up bracing her hands on Jonah's for support as they make their way down, a crop of *adult men* and Jade coming into view.

Seb, Leo, and Boy Number 3 are dressed nearly identically to Jonah (though she expects any of them would argue this point): short-sleeved button-ups with a subtle pattern French-tucked into expensive denim, the top three buttons left undone to reveal a chain or pendant, or for one of them, both. Nia tries not to look at Jade, for fear she'll blush.

"Nia, this is Seb," Jonah says, gesturing to the man closest to him, a Latino guy with a head full of loose curls, about Jade's height, "Leo," the one standing in the middle, tall and white, with short, sandy-colored hair, "and Seb's roommate, Andrew. Boys, this is Nia."

Andrew (two necklaces) is taller than Seb but nowhere near to Leo and Jonah, and East Asian, with jet-black hair that tucks behind his ears and a Marilyn Monroe mole. While the other two greet Nia with simple *hey*s, Andrew holds careful eye contact and says "Nice to meet you, Nia," drawn-out with an emphasis on her name.

He's attracted to her. And incredibly handsome. If she can spend enough of the night talking to him, it's another few hours of assured normalcy with Jade.

"C'mon, we've got a surprise for you," Seb says, clapping a hand on Jonah's shoulder.

They depart, Seb walking next to Jonah, Leo chatting with Jade, and unsurprisingly, Andrew falls in step beside Nia.

"So, you're Nia . . . ?" he says.

She laughs up at him. "Chin," she answers. "Very subtle. What would you have done if I'd had my white parent's last name?"

He grins back, his mole jumping. "Then I would've asked directly," he says. "But I thought it was worth a shot."

"I guess you got lucky, Andrew . . . ?"

"Guo," he says. "So, is your Chin Canto or Korean?"

"Jamaican, actually. Canto if you go far enough back on one side." She wonders if she should offer that her dad is Black, too, but decides against it. She's never totally sure how to respond—if someone outright asks her ethnicity (assuming it's not in a rude way), of course she includes that.

But most people read her as white and East Asian, sometimes Southeast Asian, so she's usually asked about that. And then she gets caught between her desire to honor all parts of herself and a deep fear of being one of those mixed people who goes on about how they're *actually 1/42nd blah blah blah* to monoracial people of color as if it's a badge of superiority, somehow.

"That's cool," he says. "I've always wanted to go to Jamaica."

"You should, it's beautiful. And I miss the food daily," Nia says. "Anyway . . . how did you become a Boy?"

He coughs. "I'm sorry?"

"Oh no, *fuck*." She puts her hand on his arm in apology, and he leans in slightly to her touch, his smile widening. He's *really* attracted to her. "I mean, Jonah kept calling the three of you 'the Boys.'"

Andrew laughs. "Much more fun than 'how do you know them,' I guess. I'll have to steal that from you."

"I'll trade you for 'so you're . . . *dramatic pause, implied question mark*' . . . when I wanna know what type of Asian someone is."

"Deal," he says, and extends his hand for Nia to shake. It's warm, his handshake is firm, and it leaves a tingle in her palm. Not a spark, not searing. But *something*. It's reassuring, like maybe Jade hasn't ruined her completely. "Seb and I grew up together," he continues. "Decided to live together when we were twenty-six and ended up in the same city again. How do you know the twins?"

"We grew up together, too." Nia swallows. "A mutual childhood friend introduced us."

Andrew gives her a long look, and she wonders if he's heard from Seb that Jonah was dating someone who died, and is putting two and two together.

Should she say something? Three years, and she's still not totally sure what to do when Michal comes up in casual conversation with a stranger. *Yeah, my best friend got brain cancer and died when we were twenty-six. Do you have any hobbies?*

His eyes scan her face, briefly dipping to her collarbones, then chest. His cheeks pinken slightly and he looks away, as though he's caught himself doing something he shouldn't be. But Nia doesn't really mind. "Right. And are you and Jonah . . . ?"

"God no," Nia says. "Are you and Seb . . . ?"

"No." Andrew replies easily, but not defensively, which endears her to him. "I like women."

"Me, too." Nia laughs.

"Oh," he says, and his next step puts a bit of space between them. "Are you and Jade—"

"No," she says, surprised at her own acerbity. "Jade and Jonah aren't together, either, in case you were wondering."

She gets the laugh she wanted, but it's sheepish. "I want to make sure I haven't misunderstood, here. When you say you like women, do you mean you *only* like women?"

Andrew looks ahead at the others, but something about his directness sends a shiver down Nia's spine. "No," she says, and his gaze snaps to hers. "That's not what I mean."

He nods slowly, rolls his lips together, smiles. "Good," he says, his voice low.

Good, Nia thinks, noting the flutter low in her belly. Gentle, unimpressive, even paltry compared to the dips and dives from half an hour prior, but there nonetheless. *You are a perfect distraction.*

CHAPTER TWENTY-TWO

tuesday night, july 1

They walk in to the opening notes of T-Pain's "Buy U a Drank," and Jade has to hand it to Jonah. If she's going to ring in her birthday at a straight bar, this is the best possible theme.

"I'm gonna get a drink. Want anything?" Andrew ostensibly addresses this question to everyone, but he's mostly facing Nia.

"Just a club soda with lime," Nia says. "I really outdid myself on Saturday." Her eyes flick to Jonah first, then Jade, and they fall away just as quickly. Jade crosses her arms.

"I'll go with you," Jonah offers.

Seb checks his watch. "No, stay. Your surprise is on the way. Leo, could you?"

Everybody makes their requests; Jade, like Nia, opts for sparkling water, the feeling in her stomach on Sunday morning still too easy to conjure. They're talking about Jonah's surprise, and there's ribbing about something that happened their second year of business school, but Jade isn't really listening. Instead, she's watching the placement of Andrew's hand on the small of Nia's back, how it hitches the fabric of her dress up ever so slightly, as he bends to whisper something in her ear.

Nia looks up at him with laughter in her eyes, rising up on her tiptoes to whisper something back. Whatever it is, it makes him laugh and shake his head, his hand moving from her back to her waist for a parting squeeze as he turns toward the bar.

Jade has never really gotten a handle on Nia's taste in men, but whatever it is, Andrew clearly fits.

"Jade?"

"What?"

"I asked if something was up," Seb says. The way he glances at Nia before focusing back on Jade makes her straighten her spine and drop her hands to her side.

"Oh, sorry. I'm just spacey. I'm good," she says.

He opens his mouth, but Jonah interrupts with a shake of his head. "Don't bother, Seb. Lost cause."

"I'm sorry," Jade says, "*what*?"

"Jonah fuckin' Pardo," a deep voice calls from behind Jade.

"Jordan fuckin' Ames!" Jonah calls back.

Jordan steps out from behind her, wearing a variation of the uniform he'd walked into their apartment with three nights a week when he and Jonah were getting their MBAs: a tightly-fitted plain T-shirt, jeans, and colorful shoes that Jade would need to be a much more serious sneakerhead to truly appreciate. He greets Jonah with three low-fives followed by an enthusiastic dap. Their secret handshake is ridiculous, and also delightful.

"Hey, Jade!" he says, offering her a hug hello.

"It's good to see you," she says when they part. "How's Chicago?"

He smiles, shaking his head. "Somehow ended up the only single one outta my friends, can you believe that?"

"I genuinely cannot," Jade says.

Jonah can't wipe the grin off his face. "What are you doing here, man?"

"In town for business, when I hit up Seb to tell him I'd be here, it was his idea to make it a surprise."

Andrew and Leo return to dole out the drinks, greeting Jordan with equal enthusiasm. Jade thanks Leo for her seltzer and watches as Andrew falls into place next to Nia.

His hand is on her elbow, then her lower back again. Hers is on his upper arm, his shoulder, even briefly his chest. The hair on the back of Jade's neck stands up.

It's not that he's hitting on Nia. She is beautiful, smart, witty; obviously people will vie for her attention.

It's not even that Nia's flirting back, she doesn't think. Andrew isn't leering, his taste in friends is a credit to him, no matter how much Jade ribs Jonah, and she'd have to be blind not to notice how good-looking he is.

It's watching this, knowing that an hour ago, Nia was straddling Jade's hips, shivering at *her* touch. Flushing under *her* gaze. Jade can convince herself that she's imagining finger brushes, furtive looks. Reading into hands held in difficult moments. That whatever Saturday was only happened because they were drunk.

But today? There's no talking her way out of that.

After everything, maybe *because* of everything, Nia wants her. Sober, in the full light of day.

The want Jade feels in return is bone-deep. And it's making the way Andrew's lips move against Nia's ear feel a lot like cruelty.

"Jade," Jonah says. "You look fucking miserable."

"Yeah, well . . ." she says. She could make up something

about being dragged to a straight club, but Cassie's "Me & U" is bumping and she doesn't want to be a dick to Seb. Besides, what's the point in pretending? There's that learned telepathy in his eyes, a little sadness in the furrow of his brow. If he tries for a repeat of the cab ride right now, she thinks she'll melt into the grimy floor. "I have to pee," she says, and slips away before Jonah gets the chance.

NIA WATCHES AS Andrew finishes the last of his drink, how his Adam's apple bobs as he swallows. She knocks hers back, too.

Jade is no longer with the rest of the group. Probably just off to the bathroom, but Nia prickles at the fact that she can feel her absence so immediately. She *wasn't* looking at Jade. That's the entire point of Andrew.

She even told him as much—he replied to her "I have a lot going on right now" warning with a grin and "I'm happy to be your respite for tonight."

But even with him here, with his warm, strategically placed hands, his woodsy cologne, and his whispered flirty jokes, she can't stop tracking Jade. Nia's like a broken car radio, forever tuned to Jade's frequency.

Nia sets her empty cup down on the nearest tall table and turns to Andrew. "May I have this dance?"

He gives her what should be, quite frankly, a panty-dropping smile. But unlike Jade's, his lips are uniform in color, and it just doesn't have quite the same effect. "I thought you'd never ask."

They push their way onto the dance floor, her hand in his. A couple of layers into the crowd, Andrew tightens his grip, pulling her flush against him. His hands are on her lower back, hers around his neck. He's all hard planes against her, firm and solid. Andrew's a good dancer, can find the beat and respond to the swivel of her hips in turn. If she closes her eyes, maybe she can get lost in him.

The song changes, it's Nelly Furtado's "Maneater," and he spins her so they're pressed back to front. A few exploratory grinds and his fingers dig into her hips. He meets the moment enough, she starts to whine her hips in earnest, and she thinks she can feel him half-hard against her. One of his hands splays at the front of her hips, and her eyes flutter open.

Jade.

She's several rows of dancers deep, and yet somehow her gaze snags immediately.

Their eyes lock, the expression in Jade's tense enough to match the set of her jaw. She brings her glass to her mouth, taking a long, slow sip. Her tongue darts out to catch the drop left on her lower lip.

Nia is frozen in place.

"Are you okay?" Andrew ducks to say against her ear.

Her reverie breaks, but she doesn't quite register what he's said. "What?"

She belatedly processes his words, so Andrew's "I asked if you were all right" overlaps perfectly with her "Oh, yeah. I'm, uh, fine." Their apologies overlap, too.

It's then that Andrew looks up through the mass of bodies and seems to realize where her attention has been. She looks, too, sees Jade set her drink down behind her, still watching Nia and Andrew. "I'm going to be honest with you, Nia," Andrew says. "You're cool, and a fantastic dancer, and I'm insanely attracted to you. But I don't think I want to be in the middle of whatever all that is."

Nia half turns toward him. "You're not—" she starts, but

he silences her with a soft smile and a knowing look. She averts her gaze, glancing over his shoulder, at his necklaces, finally at the place where his hand still rests so lightly that she barely registers it on her waist, before meeting his eyes again. "I'm sorry, Andrew."

He shakes his head, a lock of hair slipping out from behind his ear. "I've been there," he says. "Maybe not quite there, but somewhere similar. It's okay, but I'm gonna go." He bends to press a kiss to her temple, then disappears into the crowd.

Nia's left a little shell-shocked, heart beating wildly, keenly aware of Jade approaching in her periphery.

Jade says nothing when she reaches her, but the look in her eyes borders on withering. Nia doesn't shrink under it; her pumping heart just beats harder with annoyance, maybe even anger. "What is it, Jade?" she demands.

Jade matches her tone, her brow furrowing. "I'm not allowed to dance?"

Nia rolls her eyes. "You scared Andrew off."

"Did I?" Her face softens with a sudden flicker of amusement. "My condolences."

"You sound real broken up about it," Nia volleys.

Jade shrugs, clenches her jaw. "Maybe I wanted to dance with you."

"You could've asked."

She gives a short, frustrated laugh. "When, exactly? While he was folded over you and whispering in your ear by the bar, or when you were whining on him to a song we scream-sang together in middle school?"

Somebody behind Nia stumbles, sending her careening into Jade. Her fingers are at Nia's hips immediately, anchoring her in place. One hand skates down the fabric of her dress as it falls away, and *everything* in Nia pinches tight.

Jade squeezes her hip with her other hand, and Nia's sure it'll burn through the fabric. It'll mark her forever, tell any future lover that she once belonged to Jade. They're so close, Nia has to tip her head back to keep eye contact, feels her breasts press against Jade's upper ribs with every breath. But she doesn't even try to put space between them. "Are you doing this on purpose?" Jade asks softly. Nia can barely hear her over the music.

"Am I doing *what* on purpose?"

"Flirting with him," Jade says, but it sounds more like "torturing me."

Her anger flares. Because how dare Jade make Nia out to be the cruel one, after what she said to her three years ago? That *Toni said* coming out of Jade's mouth had haunted her for days, weeks afterward. Jade could say she knew Toni was lying all she wanted, but she still said it. And even if she said in her apology that she thought it was all bullshit, there had to have been a tiny bit of her that believed it, or at least believed it *could*'ve been true. Or it wouldn't have been worth saying. The anger heats and heats, comes to a rolling boil. "It sounds like you're accusing me of something," she says.

Jade shakes her head. "I'm not trying to," she says. "This is coming out wrong."

"Why do you even care about Andrew?"

"Oh my God, Nia. Are you serious?"

"Deadly. What could it *possibly* be to you?"

Jade groans, bringing her free hand suddenly to the nape of Nia's neck, fingers threading into the hairs there.

Nia's only surprised for half a heartbeat, until she reads the hunger in Jade's eyes and realizes that maybe this was what she wanted the moment they made eye contact through the crowd. Maybe what she's feeling isn't anger at all, or at least it isn't *only* anger. Because when Jade's eyes dip to her mouth and her own lips part, Nia's the one who pushes forward and closes the gap.

JADE'S KISSING HER back without a pause to react; some part of her knew this would happen the moment she reached her on the dance floor. More of her knew it when *you scared Andrew off* left Nia's mouth, her voice a clear challenge. All of her knew when she slid her hand into Nia's hair and watched that oval gap form between her lips in response.

The only surprise is that she wasn't the one to lean in first.

Nia sucks on Jade's lower lip, and Jade closes her fist around Nia's hair, tugging gently. Nia pulls away for a breath, exhales that same sound she made at the gas station on Sunday, and in their bed on Saturday night. Jade steals a breath, lets her fingers roam lower, hitching up the skirt of Nia's dress just slightly so she can get her hand on *skin,* presses her lips to Nia's once again.

It's like Nia suddenly remembers her hands then. They're everywhere—sliding into Jade's unbuttoned overshirt, trailing up her arm, shoulder, throat, jaw. Her touch is everywhere and her tongue is in Jade's mouth, sliding against her own, and she tastes exactly how she knew she would, even though they've never done this before.

They've never done this before.

She's kissing Nia. For the first time.

Jade moves her hand to the side of Nia's face, tilting her head back, deepening the kiss. Her leg threads between Nia's, the heat of her against Jade's upper thigh, and Nia goes pliant in her arms, her kisses turning desperate, feverish.

Finally. *Finally.*

She wants to latch her lips onto Nia's neck. Devour her.

She wants to rip this dress off her, peel off her panties, feel her around her fingers, taste her on her tongue.

Jade breaks the kiss for another breath. Nia looks up at her, eyes wide and glassy, lips swollen. "Nia," she whispers. Nia leans up to kiss her again, but Jade pulls back, brushing their noses together. "Not here."

"What?" Nia says, not like she couldn't hear Jade, but like Jade's speaking a language she doesn't understand.

"I want to leave," Jade says.

Nia blinks, her expression cracking. "Oh," she says, her hands falling away from Jade's body.

Jade catches one of them, brings it to her mouth, and presses her lips to Nia's knuckles. "I don't want to do this here, with 'Temperature' playing and Jonah's business-school buddies twenty feet away. I want to take my time with you, Nia. I want us to take our time with each other."

And even though Nia's eyes are dark brown and it's dimly lit, Jade swears she can see her pupils blown out, the flush creeping up her neck. "Oh," she repeats. She nods, her eyelids fluttering shut. "Yes," she says, but it's so quiet, Jade only knows because she can hardly stand to tear her eyes away from her lips.

"Let's go back to the house."

CHAPTER TWENTY-THREE

almost midnight, july 1

They walk out into the night, hand in hand, Nia's heart beating so hard she can't quite hear the pulse of the music. Nia expects being out in the open, with the cling of the muggy night, to be a bucket of ice water poured over them, but it's not. Jade keeps running her thumb along Nia's pulse point, and desire courses through her like a drug, the high only intensifying. They don't talk, don't even look at each other, during the four-minute walk home.

But when they reach the driveway of their Airbnb, Nia says, "Wait."

"Hmm?" Jade replies, and when Nia makes eye contact with her, she looks dazed. Cheeks slack, eyes sultry.

And she doesn't have an immediate answer. All she has is a tiny voice in her head, barely audible over the *oh my God, oh my God* and *Jade Jade Jade* playing on loop, telling her she *should* be thinking. Her thoughts swim. "We just left, without saying anything," she says finally.

A little bit of clarity creeps into Jade's expression. "Shit, you're right." She laughs. "I wasn't thinking. I can text Jonah.

Tell him we're walking Luna, or something." Jade releases
Nia's hand to go for her phone, and Nia folds her arms across
her chest.

God, what are we doing?

Wasn't she mad at Jade, like, five minutes ago? Hadn't she
promised herself she would keep it together, at least through
tomorrow? Has either of them thought this through?

"Jade," she says.

"One sec," Jade says, then holds up her phone screen to
show Nia her text has sent.

"J, what did you . . . ?" Nia says, coming to a full stop.
"What did you mean when you said you weren't thinking?"
The corners of Jade's lips turn down; her brow furrows. But
she doesn't speak. Nia can feel her pulse in her throat. "Were
you thinking when you decided to kiss me?"

Jade chuckles, taking a step toward Nia.

"It's not funny," Nia insists.

"It's a little funny to me," she says. Gently, she brings her
hand to Nia's shoulder, trailing a finger along her collarbone,
around to the back of her neck, coming to rest at her nape
once again. "Because sometimes it feels like kissing you is
literally all I think about."

Nia feels like someone has blown air into her heart, inflating it so that it no longer fits in her chest. She swallows,
closing her eyes.

"I shouldn't have said that, should I?" Jade asks. Nia half
nods, half shakes her head. Jade leans downward, resting
her forehead against Nia's. "You want to talk about what
happened," Jade says. Her voice is resigned, but not upset.
Understanding.

She could say yes, and Jade would walk inside with her,
sit down, and dig through it.

She should say yes.

"We should talk about everything," Nia says, and she opens her eyes as Jade lifts her head away. Before Jade can remove her hand, too, Nia closes her fingers loosely around her wrist, stilling her.

Jade looks at her, the dark irises of her deep-set eyes bottomless with lust, her teeth sunk deeply into her bottom lip. Usually cotton candy pink, but bruised raspberry sorbet from Nia's kiss.

"We *should* talk about everything," Nia repeats.

But what if we do, she thinks, *and I lose you for good?*

But what if we do, and I keep you, but I never get to have you like this?

What if I don't get to have you like this, and I don't get to keep you anyway?

Nia tightens her fist around Jade's arm. "But," Nia says, "I don't want to."

Jade blinks slowly, swallows. "Yeah," she says, nodding. "I don't want to right now, either. I just want . . ." Her gaze trails heat across Nia's face everywhere it touches: brow, temple, cheekbone. Mouth.

An impasse. They both know they shouldn't do this; they both know they're going to.

Nia's lips tingle under Jade's scrutiny. Jade chokes out, "*God,* Nia," and then kisses her.

It's slow, luxurious, the way her tongue slides along Nia's bottom lip, asking her to open. How their tongues tangle, even the way Jade takes her lip between her teeth. Nia can feel Jade savoring this, savoring her.

Her hands are on her thighs again, just under the hem of her dress, one inching higher. "Inside." Nia gasps on a break for breath and Jade agrees, but she finds herself pressing her mouth back to Jade's, stealing another kiss before they take a single step.

Jade smiles into her mouth, then grabs her by the hand and pulls her up the driveway.

Nia feels leaden with want, yet she floats along behind Jade, a woman entranced.

Then they're inside, and Luna's on the couch asleep. They didn't leave for the club until after Luna's usual bedtime, so when Jade stops to lock the door, the dog looks up briefly at the noise, then promptly goes back to sleep.

Nia tugs Jade into their bedroom, pushes her up against the door. She touches her waist, her back, nips where her shoulder meets her neck. "I don't even know where to start with you," she says.

"Then let *me* start with *you*," Jade replies. "I know exactly what I want to do."

"No." Nia shakes her head. "No, I want to touch you first."

Jade holds her hands up in surrender before dropping them, which isn't what Nia meant, but she's not complaining. She goes for the overshirt first, easing it off Jade's shoulders and letting it fall to the ground. Without it, there's so much skin on display—the ribbed tank top she's wearing extends maybe half an inch below the curves of her breasts, less when she inhales deeply.

Nia slides one hand up Jade's torso, shoving up the fabric of her tank to cup her breast. It fits so completely in her palm, as if molded just for her. She bends, nudging the other side of the hem up the rest of the way with her nose, taking Jade's nipple between her lips, between her teeth. There's a soft thud, Jade's head against the door. Her skin is perfect on Nia's tongue, just barely salty with sweat. She moves her mouth to her other breast, replacing her lips with her fingers, her palm with her lips. Jade moans in response, and Nia shifts her knee in between Jade's legs, giving her something to clench around.

"Please, Nia," Jade whimpers.

"Please, what?" She kisses her way back up Jade's neck, along her jaw.

"Let me touch you," Jade says. "If you don't let me touch you, I'm going to die."

"Okay," Nia says, and then Jade's hands are on her hips, urging her back, spinning her around.

Nia expects Jade's hands to slide up her thighs again, maybe curve over her chest. But instead, Jade goes for her neckline, carefully undoing the top button of her dress, then the next, holding the fabric away from her body so Nia only gets torturously glancing pressure as she unclothes her. She reaches for Jade's pants, undoing the button and yanking down the zipper, not caring that this tangles their arms together, making it difficult for either to operate. Jade gets enough buttons loose for Nia's dress to pool at her ankles, and Nia takes the opportunity to shove Jade's jeans down her thighs.

"I still get tested after every new partner, and every six months, just in case," Jade says. "Like you taught me."

Nia feels the flush in her cheeks deepen, because she hadn't even thought to ask. She's never forgotten to ask before. "I do, too."

Jade nods, and hooks her thumbs into the waistband of her own boxer briefs, tugging them off, then sits down on the edge of the bed. "Yours, too," she says, and Nia obliges.

The moment she steps out of them, Jade's hands are on her ass, bringing Nia to her mouth. She kisses Nia's right hip bone first, then her left, then just under her belly button. Then lower, and lower, and then Jade's flattening her tongue against her and Nia's crying out, arching forward.

She hasn't considered herself Catholic in a good twenty years, and even when she did, she's not sure she was ever a true believer. But with Jade's lips on her, she's pretty sure she meets God.

"Jesus fucking Christ," Nia swears, and Jade's eyes flutter open, lips spread into a smile before she closes her mouth around her once again.

Jade adds a finger, and then Nia's legs are trembling as she grabs at Jade's shoulders in a futile effort to find stability.

"I can't—" Nia gasps. "I need—"

And suddenly Jade's hands and mouth are gone. She nods, scooting back and lying down on the bed. She pats the pillows on either side of her head. "Come here then," she says, her lips curving with amusement.

Nia does as told, straddles her head, lets Jade's hands on her hips guide her into place.

When Jade's lips are on her like this, it's somehow even more intense than before. Jade crawls her hands up Nia's stomach, anchoring on her breasts. When she brushes her fingers over Nia's nipples, Nia has to grip onto the headboard for balance.

She's dimly aware of the sounds she's making, how desperately she's riding Jade's face. Jade pauses for a breath, easing Nia's hips upward.

"I wish I had my strap," Jade says.

Nia opens her eyes, looking down at her. The image of Jade, half-lidded, lips glistening, quickly becomes the hottest thing she's ever seen. "This is perfect, J," Nia says.

Jade kisses her inner thigh. "Next time then," she says, and pulls Nia back down to her.

Next time.

So easy, so casual.

Nia's face heats, her throat tightening. She blinks, looking upward. Everything is so perfect, Jade's fingers, Jade's lips,

Jade's tongue. Jade under her, so focused, anticipating and responding to her every need. "I'm close," she gasps.

"Good," Jade says.

"I haven't tasted you, yet," Nia says.

"I don't want to stop," Jade says.

"But I want to taste you," she insists.

"So turn around."

JADE HAS NEVER been a touch-me-not, but with Nia, she deeply considers it. She could do this all night, all day, forever. Devouring her with nothing in return. Getting to experience her so undone, her little noises and the way she tastes is reciprocation enough.

Nothing could have prepared her for the feel of Nia's mouth on her while her mouth is still on Nia. She forgets what she's doing for a moment, throwing her head back and bucking her hips upward so that Nia has to push them firmly down onto the bed.

"This is," Jade pants, "*so* . . ."

Nia pauses only long enough to say, "I know," and then her lips are back. Her fingers.

Jade whines, touching, kissing, licking as if in retaliation, feeling Nia's barely withheld moans shudder through her.

Nia starts to clench, to rock. On the brink once again. Everything in Jade is tightening, too, so much she can hardly take it. Nia's thighs begin to tremor, then shake.

And even though Nia's mouth on her clit and Nia's fingers inside of her is the most exquisite pleasure Jade has ever felt, it's the sound, the taste, the feel of Nia coming apart on her tongue that ultimately tips her over the edge.

After, Jade lets her head loll back into the pillow, her

arms linking around Nia's waist. Nia's cheek rests against Jade's thigh.

They're quiet for a minute, the only sound in the room their heavy breaths.

Nia sighs, rolling off, her hand on Jade's hip the only point of contact left.

Jade pushes herself up, crawling over to Nia so that they're both lying with their heads facing the foot of the bed. She curls onto her side, flattening her hand against Nia's stomach. She traces her finger from her belly button to her sternum, over to the matching tattoo. Around the symbols for Aquarius, Capricorn, Cancer. Michal, Nia, Jade. She watches the path her finger takes, even though she has it memorized.

"Nia," Jade says. "Look at me."

"I can't." Her voice sounds thick, constricted.

"Why not?"

Nia shakes her head, still facing away. "If I do, I might cry."

"Then cry," Jade says. "And I'll hold you."

She looks at her then, her eyes welling.

"Nia," Jade whispers. She presses a kiss to her forehead, her eyelids, her nose, her lips. "Nia," she says again, almost in disbelief. "You have no idea how long I've wanted this. Wanted you."

Nia nods, and the tears start to fall. Jade catches them with her thumbs, her chest tightening. "Jade," she whispers shakily. "I think *you* have no idea how long *I've* wanted this."

Jade laughs, gives her a soft kiss. "I've been dreaming of you since we were teenagers," she says.

"Me, too."

Neither of them asks the obvious question: *Then why didn't this happen until now?* because they know why, and they said they weren't going to talk about it tonight.

It hangs in the air, anyway.

Nia nuzzles into her neck, Jade presses closer to her. "Jade?"
"Yes?"
"Happy birthday."
She laughs and kisses Nia's forehead. "Thank you," she
says.
They'll have to get up at some point. To wash up, to pee,
to get in bed the right way. But they don't, not yet. They
just hold each other. Until Jade thinks she can feel the love
pressed between them. Until she thinks she can feel the vis-
ceral ache of missing Nia these past three years, radiating
through every place where they're touching.
Until she thinks she's crying, too.

CHAPTER TWENTY-FOUR

technically wednesday morning, july 2

Nia wakes to the sound of Jonah's door slamming shut.

The overhead light is still on and she blinks, rubbing at her eyes until she realizes that she never took off her makeup. Her mouth tastes of sleep and of Jade. They're on top of the covers, stark naked, Jade's arm slung across her stomach.

"Jade," she says, gently shaking her shoulder.

Jade just hums, nuzzles closer.

"Jade, we fell asleep."

She opens her eyes then. Jade's eyeliner is a little smudged. Because of Nia. There's a small swell of possessive pleasure in her belly. "Oh, shit. We should clean ourselves up."

"And pee," Nia says.

"And pee," Jade agrees, propping herself up on an elbow. "And probably drink some cranberry kombucha tomorrow, because E. coli have a doubling time of, like, twenty minutes in urine."

"I can't believe you and Michal used to think *I* was the nerd."

Jade's lips do that amused twist. "Used to?"

Nia moves to smack her arm, but Jade catches her wrist,

pinning it above her head and bending to kiss her. Long and slow, until Nia's stomach is fluttering and she can't help but squirm under her. Jade parts with a peck, releasing her hand.

They both groan when they hear the sounds of another door closing and the shower turning on.

"Jonah." Jade sighs, shaking her head. "First snoring, now he's a bathroom hog." She reaches out, tracing circles around Nia's belly button.

"I don't mind the snoring," Nia says. "It means I got to share a bed with you." The words pour out, and she only belatedly has the sense to blush.

Jade hums. "You're right. Never mind, I love his snoring." She presses a sweet kiss to Nia's shoulder, then one to the top of each of Nia's breasts.

The look in Jade's eyes is one of such utter adoration, and Nia feels the words filling her up, ready to spill out. A force behind them, this bit of hope, telling her to *just say it. Tell her. Fall, and she'll catch you. She has to. Because how could she look at you like this, how could she touch you like this, how could she be with you like this, if she wouldn't?*

"Jade," she says. *Tell her.*

"Yes?" Jade asks, pressing a hot, open-mouthed kiss to her sternum.

Tell her. Nia takes a deep breath, willing herself to say it. "Will you go with me to my mom's wedding?" is all that comes out.

"I'd love to," Jade replies easily. "Or, well, I know it's going to be tense and probably not the most enjoyable day of your life, but I'd love to be there for you."

Nia nods, and suddenly she feels like she might cry again. "Thank you," she says. *Tell her,* she thinks.

Just tell her.

"I love you," Nia says.

"I love you, Nia," Jade says back.

Her heart doesn't skip, her breathing doesn't accelerate. There's barely a reaction in her body, because when Jade says it, Nia realizes her mistake. "I love you" they've said before, countless times, in innumerable ways. Of course Jade loves her. She's never doubted that.

And now they can hear Jonah's door shutting and Jade's swinging her legs over the bed and offering a hand to help her up. The moment is passing, Nia can feel it slipping away. She's a mess, sweaty and spent and utterly wrecked, and she's *in love with* Jade. It feels like maybe she can't breathe around it. Like it's so big it consumes her, and she knows Jade loves her but she doesn't know if it's in the way she wants her to. And when she accepts Jade's hand and lets herself be pulled out of bed, she understands that she isn't going to know. Not tonight.

JADE TRIES NOT to like how Nia's reflection looks too much as they brush their teeth together over the tiny sink. It's a futile effort.

Her cheeks are still stained red from exertion, her loose curls tangled and frizzier on the left side than the right. Nia always brushes her teeth before washing her face (Jade witnessed her panic once when she did the reverse, and decided it was better to wash her face a second time than risk letting even the tiniest bit of toothpaste foam rest on skin overnight), so her makeup is a mess. Her eyeshadow is entirely rubbed off, her eyeliner smeared. Delightfully undone in a way Nia never is, in a way even Jade has never had the privilege of seeing her before.

They lock eyes in the mirror, and her silk pajama top is

low enough that Jade can see the flush suffuse through her chest first before creeping up her neck.

Jade spits and rinses, then offers to hold Nia's hair back as she does the same. Jade washes her face and pats on some moisturizer before dropping down onto the closed toilet.

"What are you doing?" Nia asks.

"Waiting for you," Jade answers.

"It'll be a while. Ten steps, remember?"

Jade just shrugs, reaching out to wrap her hand behind Nia's knee, stroking her skin.

"You could use this time to read your letter, if you want," Nia says.

"Do you want me to leave?"

"No, I—I just don't want you to feel like you have to sit there while I do this."

"I don't feel like I *have* to. We're leaving tomorrow, and I know I'll see you in August, but it's been . . ." Jade trails off, sighing. "Besides, I didn't bring the letter with me, anyway."

Nia pauses in the middle of patting her face dry to look at Jade. "You didn't?"

She shakes her head. "I always wait until the very end of the day. I have to be alone and in my own bed or I can't bring myself to do it. The second year, I actually fell asleep while trying to work up the nerve so I didn't read it until the next morning."

"That makes sense, actually. Not sure what I expected." She pulls the little dropper out of a serum bottle, tilting her head back so she can drip the product onto her face without the wand touching her skin. There's a reason for this that she explained to Jade and Michal once, but Jade doesn't remember it.

"What do you do, usually?" Jade asks.

"I keep it with me, whether I'm at home or stuck in the library or whatever, and then I read it the moment the clock strikes midnight." Nia smiles, gently spreading the serum (or maybe it's an oil?) around her face.

Jade laughs, bending forward to kiss Nia's thigh.

"What was that for?"

Once again, Jade shrugs instead of responding. She did it because she wanted to. And there's something there, something that just wanting to means, that she can't really sift through right now.

Even the thought of going home tomorrow makes Jade feel like someone's wedged a fingernail into her chest, trying to crack it like a pistachio shell. Thinking about everything that they haven't said to one another this trip, everything they missed saying to each other over the last *three fucking years* makes her feel like she actually might die. Like she'll collapse into the loneliness inside her, a planet sucked into a black hole.

"Jade?" Nia says, and Jade looks at her own hand and realizes that she's shaking.

"Sorry," Jade mumbles.

Nia puts down her tiny bottle of lotion and crosses the whole six inches of space between her and Jade. "J, what is it?"

She's still trembling, and inhales deeply, but it doesn't fix it. Nia takes her face between her hands. "I can't—" she chokes out, and sucks in another breath. She's almost hyperventilating.

"Breathe with me," Nia says, and Jade does. Tries to hold it, follows her long exhales.

"I can't go that long without you again," she says at last.

Nia closes her eyes, nodding. "I know."

"I mean, I *can't*," Jade says softly. "I can't," she says again, even softer.

"You won't, J. Whatever it takes, we'll figure it out."

"Okay," she says.

"We'll figure it out," Nia repeats. "But right now, we'll go to bed, okay?"

Jade bites her lip, nods, and makes direct eye contact with Nia for the first time in minutes. Nia still holds Jade's face in her hands. Nia's lips are parted, her brows knitted together. "Yeah," Jade says. "Bed sounds good."

A slow smile, and then Nia presses her lips to Jade's.

CHAPTER TWENTY-FIVE

wednesday morning, july 2

Once again, Nia wakes to Luna licking her hand. She ended up on the side of the bed farthest from the door, which in this shoebox room meant Luna had to navigate a narrow path to get there. It gives her the same rush of flattery as that first morning.

She gingerly pulls Jade's arm off her midsection and sits up, dangling her legs over the side of the bed.

"Not yet," Jade murmurs, reaching for her. When Nia looks back, her eyes are still closed.

"I'm walking Luna," Nia says.

Jade nods into the pillow, her eyes still closed. "Okay, you can go. I'll get coffee and breakfast."

"Thank you."

One eye opens briefly. "When I get up."

Nia laughs. "Of course." The urge to kiss Jade on the forehead overtakes her before she can reconsider it. And when she does, Jade hums, the visible corner of her lip turning upward.

She tries not to read into it as she throws on her shorts

and a T-shirt and beckons Luna to follow her out into the living area.

In the next hour she has to herself, first on the walk, and then in the shower, and especially when she hears the sound of the door unlocking, indicating Jade's return, she *forces* herself not to read into it. There's no use guessing at Jade's feelings and desires.

And, *fuck,* she probably has to suck it up and do it today. Which leaves only one thought as she scrubs her body with a washcloth: *How?*

Getting Jade alone would probably be easy enough—banish Jonah for the last dog walk before the ride to the airport, or something. But what is she supposed to say when she does? *I'm in love with you, I want to be with you, also, I'm almost definitely moving to North Carolina to be a professor? I know that I promised you we'd figure out how to keep our friendship together like ten hours ago, but actually I'd like to propose doing the riskiest thing possible? And also, I'm the one who suggested we not talk before you made me come so hard my face went numb? Like a horny dumbass? Even though that obviously was going to make how I feel for you forty thousand times worse?*

But once Nia's ready and out at that little red-painted metal kitchen table and Jade hands her a coffee, saying "One vanilla oat milk latte, *hot,* for our favorite bisexual," she gives her a smile that Nia can't help but read into.

"What does hot coffee have to do with being bisexual?" Jonah asks.

"It's the oat milk," Nia says.

"But I get oat milk, too."

"Is there something you want to tell us, Jonah?" Jade reaches over to take his hand. "You know I'll love you no matter what, but if you've finally decided to turn away from your lifestyle of heterosexual deviancy, I'll be so happy to shepherd you on your godly journey. Hashem has answered my prayers!"

Nia snorts into her hand, and Jonah sucks his teeth, glancing toward the ceiling, and takes another sip of his drink.

"So," Nia says. "What do y'all want to do today?"

"You don't have something in mind?" Jade says.

Nia shakes her head. "This page of the Google doc was left intentionally blank. We've got like five hours until we need to be at the airport. We could go the aquarium, a bookstore, walk around, whatever."

"Do you want to do the aquarium?" Jonah asks.

"I am remaining agnostic. It's up to the birthday boy and girl."

"I kinda want to just hang out with you guys, if that's okay," Jade says. "Jonah?"

He nods. "Yeah, that sounds good to me. We could go sit in the park?"

"A picnic!" Jade says, delight overtaking her face.

Nia already has her phone out, pulling up a browser. "There's a Trader Joe's right around the corner."

IT IS REMARKABLY easy, walking up and down the aisles of a grocery store, working with Nia to talk Jonah out of buying absurd portions of snack foods, pretending that this is real life. That she'll go home tonight and Nia will still be in her bed. That Nia will be up first to walk Luna again tomorrow, that they'll be at a grocery store again the same time next week.

That they know what comes next, that NYU will call Nia any moment now and she'll be back home and they won't *have* to figure anything out, because they'll just be. And she wants to let herself pretend, at least for a little while. It's her birthday, after all.

When they get to the cash register, breads and cheeses and other accoutrements in hand, Nia is bouncing back and forth on her heels.

"You good?" Jonah asks.

"I have to pee," she says.

Jade nudges her with her elbow. "Just go."

"But we're next," she protests limply.

"We'll wait for you outside."

When Nia emerges from the automatic doors, she's holding her own brown paper bag by the base and not the handles. The top of it is folded down so that Jonah and Jade can't see in.

"What've you got?" Jonah asks.

"Organic tampons," Nia says.

Jade can't help but smile. Nia barely catches her eye, and she averts her gaze quickly, probably trying not to give herself away. But the corner of her lip twitches, and Jade knows.

She *really* knows when they're back at the Airbnb and Nia insists that she and Jonah take Luna to find a place to sit in Piedmont Park and drop her a pin while she fixes her hair.

Jonah, of course, appears to be genuinely unaware. They lay out the picnic blanket that was fortuitously stuffed in the back of the linen closet, and he says, "You know, I really thought her hair looked fine."

"Jonah, seriously?" Jade asks, raising her eyebrows in disbelief.

"What?"

"She's not fixing her hair."

"Ohhhhh," he says, and for a moment Jade thinks it's clicked. "She's putting in a tampon."

246 RACHEL RUNYA KATZ

"You have lived with me for your entire goddamn life. How long do you think it takes to put a tampon in?"

"Hey, it's not exactly something I've timed before!" he protests.

She shakes her head, patting him on the shoulder. "Happy birthday, bud."

He glares and shrugs her off, mumbling "happy birthday, Jade" anyway.

They watch Luna roll in a patch of dandelions, try to catch a fly, then bark at a pigeon. On the second bark, her voice cracks, pitching down. Jade and Jonah *aww!* in unison.

And then Nia's voice comes from behind them, a shockingly on-pitch rendition of "Happy Birthday to You."

They turn, and Nia's presenting them with a cake with white frosting, rainbow sprinkles, and block-number 2 and 9 candles that she shields with one hand to keep them lit. She sets it down on the blanket between them, so they can see the handwritten purple icing:

Happy Birthday Ja-

de and Jonah!

She blows out the candles in tandem with Jonah, and Nia barely waits for the flames to go out before saying, "I ran out of room, I'm—"

"If you apologize," Jade says, "I'm going to shoot myself."

Nia snorts. "A bit much, J, but point taken."

"This is so nice, Nia," Jade says, pulling out the number 2 to get a taste of the buttercream. Shockingly good for a store-bought cake. Nia blinks at her.

"Thank you, Nia," Jonah says. "When did you have time to get this?"

"Jonah, seriously?" Jade says for the second time in ten minutes.

Nia chuckles, sitting cross-legged on the picnic blanket. "I guess I was slicker than I thought."

"You were not," Jade says, and Nia pretends to pout about it. "But I love it." She scoots closer to Nia, letting their knees brush.

"There were never any tampons?"

"No, Two, there were not."

Jonah laughs. "Okay, I realize how stupid I seem right now, but you said the one thing that would make me stop paying any attention."

"That was the point, I think," Jade says.

"Well, thank you for surprising me, at least," Jonah says.

Nia leans forward to pat his knee. "Anything for my third-favorite Pardo."

"Still? Even after all the vomit? Even after you cleaned her shit?"

Nia nods, grinning. "Still."

"ANYBODY WANT A FREE PUPPY?" Jonah whisper-shouts.

Jade unwraps a hunk of brie, her heart the fullest it has been in three and a half years.

AN HOUR (and most of the baguette, half the cheese, and a quarter of the cake) later, the three of them are too full to continue. Luna's asleep, half her body on the blanket and half in the grass, and Jade is lying down with her head in Nia's lap, trying to make a daisy chain.

Jonah didn't even blink when she first did it, nor did he react when Nia started running her fingers along Jade's arm, down her shoulder. And Nia doesn't think it's an oblivious thing, more like a *whatever it was with Jade* thing. Like he sees them, and has seen them, and this isn't surprising to him at all. Like maybe, maybe, he's talked to Jade, and knows something even Nia isn't sure of.

"This is making me feel so incompetent," Jade says as she completely rips through yet another stem. "It was so easy when I was a kid."

"I think your fingers were smaller," Nia says.

Jade smiles up at her. The freckles on the tip of her nose and the high points of her cheeks are darker than the ones on the rest of her face, darker than they were when Nia picked her up at the airport six days ago. "Sure." Jade laughs. "We'll go with that."

"You're allowed to be nice to yourself," Nia says softly. "Even for small things."

Then Jade really grins. Her smile seems even bigger, with Nia's perspective from above. She can see how much her nose scrunches, her eyes crinkle, her cheeks round. How it takes over her entire face. "I love you, Nia," she says. "You know that?"

Nia's heartbeat triples in time. "I know that," she says. "I love you, too." And Jonah doesn't blink at that, either.

"Birthdays are weird as a twin," Jade muses.

Jonah furrows his brow. "What? I don't think so."

Jade rolls her eyes. "Okay, birthdays are weird *for me* as a twin. Like, growing up, it's this day that's supposed to be all about you, and you see all your friends have their time to feel special, and then you have a joint party where the theme is some sort of weird compromise between Pokémon and the US Women's National Team and there're a bunch of kids you never talk to and also your grandparents and maybe also mother are clearly more excited about your brother, because he's the bloodline or whatever shit they'd never admit to believing," she says. She's still focusing on her daisy chain, three whole flowers long now, and she bites her lip, releasing it with a short laugh.

"I had to share them, too," Jonah says, his tone a little sharper than Nia would deem necessary.

"Oh my God, Jonah, I know that. I'm not blaming you."

They're all quiet for a moment, and then Jonah just nods and says, "Okay."

"It obviously got better as I got older, because, like, who really gives a shit about birthdays after a while. I've just . . . I don't know. I've been thinking about it more recently, I guess. Because Michal"—Jade takes a deep, shaky breath—"was really good at making me feel special on my birthday. She'd do something a little extra, you know? Bring something to school, or whatever, to make sure I had some moment that day that was just for me."

Nia smiles at this, even as she can feel tears welling. Jade's right, Michal was *really* good at that kind of thing. She could zero in on whatever your biggest insecurity was, whatever thing was most painful, and do her best to assuage it. Without you having to say anything.

She makes eye contact with Jonah, but instead of finding an expression that mirrors her own, his brow is lowered, his jaw set.

"Well, she really did something extra for me one year," he says. The way he laughs gives Nia a distinct sense of unease.

"Okay, unnecessarily crude, but I'll accept the wordplay. Wait," Jade says, sitting up. "You and Michal didn't start dating until September. And . . ." she trails off.

She died at the beginning of June, Nia hears, even though she doesn't say it.

The way Jonah's lips curve tip Nia's unease directly into dread.

"We started sleeping together in June," he says.

Jade narrows her eyes. "I have a hard time believing that Michal was having sex with anyone, let alone you, for three whole months without telling me and Nia."

Jade looks at Nia, and whatever she sees on her face makes her own expression drop.

"Oh," Jade says.

"I did tell her she should probably tell you," Nia says, to which Jonah gives a distinctly mean laugh. Nia can see that the train is headed for derailment, and she's not sure she can get to the brake in time. "Jade—"

"But I was fine with Jonah and her dating!" she says, more to herself than them. She's looking straight ahead. "Why wouldn't she have *told* me?"

"Well, Jade, she told me lots of things she might never have told you, because I was her boyfriend, not just her friend."

Nia's stomach bottoms out, and from the look on her face, so does Jade's. "Jonah, that was below the belt," Nia says.

"Was it?" His tone drips with false aloofness.

Jade's expression moves from shock to hurt, but only briefly. Just as quickly her smile turns cruel. "Nine months is a *casual* relationship, Jonah. High schoolers date longer than that. I was 'just her friend' long enough for her to say that if any Pardo was the love of her life, it was me."

He looks away, a muscle in his jaw ticking.

Nia has no fucking clue what to do.

"Sure," he says. "You can say whatever you want, Jade."

"It's in my twenty-sixth birthday letter. I can show you, if you want. You can check her handwriting against her journals, which only Nia and I have, because she didn't want her parents to go through them. Did you even know they existed?"

"Jade," Nia says softly. "Please stop."

"It's fine, Nia," he says. "She's just upset because everything she wants, I get first."

Nia freezes, eyes wide. He can't *possibly* be talking about . . .

"Oh, please. I never had even remotely romantic feelings for Michal. Some friendships are just bigger than some relationships, and I'm so fucking sick of everybody in this world, including you, acting like that's not the case. Why is my love with her not as big, not as important, just because sex was never attached? Can you explain that to me? Why do you matter more, because you happened to have a desire to put your genitals closer to hers than I ever wanted to? Do you not see how incredibly fucking shallow that is?"

He smiles, and then Nia knows exactly what he's going to say. Exactly what he's been gearing up to say, since he made the weird *extra special* joke, for some reason Nia can't quite parse right now.

"I wasn't talking about Michal."

CHAPTER TWENTY-SIX

wednesday afternoon, july 2

Jade is so angry that the confusion takes a moment to register. "What?" she says, pinning Jonah with her stare.

The second he'd said it, he had looked away, but now he meets her gaze head on, the same anger she feels flaring in his eyes. "I said, I wasn't talking about Michal."

Jade laughs. "Okay, sure, because I have a wealth of friends who you've slept with, right."

She turns to look at Nia, but Nia is staring at Jonah. Her neck has splotches of red, her lips are pressed together, and she is wearing what Jade can only describe as the purest look of fury she's ever seen.

Jade looks back over her shoulder, and now Jonah is looking at Nia, instead of her, his eyes softening apologetically under her glare.

Then, she understands.

"Nia?" she says, and she can hear the pain in her voice before she feels it. And then it's in her chest, at her core, hitting her with the force of a bowling ball.

Neither says anything, but she keeps staring at Jonah until he nods.

"When?"

"A couple weeks before graduation in high school," Jonah says.

It takes her a second, but then she turns to Nia. "That party that Ari Torres invited me to. I was convinced you were mad at me for leaving you at home with Jonah, but that wasn't why you were avoiding me."

"It was eleven years ago, J," Nia says, and it's like Jonah fades into the foliage of the park. All Jade can think about is this.

"You kept it from me for eleven years," she hears herself say. And part of her knows she doesn't really have a right to be upset about this, that it shouldn't actually change anything. But it feels so *big*. All this time she thought Nia lost her virginity to a girl named Sophia her freshman fall at NYU, but really, her best friend and her brother had lost their virginities to one another, if her math is right, and she didn't know.

"I honestly don't think about it at all," Nia says, her voice small. "I didn't really think he did, either."

"But you had to have thought it was a big deal at the time, and you didn't tell me," Jade says. "Did you tell Michal?"

"Yeah, I did. I was really worried about telling you, because I wasn't sure how you'd react. And so she—well, *we* decided I wouldn't, since it was a one-time thing."

Shameful heat creeps up Jade's neck. "I would've understood! I mean, I was seventeen, and it's my twin brother, so yeah, maybe I wouldn't have immediately been stoked. But eventually, I would have."

"You're not reacting great now," Jonah says.

She whips toward him, the heat turning to blazing anger. "Don't fucking start, Jonah," she seethes. "It's so misogynistic, you talking about having sex with Nia like it's us competing

254 ♪ RACHEL RUNYA KATZ

for a soccer trophy when we were kids. You cannot tell me shit right now. Maybe ever. And, not that I owe you a single thing, but I'm upset that nobody ever told me, not that it happened."

"I wasn't just afraid you'd be upset," Nia says. When Jade turns, she's looking at her hands. "I was, but it wasn't just that."

"Oh?" Jade asks, but Nia doesn't say anything. Doesn't even look up.

She's just so *frustrated*. How is she the odd one out, here?

Nia and Michal were *hers*. A life of sharing so much with Jonah, and they were the only part of this world that felt like it was just for her. Then Michal started dating Jonah, and she told herself it was fine, it was different. Because she and Nia were still her true loves, and Michal made sure they knew it.

But now, hearing that there was a secret between the three of *them* that was kept from her for more than a decade . . .

Maybe she shouldn't have been fine with it. Maybe she should have had her hackles up, because even with the one thing she thought was sacred, Jonah has still found a way to make her second best.

Jade's crying now, wiping forcefully at the tears with the back of her hand. "God," she says as she chokes back a sob. "I feel like I have *nobody* left."

She doesn't realize what she's said until a sound tears out of Nia—a garbled noise that is almost like a *what?* but more like she's been hit by a car, all the air whooshing out of her.

"No, I didn't mean that," Jade scrambles to backtrack. "I didn't mean it like that. And I know you'll probably be back in the city soon—"

"I'm taking the offer, Jade," Nia says. There are tears in her eyes, too, and she tries to blink them away.

"What?"

"I'm taking the position at UNC," she says. "I'm not moving to New York."

"But you haven't heard back from NYU yet, and there are other universities," Jade protests.

"I want the position. I want to work at Radical Healing. I want to be able to buy a home on an academic salary. I want to live there. I like it, Jade. I don't want to move back to Brooklyn."

But what about me? she thinks. "When did you decide you were going to take it?" she asks.

Nia averts her eyes, picking up Jade's abandoned daisy chain. "The third day of the visit," she says.

"A week ago," Jade says slowly, swallowing. "And you told me the next day that your dream was still New York. Why wouldn't you just tell me the truth? God, do you not think it's worth telling me *anything*?"

Nia looks at her then, and Jade's tears are spilling now, but she makes no move to wipe them away. "I told you about Michal's birthday letter. About her wanting this trip."

Jade nods, closing her eyes. "But would you have if I'd responded quicker?"

Nia doesn't say anything. Jade counts her breaths.

"You don't trust me, Nia. Not with the important stuff."

Nia's eyes narrow, her jaw clenches, and Jade can feel the impact of the blow before it's even delivered. "The last time I tried to tell you something important," Nia says, "we didn't see each other for three years."

"THAT'S NOT *FAIR*," Jade says, and maybe it isn't.

Nia was the one who asked for time, she knows that. She put the ball in her own court, and then cowardly chose not to use it.

And maybe how Nia found out was wrong, but when she confronted Jade about Toni, Jade fucked up *bigger*. And even now, even after last night, she clearly doesn't understand just how bad. Because if she did, she wouldn't be telling Nia a thing about fairness.

"Guys, we—" Jonah says.

"Shut. Up," Nia says. It's pure reaction—she'd been so caught up in Jade that she'd completely forgotten he was here.

"I'm sorry," he says.

"You should be," Nia replies. "Can you leave? Just give us a few minutes."

He gives her a look that is both remorseful and trepidatious. "It's two-thirty," he says.

She releases a sharp groan, frustrated tears squeezing out of her eyes. "I really hate you right now," she chokes out.

"I know," he says, his voice low and quiet.

He hates himself, too, Nia realizes, and that's the problem. She resents that she notices, wishes she could turn it off. She doesn't want to be empathizing with him right now. She wants to be able to latch onto her anger. It's better than the alternative.

"Do we have to go?" Jade asks. Her eyes are fixed on Nia, and her gaze burns into her.

Nia nods, closing her eyes.

"But we haven't . . ." Jade trails off. "Jonah, go pack up the car," she says.

He nods, standing. "What about—"

"I will take care of Luna," she cuts him off. "You deal with the rest of it."

And he does. It's kind of amazing, actually, Nia's never seen him so compliant with Jade's direction. He must really be sorry.

He packs up all the food, and they clear the blanket, Jade tugging on Luna's leash to get her to follow so that Jonah can roll it up.

All the while, Jade looks at Nia, and Nia stares back, feeling like someone's inserted a pin in her heart, like one of those balloon magic tricks. If she shifts slightly, or the next one goes in at the wrong angle, that's it. She'll pop.

Jonah disappears, and Jade steps closer to her.

Instinctively, Nia takes a half step back. A bolt of pain shoots across Jade's face.

"How do we fix this?" Her voice is strained, earnest, her brows knitted together.

"I don't—" Nia swallows. Her throat is thick, scratchy. She might start sobbing. "I don't know."

"Please, Nia. If you need a moment, I can do that. You can call me. Or, fuck, I'll fly to Palo Alto. But if you want time again, it can't be like before. I thought I lost you, and I don't . . ."

Nia shakes her head. "You didn't lose me."

"But I didn't have you," Jade says.

Nia blinks slowly. *In what way did you want me?* she wants to scream. "Jade, do you have *any* idea what it sounds like to me when you say that?"

"Is this . . ." Jade says, pausing to rake her teeth over her bottom lip. "Should we not have slept together?"

There it is, that misplaced pin.

I guess not.

She turns away, because they really have to go, and because she would rather die than have Jade see what her words can do to her.

"Nia—"

"I need to take you to the airport, or you'll miss your flight."

"Fuck the flight," Jade says, her voice cracking. "This is more important."

Nia starts walking, and somehow, she can *feel* when Jade follows.

"Please—you're still upset," she says. "You're still mad at me for believing Toni over you? I'm not accusing you, I just want to understand. I want to fix this, and I need to understand."

Nia shakes her head, not trusting herself to engage. "I need a couple minutes."

"Okay," Jade says. "Okay, I'll stop."

They don't really have a couple of minutes, though. Because in a block and a half, they're outside the Airbnb and the car is already loaded up, Jonah leaning against the passenger-side door, keys in hand.

He passes them off to Nia, and they board in silence, Jonah and Luna in the back, and Jade up front. Nia pulls up the directions on her phone, and then they're off, twenty minutes behind schedule.

Everything she wants to say hangs in the air. It's suffocating.

It's a twenty-minute drive, but she feels each and every millisecond.

At the airport, there's no time. Nia had planned carefully: drop the twins off at 2:45, get the car returned by 3:15, in line at TSA for her own flight by 3:30. It's 3:07 when they pull up, and Jonah rushes to transfer Luna from lap to carrier and trots around to the trunk.

Nia is staring at the SUV in front of them, but she can hear that Jade hasn't opened the door, can feel her eyes on the side of her face.

"You need to get out of the car. You're supposed to get there extra early when you have a pet with you," Nia says.

"Nia, I can't get out of the car like this. We can't end on this note."

Nia takes steadying breaths, gathering her will to respond, but Jade beats her to it.

"Tell me I can come see you, or at the very least call," Jade says. *You promised me that we'd figure it out,* Nia hears underneath it.

Part of her wants to say yes, to tell Jade that it's all okay. They'll talk, they'll be fine, they'll go to the wedding together. But she can't.

All Nia can think about is sitting on that picnic blanket, Jade thinking that *she* was the one being unfair.

Jade doesn't get it. She just doesn't get it. And maybe that means that she'll never love Nia the way she wants her to. Maybe that means that Nia has been stupid this entire trip, stringing herself along. Maybe it means that the mess they're in is her fault for not accepting that sooner.

But right now, in this moment, it means that Nia can't bear to be misunderstood by Jade for a single second longer.

"Toni was right," she says quietly.

"What?"

Nia makes eye contact for the first time since they got in the car. "What you said three years ago—what Toni said about me. She was right. It's not why I told you about Cheyenne. But she was right, and so was Anabelle, and probably whoever else." Nia's hands tremble, and she folds them together in her lap to disguise it. "I know exactly what I want, Jade. *We* don't need to figure it out, *you* need to figure it out."

"Nia," Jade whisper-gasps.

"You don't get to sleep with me because you're annoyed that some guy wants to, and then say maybe we shouldn't have done it. Say that you don't have anybody left."

Jade shakes her head. "That's not at *all*—"

"I don't," she swallows. "I don't want an explanation right now. I just want you, for once in your life, not to run away from this problem."

Jade gapes at her.

"You need to get out of the car, Jade," Nia says.

And this time, she does.

CHAPTER TWENTY-SEVEN

june, three years ago

Jade squinted at her phone. Even though it was well into day-light hours outside, her blackout curtains were drawn, and she still hadn't gotten out of bed. She was awake, of course. Had been for hours. But in the darkness of her room, her phone screen seemed to be the same wattage as the sun.

NOT LONG NIA

Hey, J. I need to talk to you
about something important.
Can you meet at our bench
at 10:30? I'll bring food and
coffee.

The notification buzz might as well have been ominous organ music. They'd spent every single day together since Michal died. The rest of their texts from the last three weeks were just times and places, mostly after 10:00 a.m. for Jade's sake, but sometimes earlier if Nia felt like she couldn't han-dle being awake and alone.

Honestly, what could she have meant? In Jade's mind, everything important had already happened.

Maybe Toni said something to her while Jade was in the bathroom last night, or Nia had said something to Toni. She had been distant and weird, leaving Jade and Jonah's apartment only twenty minutes after Nia did. She'd been distant and weird a lot, recently. But to be fair to her, so had Jade.

It was hard to want to be around anybody but Nia, maybe Jonah sometimes. Her parents got all weepy whenever they looked at either of them, and while she knew that they loved Michal, too, it wasn't the same. Part of their grief was empathy at the abject horror of losing a child in the broad sense, and she was stuck feeling like she was expected to offer *them* comfort, while Jonah sat silently in the corner. All the responsibility on her, all the focus on him. Nia's parents were hovering, as though she hadn't acquired the ability to self-soothe at six months old, like everyone else. But Nia got it, and Nia's grief was purely about Michal, too.

So, she couldn't be too hard on Toni. Most people their age didn't know what to do with the kind of loss that she was going through, and those who tried usually missed the mark by miles.

She texted back a **sure, see you soon** and dragged her heavy limbs out of bed and into a shower and a clean change of clothing. Her eyelids seemed to be in a permanent state of pink and puffy. Nia's, too, though her eye makeup concealed it better. Part of Jade wished she could do the same, just so interacting with strangers wouldn't elicit sympathetic looks, but also it seemed to take all her available effort to shower in the morning and brush her teeth twice a day. She was hollow, more consciousness than physical person, unless she was with Nia.

Two days before, between sobs on the same Prospect Park

bench she was headed to now, she'd asked Nia when it would stop. When she was supposed to be able to get through the day without crying. *I don't know,* Nia had said. *But it hasn't even been three weeks, J. It'll happen eventually, but I know it's not yet.*

Jade made it to their bench near the Brooklyn Botanic Garden as if in a daze, realizing she wouldn't have been able to recount a single detail of the walk if pressed.

Nia was already there, of course, a second coffee and breakfast burrito saving the seat beside her. Her hair was messily pulled back in a claw clip that looked like it was going to slide out any minute, and the dark circles under her eyes were deeper than yesterday. Beautiful as always, but unkempt in a way Nia never was. The seam of her lips was a tense line, and her knee bounced with nerves as she offered the food and iced coffee to Jade.

"Thank you," she said, and took a sip. It was good, but not as good as their usual place. The barista whose shift most often overlapped with their trips referred to the three of them as their "favorite throuple." They noticed immediately when Nia had moved to Madison, and acted out the five stages of grief over the throuple breakup that wasn't, even though there were four people in line behind Jade and Michal.

Neither Jade nor Nia had been willing to brave it without her.

Nia nodded, and brought her own cup to her lips. She drank hers hot, even in the middle of summer. Either she'd eaten her food already, or she hadn't eaten at all. That, combined with the continued bounce of her knee, begot imagined organ notes, heavy on the pedals, once again.

"What did you want to talk to me about?" Jade asked, since Nia still hadn't said anything.

Nia took a deep breath, inhaling and exhaling through her nose. "I don't really know how to say this, J."

Jade felt her stomach drop. "Did you . . . are you sick?"

Her lips parted, a little oval of shock appearing between them. "Oh. Oh, no, *no*. That's not what the text was about. God, I'm sorry I made you think that even for a second," she said.

"It's okay," Jade said. Her shoulders sagged with relief. "I'm glad . . ."

"It's not good, though," Nia said. "What I have to tell you. It's not *that,* but it's not good."

Jade shrugged, then took a bite of her burrito. "Aight, then. Shoot."

Another deep breath, and another. Jade had enough time for three more bites before Nia got any more words out. "Toni's cheating on you with one of the veterinary nurses at her office."

She rushed the words out, slammed so hard against one another that it took Jade several seconds to unstick them in her head. When she finally did, all she said was, "Oh."

"I'm so sorry, J," Nia said. She squeezed Jade's knee, and when she took her hand away, Jade moved her leg as if chasing it, her thigh knocking into Nia's.

"I . . ." she started, trailing off. "You're sure?"

Nia looked at her hands, picked at a hangnail. On instinct, Jade reached out to stop her. As soon as she'd separated Nia's hands, Nia threaded her fingers into Jade's. "I'm sure," she said.

Jade searched for words. Searched for feelings, even. She kept drawing blanks. "I don't . . . know what to do with that information," she said at last.

Nia furrowed her brow, tilting her head away from Jade slightly. "You have to break up with her," she said, like it was easy, obvious. "I can go get your stuff from her place, or you could send Jonah, or something."

Jade shrugged. All she could think of was the conversation she'd had with Michal at Disneyland, about Michal getting to see her with Toni. That can't just be . . . over. "I'll talk to her," Jade said. "I can't throw away our entire relationship over one mistake."

"It wasn't just one mistake," Nia said softly. She ran her thumb over the back of Jade's hand. "It's been going on for months, Jade."

"Cheyenne?" Jade asked. When Nia nodded, she closed her eyes and shook her head. Dimly, she knew it wasn't good that she could guess immediately, but it was still too much for her to grasp. "I've been really distant the last few months, with everything. I guess . . . I guess I haven't been a very good partner."

"Jade," Nia said, her voice strained with tender consternation. "You can't blame yourself for your partner cheating on you while your best friend was dying."

Jade unthreaded their fingers then, propping her elbows on her knees and dropping her head to her hands. "There has to be some reason. Something I did."

"There really doesn't have to be a reason beyond the fact that Toni fucking sucks. She made up an entire story about an emergency veterinary clinic just so she could fuck her nurse."

Jade let out a gust of air. "Wow, okay. How did you find out?"

Nia bit her lip, looking away.

"Did Cheyenne tell you?"

She shook her head. "No. I, um . . . I looked at Toni's texts last night."

"*What?*"

"I know it's bad, I know. But I've just . . . I thought something was going on for a while. She's been so weird with you, and extra weird to me and Mich and Jonah since, like, December. And then she was making this moony-eyed face at her phone, and left it on the coffee table without locking it when she went to help you in the kitchen, so I checked. I recognize that it wasn't a good thing to do, but I was right, J."

Jade blinked, trying to process what Nia was saying. "Jonah was still in the living room when we went to make popcorn," she said eventually.

Nia stared at her. "Yes, that's true," she said slowly.

The first emotion cut through Jade's numbness. It seemed closest to anger. "Are you saying you and Jonah conspired to look through my girlfriend's phone?"

"It wasn't like that," she whispered.

"Oh? So, he tried to stop you?"

Nia said nothing, but she didn't have to. If anything, he'd probably encouraged it. Jonah and Toni had never gotten along. Jade mostly hadn't minded—she and Jonah didn't always get along, either. But this was another level.

"I can't believe you'd do that, Nia."

"Look, I'm not going to try to defend myself here. That was objectively not the healthy way to do this. I should've asked her, or maybe come to you with my suspicions first, or something. But I felt like I couldn't say anything if I hadn't gotten proof. I'm sorry I meddled like that, instead of just being straight with you. I'll even apologize to Toni for going through her phone, if that's what you want. But I'm not sorry for telling you, Jade."

The anger swelled, filled Jade up to her extremities. Honestly, she could've handled hearing it from Toni herself, or maybe even Cheyenne, better than from Nia. But Jade still felt thoroughly cracked, like Nia and the comfort that Michal had known Toni were the pieces of duct tape keeping her from completely shattering. The idea that Nia might judge her for hanging on was too much to bear.

So, she reached for the worst thing she could think of, the worst thing Toni had said to her, during their biggest fight. When Jade had asked for more support, and mentioned that Nia had encouraged her to speak up when her needs weren't being met.

"Toni said you would do this. That you would make up whatever you could to break us up. Because you hate her, and you're in love with me."

She said it, even though she knew it wasn't true. The regret was instantaneous; it came before the nausea, before she caught the absolutely stricken look on Nia's face.

But it was still too late.

Nɪᴀ ʜᴀᴅ ᴘʟᴀʏᴇᴅ this out in her head a hundred times in a hundred ways. She'd prepared for denial, she'd imagined tears, she'd wondered if she'd have to talk her down from veterinary clinic vandalism.

In none of her myriad of fabricated scenarios had she imagined this unrestrained cruelty.

After a moment, her shock waned, replaced with a lump of sadness so thick she thought she'd choke. Tears sprung to her eyes, and she tried to dab them away with the knuckles of her thumbs. No use, probably.

"Nia," Jade said. She reached her hand toward Nia's shoulder, but Nia jerked away.

"Don't fucking touch me," she muttered, her voice shaky. "I should've . . . I should've known you wouldn't believe me." She pulled out her phone, going to her photos app and selecting the last seven pictures.

"I'm—"

"I just sent you what I saw," she said, pushing herself up off the bench. "Look at it, or don't. Stay with her, or don't. I don't care anymore." The harshness of her tone belied the feeling in her chest, like her sternum was being carved with a spoon.

She looked at Jade, wanting to see if her words landed. Jade looked back, her gaze comprised only of remorse. But really, at this point, it didn't matter how sorry she was. There are some things that can't be unsaid.

So, Nia turned on her heels and left. Back to her mom's new apartment in Williamsburg, made tinier by her dad's extended visit. She was grateful for the gesture, but their collective helicoptering suffocated her, no matter how well-meant. The only person she'd wanted to be with the past few weeks was Jade, and now she wanted to be completely alone.

Her mom's place was empty, so she scrawled out a note, bought the earliest flight she could find—a $377 one-way ticket to Madison that left in an hour and forty-five minutes—threw all her shit in her suitcase, and called an Uber.

She made it home like a reanimated corpse and fell asleep on top of her covers, all her clothing and makeup still on.

She slept until noon the next day, and when she woke, her phone screen was alight with notifications.

Stoney Baloney
> i went to look for you this
> morning but helen and kevin
> said you were already gone,
> and you aren't answering
> your phone

maybe i should have gone
yesterday, but i wanted to
end things with toni first. to
show you i believe you

nia, i am so sorry. i didn't
even look at the pictures you
sent, i swear. i believe you
without them. toni and i are
done

and what i said was so
horrible. i don't even know
why i said it, toni only said it
to me because she was mad.
i know it's not true, and i'm
so so sorry

Nia felt her heart breaking, as if she were still sitting on
that bench, hearing Jade say it all over again. Because sure,
Jade could say that she didn't *think* it was true, but it *was*
true—at least in part. So Nia wasn't really sure that what
Jade actually thought made a difference.

Nia
I need time, Jade. I'll
contact you.

And then she turned off her phone.

CHAPTER TWENTY-EIGHT

july in brooklyn

If Jade thought that she and Jonah had grown apart before the trip, they're entirely different species of plants now. In different habitats. On different planets.

Jonah's consulting career has always meant an inordinate amount of travel—once per month at minimum, but every now and then, he'll be on a project that requires him to fly out every week. His travel routines are cultivated down to a science so that he can cut everything as close as possible and minimize the amount of time he spends away from his own bed. He'd never say it, but Jade has long suspected that part of it is to minimize the time away from her, too.

Since they've been back, he's arranged flights so that he leaves the night before his first meeting and comes home the day after his last. Stretching two-day trips into three, four. Even when he is home, they're ships passing in the night—him up earlier than she ever is and apparently choosing to buy breakfast near his office every morning to avoid any refrigerator run-ins.

Jade, for her part, continues to go directly for Luna's leash when she gets home from the studio, allowing time for

Jonah to retreat into his room before they come back from their nighttime walk. Which never used to be her responsibility, since she usually did the midday one, too.

The first few days after the road trip, he tried to talk to her. When she and Luna returned, he'd be on the couch, elbows on his knees, that earnest and eager look on his face. And Jade just couldn't take it.

You need to stop trying, she told him on the fifth day. *If we talk now, I don't know what I'll say to you. But whatever it is, it won't be something we can come back from.*

That hint was big enough for even Jonah Williams Pardo to take.

Tonight, Jade unlocks the door to a quiet apartment. Jonah closed off his bedroom when he left for LaGuardia on Monday, and the sun's still out, so there's no potential strip of light under the door to tell her whether it's actually empty or just cavernous with the space she asked for.

"Hey, baby girl," she says as Luna trots over to her, sitting when Jade motions for her to do so. Jade slides her leash off the hook beside the door and clips it onto her collar. Luna looks up at her, mouth wide and tongue out in excitement, tail wagging against the floor. Jade tries not to think about how it took Luna a week to get back to this, to stop going to the wrong side of the bed in the morning, to stop looking behind Jade with the expectation that someone else would be at the door.

They walk their usual route, and Jade tries to let every thought that wants to nest fly by instead. How ironic: she kept her promise to keep afloat—to not give in to the avoidance that's always threatening to overtake her—on the trip, and the moment she got home, she let herself drown.

"Let" is generous. Jade has practically encased her own feet in cement and thrown herself into the East River.

She stops for Luna to smell each tree, nip at each dandelion. In the park, she finds a stick, and throws it until her arm aches. Like so many days of these last few weeks, it's dusk by the time they turn toward home.

A block away, she reaches for her pocket instinctively. But she left her phone on the catchall table in their doorway. Otherwise, she'd spend the whole walk staring at the **i'm so sorry. you'll always have me, just let me know whenever you're ready to talk** she sent a few days after they got back, to no response.

She unlocks the door to a quiet apartment once again.

Quiet, but not empty. All the lights are on, and Jonah is on the couch, still in his work suit, his carry-on beside him. He stares at her. Eager, earnest, a little angry, maybe.

Jade could unlace her shoes, grab a tub of the pasta she made yesterday, and close herself off in her bedroom. But her head bobs above water long enough for her to say, "Yes, Jonah?"

"I need to talk to you," he says.

"I don't want to talk to you," she replies.

He lets out a gust of breath. "Well, too fucking bad."

"What? Are you gonna strap me to a chair and make me listen?"

"No. You're going to sit down and listen, and *talk,* because you have to."

"Do I?"

"Yes, you do. It's been weeks, and you're all . . ." The look on his face makes Jade's blood feel frothy, like everything she's shoved down might bubble up out of her.

Jade circles the couch, planting herself in the velvet armchair she got when their upstairs neighbor moved. It's mostly for decoration, but she doesn't think she could handle sitting right next to him. "Okay, I'm sitting." She sweeps her arms out, telling him he has the floor.

"I'm going to talk first," Jonah says.

"I'm waiting," she snips.

He clenches his jaw, then brushes past this. "I'm going to apologize, but first I'm going to explain myself as best I can, and I need you to listen. If you tell me to fuck off or need to yell at me or whatever, you can do that after. But let me do this first."

Jonah pauses, his eyes fixed on her. She wants to tell him no, that it's too late. That she wants nothing to do with him. And if she opens her mouth, she probably will. Instead, she nods.

"I have trouble when you talk about Michal, sometimes," Jonah says. Jade snorts, and that jaw muscle ticks again, but he brushes past this, too. "I have trouble because I know what your relationship with her was like, and what my relationship with her was like. You said I was shallow for thinking that my love with her was bigger just because sex or romance was involved. And you'd be right, if I thought that.

"But I don't think that. I *know* that her love with you and Nia was bigger than her love with me. You don't have to tell me that she told you so in her letters—I know it because she actually *gave* you letters. I know it because one of her nicknames for me was Two, as in JWP II, even though I was born first. Because you were always most important to her. She was obvious about it in every single way. Even the last conversation she had with me was mostly about you and Nia.

"She loved me, I know that. But I don't think she was in love with me the way I was with her. Maybe she could've been, if she wasn't dying, or if she let herself. But she wanted to save all her best love to be shared with the two of you. And I didn't want to resent her for that, so I let myself resent you instead.

"I'm jealous of you. Of who you were to her. It's why I

let Avuelo, and Mom and Dad, and maybe everyone else, to some extent, treat me like I was worse off. Because I was embarrassed not to be, and envious that you had her in a way I never could, and that you could share in that with Nia. Which was stupid, of course, because it made you resent me, too. And you were all I had, so that meant that I had nobody," he says. He takes a deep breath, wrings his hands together.

Jade blinks. Her stomach roils, guilt simmering with her anger, her frustration, her sadness.

"When you talked about how special she made you feel," he continues, "it hurt me, and I interpreted it as you rubbing it in my face on purpose. Which you obviously weren't, because then you actually did rub it in my face, and that was so much worse. That's why I said what I said about Nia. I wanted to beat you, and I wanted you to hurt like I was hurting. It was fucked on so many levels, I know that. And I'm sorry." He swallows, looking her dead in the eye. Expression somber, eyes just barely glassy. "I'm really, really, really sorry, Jade. There aren't words for how sorry."

She nods slowly, raking her teeth over her bottom lip. "Okay," she says. She crosses her arms and presses her fingers into her ribs.

"You can yell now," Jonah says.

Jade shakes her head, sighing. "I don't want to yell."

They're silent for a long moment.

She takes a deep breath, tries not to think about Nia counting out her exhale. "Why wouldn't you . . . ?" She trails off before the "tell me" because she knows she'd never have been receptive to it before all this. Guesses that he might not have been able to put it into words. "I know that you loved Michal," she whispers. "But you just kind of . . . stood there, stoic, through everything. I think you shed maybe one tear at the funeral. It's hard to watch you like that, when I'm not only falling apart but fucking *disintegrating,* and then you're being offered comfort by everyone but—" She clamps her mouth shut before the "Nia." Even now, there's so much she cannot make herself say.

"It's different for me. I know we were raised in the same house, but we weren't always treated the same."

"You don't have to tell me that," she bites out.

"I don't, huh? I don't have to tell you that the attention, or favor, or whatever you want to call what they showed me because I was the son was also a lot of fucking pressure? That even our relatively liberal father cradled you when you fell but told me, 'Brush yourself off, and don't cry, little man'? I know you're a stemme lesbian or whatever, so maybe you have better access to masculinity than a lot of women do, but it was never forced upon you."

"I . . ." She loses her train of thought, stuck on the fact that he can accurately categorize her gender expression and a little ashamed to be surprised at all of this.

"What I'm trying to say," he says, "is that I don't really know how to cry. So, when I'm not showing my emotions in the same way you are, it's not because I'm not feeling them." He gives a wry laugh. "Another thing I'm jealous of, I guess."

"I'm sorry," she says eventually. "About what I said to you on our birthday. I was trying to be cruel."

"I deserved it," Jonah says.

"Not to the extent I took it. Like you said, I wanted you to hurt, too." Jade takes a deep breath and looks upward, blinking back tears. "I feel so stupid that I couldn't see this."

"I didn't exactly make it easy for you," he says.

"You never have, but you're my brother."

He sighs so loudly it's almost a groan. "That's—that's good," he says. "I was worried you didn't want to be my sister anymore," he whispers.

"*Jonah,*" she says, and she bursts into tears. "That's not even a possibility."

His expression is one of both pain and relief, and she's not sure which makes her heart twist more. "You just folded in on yourself, shut everything out, me most of all. I've never seen it, and I . . . I don't know. I thought maybe I pushed too far. That maybe we couldn't come back from it. And I need to try to make things right with Nia, but I felt like I couldn't do it without talking to you first. And my therapist seemed to think that made sense."

"You're in therapy?"

"I've been going three times a week since we got back."

"Yeah?"

"Yeah," he says. "Jordan saw him through business school and sent me his number, and it's . . . 'good' feels like the wrong word. It's the hardest thing I've ever done, but I need it."

Jade's crying turns ugly—she's hiccupping, wiping ineffectually at the snot dripping out of her nose—and Luna drops her worried face onto Jade's knee. "I was mad at you. Maybe I *am* mad at you, but that's not why I couldn't talk to you." She hiccups again. "I couldn't—I can't think about the trip. Because I knew if I did, this would happen.

"I'm not . . . I don't know how to be a whole person anymore. I can't think about anything for too long, or it feels like I'm being run over by a car in slow motion, except all my neurons are firing at normal speed. I haven't even opened my birthday letter."

"Yikes," Jonah says, and it makes her laugh a little. "Have you talked to Nia?"

Jade half nods, half shakes her head, hugging her arms more tightly around herself. "I sent—" she starts, but the words get caught in her throat. "I can't talk about this," she whispers.

Jonah frowns, his brow furrowed. He scrapes his hand over his chin.

"You look like you want to say something," Jade says.

"At the risk of you finally telling me to fuck off," he says, "you need to let yourself be in love with Nia."

Jade chokes. "What?"

"I don't know if you're afraid of being happy or afraid of losing her, too, or just loyal to something I can't see or understand. But you've been in love with her since we were kids, and I don't know exactly what happened after Michal died or after I went to pack our stuff, but she clearly feels the same way."

"I'm not—I haven't . . ." Jade sputters. "I've had girl-friends."

"I'm not saying you didn't love them, too. But also, they've all had a problem with Nia, in one way or another."

"They've had issues with Nia and Michal, how close we all were," she protests.

"Jade," Jonah says, not even attempting to restrain his eye roll, "Michal was never the issue."

Her jaw drops. Twice. The words can't seem to form, in her brain or on her tongue. She wipes her nose again. "Oh," she says.

Jonah nods, a glint of amusement creeping into his eyes.

"I feel so stupid," she says for the second time in the span of ten minutes.

"You should. I mean, if I realized it, and you didn't . . ."

"Shut up. We're not there yet," Jade says, but she's laughing.

"Did you reject her?" Jonah asks. "Three years ago, is that why you stopped seeing each other?"

Jade shakes her head. "No, I . . ."

Except is that not what happened, in essence? She'd repeated what Toni said to her; sure it was a lie, because it was the easiest thing to reach for when she thought Nia was ripping the tattered remnants of her life further apart. But if it was true, how could Nia read it as anything other than rejection? An extremely callous one, at that.

"Fuck, I guess I did," she says softly. "I didn't mean to."

"I'm not going to tell you what to do, I know I have no leg to stand on," Jonah says. "But maybe sending a text wasn't good enough."

"I know it wasn't," Jade says, swallowing. "I might be too little, too late."

The corners of his lips turn down sympathetically. "Jade, it's *Nia*. That can't be true. If you want to be with her, I think all you need to do is say so. And maybe grovel a little."

"But how would that even work? My life is in Brooklyn, and she's about to settle down in North Carolina. To work in academia."

Jonah's laugh sounds a little pitying, and Jade bristles. "No offense, but I don't really think it is. You can do ceramics anywhere. I don't know what to tell you about her being a professor, but your only close friend who is still in New York is in a cemetery. *I'm* in Brooklyn, but I'm not your favorite person right now and I know you were trying to move out before Michal died and Mom begged you to stay."

She just stares at him, and whatever he sees on her face makes him belly laugh.

"Dad told me that one. I'm not *that* good at reading you."

"Luna," she says.

"If you move to North Carolina, you can take her with you. I can't handle a dog on my own with my schedule, I know that. And besides"—he grins—"she likes Nia best."

Jade draws her feet up into the chair, wrapping her arms around her knees and pulling them toward her chest. "I just—I can't take that risk. We promised we'd be friends forever, the three of us. Maybe there've been times when that's been muddled, but I could always make myself get past it, because I knew that wasn't how it was supposed to be." Jonah frowns, but this only makes Jade want to press on. "I've already lost Michal. My relationship with you is fucked up, I have a lot of resentment toward most of our family that I'm not quite sure how to heal from. If Nia and I . . . if we . . ." *God, just say it.* "If we were in a relationship, and it ended, it would kill me."

"And letting it go on like this wouldn't?"

Jade sucks in a breath, and she loses whatever progress she'd made in slowing her tears.

"I survived Michal's death. I know it's not the same, but you are a much stronger person than I am. If you needed to, you'd survive it. But you might never need to."

Again, she stares. It's all too much for her to process at once, but that last bit slices through the haze.

"Can I make you dinner?" he asks.

It's all she can do to make herself nod.

He gets up and pats her shoulder on his way to the kitchen. "Go read your letter, Jade. It's time."

My Sweet Jade,

First, HAPPY 29TH BIRTHDAY!

I dedicated some portions of Nia's letter for this year
to groaning about how many times I've written birthday
greetings and my ensuing hand cramps. I think I've gotten
it out of my system, and I'm sure she'll tell you all about
it, so I'll spare you the same complaints. You may wonder if
it really counts as sparing you if I open with this, and I can
assure you, it does. Despite all appearances, I have exercised
superhuman restraint in these letters.

Also, mazels on finishing your PhD!!!! I know in all
likelihood you finished a year or two ago, but just in case it
took a little longer, I wanted to build in some buffer time. I
am so impressed with you. I know it's been hard, and that
diversity committee drove you nuts, but I hope you've found
a job that uses your degree and makes it feel worth it. And
that you've kept up your pottery hobby. She won't say it
because it's inappropriate, of course, but I think some small
part of my mother is excited to inherit the matching set of
mugs and bowls you made me.

My best guess is that you are either toward the end of
the kicked-bucket-list/end-of-twenties road trip or have
just returned. I'm sorry for getting Nia to do the dirty work
of convincing you, but her birthday comes first and I know
you can't really say no to her. I hope you gained something
from it—I am so deeply sorry I wasn't there to hold your
hand at KKBE or to deal with whatever head-in-the-sand
bullshit Jonah managed to say when he got uncomfortable.

I hope Mickve Israel wasn't too hard for you guys to do, but I'm giving you my grace and understanding in advance if it was. Finally, I really hope you shared a room with Nia and not Two. He's recently started snoring like a motherfucker. I think trying to fall asleep second in a bed with him (I know, ew, I've been in bed with your brother, SORRY) should be classified by the UN as a form of torture.

I said this to Nia, but on the teeny-tiny off chance that I was wrong, and you managed to go on the trip last year or the year before, I hope it all the same, and that you'll forgive my tardiness.

I hope that it brought you some peace. I hope that it brought you and Nia closer together, as hard as that is to imagine as a possibility. If I were to believe in fate, I'd believe in it for the three of us. That bowling alley had to come into existence just so I could have my birthday there and introduce you. For you bitches to be mine forever, but also each other's.

I'm feeling quite sentimental, as you can see. My mood goes up and down as I write—sometimes a letter has a mission, like Nia's did this year, and I find the words much more easily. I laugh as I go, I imagine how you'll react. But sometimes, like this one, they're almost aimlessly reflective. The words get stuck in my brain exactly where the tumor once was (I can make unscientific yet poetic claims like this because I'm dead and can't hear you correct me), and I find that when they do come, they bring along a deep melancholy. I think right now I'm genuinely appreciating the loss of the road trip, the fact that I was robbed of sharing this experience with the two of you. How strange to grieve my own death.

Please also wish Jonah a happy birthday for me. But not until after you soak up this love from me to only you. You deserve to have a bit of the day that's just about you.

Loving you with all my heart, always,
Michal

CHAPTER TWENTY-NINE

july in palo alto

Nia fell apart when she got back to California, but not as much as she might have expected. Perhaps waiting an extra twenty minutes to get out of a Kia Soul idling in the Enterprise Rent-A-Car lot because she was crying too much to be seen took care of some of the meltdown in advance.

Even so, she got back to her apartment around 8:00 p.m. and fell asleep on top of her covers in her makeup and clothes the way she only has once before. The déjà vu when she awoke the next morning was stomach-churning.

At first, she cried, but mostly she slept. And when she was awake, she busied herself with laundry and dishes and plant care. Listened to political podcasts because that was somehow less painful than being left alone with her own mind.

And then she got Jade's text.

you'll always have me

It was so very Jade. Something she meant with her whole heart, and yet so ambiguous it might as well have been nothing.

If it was **you'll always have my friendship**, Nia could've worked with that. She would have been utterly crushed, but she could've pieced herself together, called Jade to figure it out.

If it was **i'm in love with you, too**, she probably would've been on the next flight to New York.

Even **i've made up my mind, can we call?** and she'd have picked up the phone.

But no, it was **you'll always have me**, so Nia just stared at the screen for a full minute before closing the messaging app, opening her email, and officially accepting the offer at UNC.

The timing could be worse, she supposes, because a couple of weeks have passed and now she's in the throes of planning—fittings for her maid of honor dress (cream, because say what you will about her mother, she's not delusional enough to be the one wearing white), apartment and house hunting in Durham and Chapel Hill. Does she want to be able to walk or bike to campus or is it more important to be closer to her community work? She doesn't have time to U-Haul between the wedding and the start of grad classes, but she didn't want to pay a moving company enough for them to pack everything for her, so her apartment is a vortex of boxes, clearings just wide enough to walk around with only moderate stumbling.

Now is the only time in her life where this level of chaos has been welcome.

It prevents her from mapping commutes from her saved homes on Zillow to ceramics studios.

It doesn't prevent her from looking at which studios have job openings.

It definitely doesn't prevent her from opening up the **Stoney Baloney** text thread and staring at her unsent **That's all you've got?**, but it keeps her staring to once every few hours.

She's out of jelly but too close to the wedding and the

move to buy more, so she fixes herself a peanut butter and honey sandwich and finds herself swiping over to the text thread as she makes her way to the couch.

Maybe she'll send it. Jade needs to make the decision herself—it can't be like the trip, something that she's been trapped into by obligation, even if she came around to wanting it—but maybe it's the nudge Jade needs.

Her thumb hovers over the tiny blue arrow. It's the closest she's ever come, and her finger trembles with the temptation.

But then a banner flashes across the top of her screen, announcing an incoming call from Jonah, of all people.

"Hello?"

The receiver picks up his deep inhale in crisp clarity. "Hey, Nia. It's Jonah."

"I have caller ID," she says.

He sighs. "Everyone is so sassy today."

"Sorry," she mutters.

"Don't," he says, sighing again. "I deserve it. And that's why I'm calling. I want to apologize."

She drops down onto the couch, folding her legs underneath her. "I'm waiting," she says, and bites into the sandwich.

Jonah's laugh comes through the receiver a little muffled. "You and Jade," he says, and she can hear in his voice that he's shaking his head.

Nia's stomach drops, hearing her name. "How is she?" she asks. She can't help herself.

"How do you think?" he replies. *Whatever it was with you and Jade.*

She wishes she had any goddamn idea, but she knows that's not the right thing to say. Having Jonah in the middle of things has never helped. She gives a noncommittal *hmm* instead.

"I'm so sorry for how I behaved at the picnic," he says.

"I mean, in general, but especially that I brought up us sleeping together in high school."

"It was pretty fucking awful," Nia agrees. "And incredibly immature."

"I know," he says. "And it caused a fight between you and Jade."

"I don't think you can really say you *caused* that," Nia says slowly.

"Maybe not. But what I said triggered it, or worsened it, or whatever," he amends.

Nia nods, then realizes he can't see her. "Fair," she says.

"And I *am* sorry. I'd explain why I did what I did, but I'm pretty sure you could see exactly what was going on with me even before I understood it." He pauses to chuckle, and despite herself, Nia smiles. "It was very messed up for me to say it at all, since we'd agreed to keep it to ourselves, but it was extra wrong for me to do it like that, as though it was another thing Jade and I were competing over. Jade's right, it was sexist, but maybe more than that, it was a gross way for me to talk about something that was actually really special to me. I don't mean that in an 'I was in love with you' way—I think we both know that's never been us. But sex is weird and embarrassing when you're that age and I'd just broken up with my girlfriend because I felt like I wasn't ready for it. You were so nice and understanding about everything, and I actually had fun. I don't know if I would've been able to if it had been anybody but you. I am really, really sorry that I did something that could have ruined that memory for you," he says.

"That," Nia says as she blinks back tears, "was a really good apology, Jonah."

"I practiced with my new therapist," he says.

"Ah," she says. "Well, thank you. And I hope you stick with the therapy. It'll be good for you."

"Wow, thaaaaanks," he says.

"It's not an insult."

"I know, I know. I think I'm not totally . . . comfortable with the idea yet."

The line goes quiet for a little bit, and Nia almost checks to see if the call has dropped.

Eventually, he says, "If there's anything I can do to help make things right with you, please let me know."

"Just try not to do it again," Nia replies, laughing a little. "And stay in therapy."

"I heard you the first time."

"I know." She sighs. "Actually . . . I think I need a date to my mother's wedding."

Jonah goes quiet again. Then he says, "I'm not the first person you asked, am I?"

"No, you aren't."

"If things were different, would I still be your best option?"

Nia doesn't answer.

"I will clear my schedule and make sure I have the right suit dry-cleaned. I'll be ready to go, but feel free to cancel on me last minute, okay?"

"I won't," Nia says.

"There's no late fee, promise. I'll leave halfway through the ceremony if you want."

"Okay, Jonah. Thank you for detailing the fine print aloud," she says.

"Anytime. I'm sorry, Nia. And I love you."

"I love you, too, Jonah," Nia says, out loud for the very first time in her life.

288   RACHEL RUNYA KATZ

"I'll see you next week?" he asks.

"Yes," she confirms, and then they say their goodbyes.

For a few minutes after she hangs up, Nia sits on her couch, eating her sandwich in small bites that take her minutes to chew, and staring at the nail holes scattered across what used to be her gallery wall. Having Jonah there will be good, she convinces herself. He's on her side, and she would really rather not do it alone. And she wants to have a relationship with him, still, even if she and Jade never figure it out. Asking him was the wise choice.

She isn't just breaking her own heart in advance, yet again.

Nia finishes her sandwich, then opens the text thread with Jade, hitting the back arrow until **That's all you've got?** disappears.

I'm going to the wedding with Jonah, she types and deletes.

I miss you, she types.

What do you mean by "always" and "have" and "me"?

I'm honestly so mad at you, Jade. I give you such a pass about everything, because I know you like sticking to your promises and have trouble reframing things once you've decided something—like understanding that Toni wasn't a good partner, or that Jonah is hurting, too. I give you such a pass because I've been in love with you and I thought you only wanted to be friends. But now we've had sex, and I have so much trouble believing that you would be that careless with me, no matter what you thought. You had to have known. It felt like you knew when you touched me. It felt like the words were etched into my skin, and it felt like you were saying them back. That's mean. That's cruel of you to do to me when you didn't know what you wanted, when I've wanted you for so long.

Delete, delete, delete.

I know I should have told you sooner, and I'm sorry. It's all my fault.

She deletes that, too.

I love you, Jade, Nia writes, and even though she doesn't press send, she can't bring herself to erase it, either.

CHAPTER THIRTY

august

Jade watches from the foot of Jonah's bed as he undoes a third tie and loops a fourth around his neck. It's a pink-and-yellow floral pattern set against a deep blue background. Just like the last one.

"You have to be playing at this point. Those are fucking identical," Jade says.

Jonah doesn't spare her a glance as he folds the collar over this one after he secures the knot. "You know, it's Wednesday night. I could be in sweats right now."

"If you were in sweats, then you wouldn't be able to go to Helen's wedding."

His eyes snap to hers in the mirror. "I'm *not* going to the wedding," he says.

Jade fiddles with the buttons on the sleeve of her suit jacket. "You don't know that," she says. "This could go so poorly."

"It won't," Jonah insists.

"I'll hate myself if I'm the reason she has to go to her mom's third wedding alone. I need the backup."

"I'm picking ties, aren't I? What more do you want?"

Jade rolls her eyes. "I want you to display some sense of urgency."

"But there isn't any."

"*Jonah.*"

"How's this one?" he asks, ignoring her complaint.

"It looks very nice. Just like the last one did."

"It's the same but a quarter-inch thinner."

Jade groans and Jonah laughs, offering his hand to help her up. She accepts it, smoothing her slacks once she's on her feet. "Are you ready?"

"The better question is are *you*."

"I'm not, but I'm not going to be," she says. "I think I just have to do it."

"You do," Jonah says.

"You'll be in the café on standby?"

"My kindle is charged and ready. But seriously, Jade, I'm not going to this wedding."

"But if she says—"

"If we have this conversation again, I'm not paying my half of the rent this month," Jonah interrupts, and walks out the door.

Nia instructed Jonah to be outside Gene's brother's restaurant—a trendy/cozy Italian joint in Prospect Heights and the venue for the wedding—at 5:30. Jade drops Jonah at the coffeeshop around the corner, reminds him repeatedly to keep his ringer on while he waves her off, and makes it to the meeting point by 5:15.

Even in her linen suit, the claggy August heat stifles. She considers removing her jacket, but her bodysuit is backless and the sun beating on her bare skin might actually make things worse. And besides, she just ironed the jacket. Might as well minimize the wrinkles while she can.

The wait passes excruciatingly slowly, but Jade can't

bring herself to pull out her phone. Can't bring herself to look anywhere but right at the Closed for Private Event sign on the door of the restaurant.

After a minor eternity, it swings open. Nia steps out in a floor-length silk dress, off-white and curve-skimming with a long slit for her right leg. The neckline is high and square and as she turns, Jade gets enough of a glimpse to see that it's backless.

She expects Nia to scan around for Jonah, maybe skip past Jade once or twice before she realizes that it's her here instead. But she doesn't. She hones in on Jade as if she knew she would be out there before she'd even opened the door, despite her standing beyond the view of those inside.

During the few steps it takes for Nia to reach her, Jade feels her breath hitch, her heart hammer, her skin tingle. It's not just nerves over what she's about to say; it's also her physical reaction to the sight of Nia after so long.

The sun glints off whatever shimmer she's applied to her cheek and collarbones. She's glowing. So beyond beautiful. Beyond—because Nia could be the most attractive person who has ever lived, who *will* ever live on this earth, and it still wouldn't be enough to explain how she looks to Jade. Now that she understands what's always been between them, she can finally admit that.

Nia comes to a stop a few feet in front of Jade. "You're not Jonah," she says.

"My favorite three words to hear," Jade jokes. What passes over Nia's expression can only be described as a wince, and Jade instantly regrets it. "That was fully a joke. I'm— *Fuck.* There's some stuff I need to say to you."

Nia folds her arms across her chest. "Okay, then."

Jade laughs nervously. "I need a couple deep breaths first," she says. Nia's face softens a fraction, and Jade inhales, holds, exhales to the counts Nia taught her. "I've practiced this in my head so many times, but I feel like I can't remember a single thing I planned. So, I'm just gonna go, and it probably won't be very eloquent, but I'll do my best.

"What I said to you on our bench after you told me about Cheyenne was horrific. I knew it was bad then, but I thought it was bad because I'd trusted my girlfriend over my best friend of sixteen years. And that *was* bad, but it was not nearly as bad as what amounted to me throwing your feelings for me in your face in defense of a woman who cheated on me while our best friend was dying. Which means that even though I technically apologized, I didn't do it properly. Nia, I am so sorry for doing that to you. If I had known you were actually in love with me, I never would have. If I'd known it was true, a lot of things would've been different. But that doesn't matter. Because you knew it was true, and I was being cruel. I'm realizing that cruelty is something I reach for sometimes—only ever on purpose with you once, but with Jonah when we fight. I promise I'll never stop working on it." Jade pauses to inhale. The words are coming quickly, so quickly that she barely has a chance to think, let alone breathe.

In the space it takes for Jade to catch her breath, Nia looks her over. "Is that all you came here to say?" she asks.

"God, no. I'm sorry this isn't—" She cuts herself off. "That was only about that first fight. I'm also sorry for saying I have nobody left, and when I said it, and how I tried to apologize for it. It was . . . a poor choice of words, and poor timing. The reality is, there's some truth in it. Because you were really all I had left, and for the past few years we haven't had each other in the way we once did, or the way I've come to understand we both wanted. I'm lonely, Nia. I miss you. I've been missing you for literal years. But I shouldn't have said that right after sleeping with you, and I should not have sent that text. It was easier than sorting through why it felt like my heart had fallen out of my chest and then been shoved back in like a misshapen, dog-chewed puzzle piece.

"I also want to make it very clear that I am not sorry for having sex with you. That was . . ." Nia makes eye contact with her and holds it. Her expression so carefully impassive, lips pressed tightly shut. "I don't know what the words are," Jade continues. "The only thing I'm sorry about is deciding it was okay not to talk first."

"I was the one who said I didn't want to talk," Nia reminds her.

"Yeah, I know. But you knew what you wanted, and I didn't, and so I shouldn't have agreed," Jade says.

"I think"—Nia averts her gaze again as she speaks—"I think I was afraid that if we talked first it wouldn't happen. Like it was my only chance."

Jade nods. "I think I felt that way, too. I just didn't appreciate how careless I was being until we were standing there in that park." She swallows and reaches into her pocket, her fist closing around the slip of paper she folded there. "Nia, I am in love with you. Love doesn't feel like a big enough word, because I've told you that I love you so many times before and I've never meant it the way I mean it now, but it's the best I've got. There're so many ways you can love someone, and I thought I knew the ways I loved you, but, God, I didn't. I think I've sort of always been in love with you, at least a little bit. I remember thinking about how smart and kind and funny you were and also your lips, like, a whole lot when we were ten. I just didn't really understand it then, and then later I never gave myself a chance to. Because I'd promised to be your friend. Any stray thought or feeling I just ignored in the name of that promise, because I didn't really think you felt the same way and even if you did, how could anything be worth risking what we have? I was scared, I guess.

"Except now I realize I might be ruining what we have by not being honest with myself. And that even if I weren't, I want to be with you so badly that I'm willing to take the gamble." She pulls the paper out of her pocket, unfolding it so that Nia can see. "I bought this. It's a one-way ticket to RDU at the end of September. I know you're moving before that, and I'll help if you'll let me, but I wouldn't be able to get myself together to move permanently until then. And I bought trip insurance so you don't have to take this as pressure, but I wanted you to see how serious I am. I'll leave Brooklyn for you. I'll go to faculty dinners, I'll listen to you bitch about the DEI committee, I'll review your lecture slides. I'm going to make a change regardless—Jonah and I need the space to grow, and it's time for us to live apart. But I want to make *this* change. The one where I get to be with you.

"I know I might be too late. I get that. I made sure that Jonah is nearby and dressed the part so if you say so, you'll still have someone by your side tonight," Jade says.

And then she stops talking.

And waits.

And waits.

And waits.

NIA STANDS THERE, letting Jade's speech wash over her, as she gathers the courage to respond. Because hearing Jade say she was scared made Nia realize for the first time just how fucking terrified she's been. Not just of Jade not feeling the same way, but of *this*. Of Jade being in love with her, too, and having to figure out what happens next. She dwelt in her seemingly unrequited crush for so long that she nestled into the uncertainty, found comfort in the maybe.

Part of her thinks that this all might be a joke, or a dream. Having what she's wanted for so long, Jade putting her heart in Nia's hands and telling her she'll trust her with it, Jade pulling out an airplane ticket, speaking of commitment, feels surreal. It's nearly *un*real.

Nearly, but not quite.

If there's one thing that does it—tells Nia that her best friend who she's been in love with for the better part of two decades is really standing outside the venue of her mother's third wedding to a man Nia has met all of four times and telling her that she is not only in love with her but is also ready to leave the city she's been in her entire life to start over with her—it's that last bit. The part about Jade making Jonah be ready for the night, too, just in case.

Because it's so Jade. She told Nia that she wouldn't have to go to this wedding alone, and she's going to make sure of it, even if it means planning around the worst possibility for herself.

It also means that she took that possibility seriously. That she didn't take Nia's love for granted, didn't assume that her declaration of love would be enough just because she meant it.

It's that bit that allows the joy to spread through her, to prickle across her skin along with the inevitable threatening sweat from leaving the air conditioning for so many consecutive minutes. It pushes the fear away, makes it so she can't hear it.

Nia looks up (she's in heels, but so is Jade, so it doesn't help much) and feels her lips pull into a grin. "Okay," she says.

Jade's lips twist like they want to smile but she can't let them just yet. "Okay, what?"

"Okay, you can be my date to the wedding," Nia says.

The smile takes over, and Jade steps toward her.

"And if there's another family wedding—hopefully not my mother's, but even if it is, to that one, too," Nia says, and Jade threads her fingers into the hair at the nape of Nia's neck. "And to faculty dinners," she continues, as Jade's eyes track down to her lips, "and to ceramics studio socials, if that's a thing, and . . ."

Nia stops talking when Jade's gaze meets hers, as if she wants one last moment to make sure that this is what Nia wants. She nods, and Jade closes the space between them. Not just their lips, but their bodies, too, her free hand finding its way to the bare skin at the small of Nia's back.

They're both smiling into it, Nia can tell from how messy the kiss is at first. Their teeth click and they're laughing and then Jade's tipping Nia's head back gently and her lips are soft against hers and they're not laughing anymore.

Nia slips her hands into Jade's jacket and finds that her top is backless, too, which is good because she'd probably die if she didn't get to feel some skin.

Jade pulls back a little bit, brushing her nose against Nia's. "We have to go inside, don't we?"

Nia nods. "We do. But I want one more," she says, and presses her lips to Jade's.

It's slower than Nia expects it to be, like Jade wants to stretch Nia's "one more" as long as she can. Nia doesn't mind at all.

"I like this suit," she says, stroking Jade's lapel when they finally separate.

"Thank you," Jade replies. "This dress is fucking incredible."

"There's about a pound of boob tape keeping my tits where they need to be," Nia says.

Jade laughs. "Incredible," she repeats.

"I'm going to have to rub oil on them later so I don't rip my skin off when I remove it."

"This is only making me appreciate the dress more," Jade says. "And I'll help you take it off—oh God, that sounded like a line. It wasn't supposed to be."

"I know," Nia says. "And thank you. We should go inside, and you should probably tell Jonah he isn't needed."

"Right, yeah," she says, retrieving her phone from her pocket with one hand and holding the door open with the other. A moment later, the door swings shut behind them, and Jade laughs, still looking at her phone.

"What?"

Jade shows the screen to Nia. Below her **went well, you're off the hook** is a selfie of Jonah on their couch in sweats, taken at a high angle so that the poorly rolled joint on the coffee table is in frame.

"He had more faith in me than you did, I guess," Nia says.

"No, he had more faith in *me*," Jade says.

"Well, I'm about to say your second-favorite three words: Jonah was right."

Jade bites her cotton candy bottom lip, but the smile wins out.

"Is that Jade Pardo I see?" Nia's mother's voice comes booming, her head sticking out from the bathroom-cum-bridal-suite.

"Hi, Helen," Jade calls back. "It's good to see you."

"Are you Nia's date?"

"I am."

"As a friend?" she clarifies.

"No, not as a friend," Jade says.

"Don't tell Gene," she yells, "but that makes me happier than the wedding."

"Mom, I don't think that's good," Nia says.

"I'm *joking*!" her mom shouts back. "Can you zip me?"

Nia looks at Jade and parts her lips to apologize, or maybe to excuse herself.

"Go," Jade says. "I'll be here the whole night."

Nia helps her mom, and they hide away in the kitchen until all the guests have arrived and then they sneak out the alley door and around the block for their entrance. Gene walks down the ten-foot-long aisle, followed by Nia with Gene's adult daughter, Clara, at her arm. Finally, her mom. The ceremony is short and sweet and ends with a kiss that forces both Nia and Clara to look away.

And when she walks back down the aisle, Jade is looking at her with what can only be described as hearts in her eyes.

When it's time for family photos, they get through two shots before her mom is shouting for Jade to join, too.

"Are you sure, Helen?" Jade asks.

"What, are you planning to break up before I get them printed?" she replies.

"Mom, oh my God," Nia says. "Gene, Clara, this is Jade."

They exchange greetings, and Jade slots in next to Nia, her hand going straight to her waist. She can't conceal the shiver that zips through her, and Jade looks down, her smile spreading.

Nia is so stupidly in love.

She hears the shutter click several times before they look to the camera.

It's a beautiful wedding. There's terrible dancing and food so good they'll be thinking about it for months. Nia and Jade take a shot and then exchange numbers with Clara, who really is lovely, even if it's Nia's first time meeting her.

They leave exhausted and happy and when they make it back to Jade's apartment, Jonah has found a way to make both himself and Luna scarce.

Jade doesn't have any body oil, so she pulls olive from the kitchen cabinet and helps Nia to saturate the pound (conservative estimate) of boob tape until the adhesive starts to slip. It may not have been intended as a line, but Jade joins her in showering it off after and they end up with their lips all over one another in the bathroom and then in Jade's bed. They spend hours like that, touching and tasting, talking and laughing, and crying, too. Happy, relieved tears.

When the first brush of daylight creeps in, and they still haven't slept, Nia is spooning Jade, both facing the window.

"Nia?"

"Yes?"

"I love you," Jade says. "In all the ways."

"I love you, Jade," Nia says back. "In all the ways."

EPILOGUE

My Dearest Darling Nia,

HAPPY 30TH BIRTHDAY!

    Now that I've gotten that out of the way, I have some business to attend to. If you are in a happy, loving, and committed relationship with one Jade Williams Pardo, please skip to the starred paragraph. If not, continue reading.

    YOU NEED TO TELL HER. YOU ARE THIRTY YEARS OLD AND YOU'VE LOVED HER FOR AT LEAST HALF YOUR LIFE, IT'S TIME.

    You may have any of the following hesitations or hang-ups:

Q1: But Michal, what if she doesn't love me back?
A1: Terrible question, Nia. She does. There is a slight possibility that she hasn't fully realized the extent of her feelings yet, but if you tell her yours, she's sure to.

Q2: But how can you be sure?
A2: Even worse question. I listened to and watched the two of you for most of my life.

Q3: What if we date and it doesn't work out?
A3: This is your least dumb question so far! The answer is that it will work out, because I'm pretty sure you're both ruined for other people, anyway. And even though there may be a vanishingly (infinitesimally, microscopically, etc.) small chance that you wouldn't work out as romantic partners, torturing yourself by never trying is way worse.

    Hope this helps!

    I'm trying to make this fun but please know that I am so completely serious. I know that it'll be difficult, and scary, and all of that, but you need to do it. Give yourself a chance to be happy. I'd say for me, but that would be pointless guilt. The real reason is for you, and for Jade. You'll be okay, I promise.

***I'm so glad that you finally got your shit together! I'm proud of you for telling her, or her for realizing and telling you, or however it happened. Selfishly, I hope that the road trip helped in some way, just so I can pretend that I'll have had a real part in this. "It was all because of your dead Auntie Michal," you'll tell your future kids together, "who told me I had to ask Jade to go on her bucket-list road trip before we turned thirty." You are very welcome, Nia.

I hope you're well. I hope you love being a professor and/or therapist. I hope you know how much better you make the world by being in it. I hope you're letting Jade take care of you the way you take care of everyone else. Most of all, I hope you feel all the love I have for you all the time, even though I'm gone. It's there, I promise.

> Loving you with all my heart, always,
> Michal

My Sweet Jade,

HAPPY 30TH BIRTHDAY, YA FILTHY ANIMAL!

If you and Nia are finally together, I trust you know how this letter is going to go. Please skip to the starred section. I'm sorry to do this twice, I just want to be extra sure. If you don't know what I'm talking about, continue reading.

I hope you've come to understand this, as I'm sure you and Toni are long over: you are in love with Nia. I have tried not to bring him up this early in your birthday letters so they can be special and just for you, but, Jade, this is something that Jonah and I have talked about. <u>Jonah</u>. If you need additional evidence:

"That little girl is a lesbian and likes your other friend"—Debbie Sarfati after our first playdate (fun fact: this is how I learned the word "lesbian." Obviously, I knew about families with two moms and all that, but I didn't know there was a different word for it. Sorry I wasn't shocked when you came out in eighth grade).

The point is that you've been in love with Nia forever, and I highly doubt that has changed. My guess is that your number-one hesitation is that we promised to be best friends until the end of time when we were, like, eleven. I hereby amend the contract: you may be best friends and also committed life partners if you so choose.

If that's not enough for you, please consider the fact that she definitely loves you and also I'm pretty sure you were made for each other (I will cool it with the mysticism, but remember I know your FULL natal chart). You need to tell her how you feel.

I'm going to tell you what I told Nia: Don't do this for me, do it for you and for her. It'll be worth it, I promise.

***Mazel tov!! It's been a long time coming, and I bet it feels amazing to finally be with your person. Actually, I know it does, because for me it was the two of you. Not in the same way, but just as big. I hope this also sheds some light on why I've never been super stoked about your previous girlfriends. Let me have this victory lap. I can't feel your judgment; I'm dead.

I hope you feel fulfilled in your life. I hope you're mostly content even if you're not always happy. I hope that you have started to work through some of your problems with Jonah, and that he's started to stand up to your parents on your behalf. Please wish him a happy birthday for me. I hope you know how special and important and loved you are. Most of all, I hope you get to feel the beauty of being alive, with all its pain and weirdness. I hope you know how much I love you.

Loving you with all my heart, always,
Michal

AUTHOR'S NOTE

The fall of 2019, I went on Shalom Y'all: A Southern Jewish History Road Trip with a group of twentysomething-year-old Jewish folks. It was an impactful trip; I felt connected to the group and my Jewishness, but I was also forced to confront a lot of uncomfortable Jewish American history that I hadn't been taught. Maybe I hadn't learned because I am Ashkenazi—my Jewish family has only been in the US since the twentieth century and assimilated to whiteness relatively recently. Maybe it was because, despite being born in the South, I was raised in the Midwest and the Pacific Northwest. Maybe it's because a lot of public school education in this country is woefully incomplete. Probably a little bit of all three.

Regardless, the experience of davening in a building constructed by enslaved Africans as a descendant of the transatlantic slave trade myself has lived as a part of me since. I created Jade and Jonah because I wanted to explore all the complicated emotions that came with that experience. Bringing them closer to it by making the synagogue part of their literal, personal ancestry allowed me to intensify it further.

While the Pardo and Sarfati families are entirely fictional, the synagogues that Nia, Jade, and Jonah visit and the Atlanta tour they go on are real. I wrote those chapters using the notes I took during Shalom Y'all and with a lot of further reading, starting with online resources provided by KKBE, Mickve Israel, the Temple, the Breman Museum, and the New Georgia Encyclopedia. I also consulted Leonard Dinnerstein's, Nancy MacLean's, and Eugene Levy's articles about the Leo Frank case.

Of course, the history and intersections of anti-Black racism and antisemitism in the American South cannot possibly be summarized in three chapters of a novel about two characters falling in love. If you found it interesting, I hope you'll consider reading more from actual historians. There may not be as many kissing scenes, but it'll be worth it anyway.

ACKNOWLEDGMENTS

The second time around, my network in this part of my life has expanded so much that I'm bound to miss some people. My apologies in advance.

Jessica Mileo, thank you for your support, belief, editorial insight, and advocacy. You make all the hard parts easier. Thank you, Claire Friedman, for being an excellent step-agent in all the same ways.

Vicki Lame, thank you for making this book the best it could be. Forever in awe of what a "rambly" email from you can do. Thank you, Vanessa Aguirre, for everything you do to pull my books together. Thank you to the people at Griffin who made the inside of the book happen correctly (when intended) and beautifully: Chrisinda Lynch, Kelly Too, Layla Yuro, Carly Sommerstein, and Janna Dokos. Thank you to the people who made the gorgeous jacket: Kerri Resnick (designer) and Natalie Shaw (illustrator). Finally, thank you to the marketing and publicity folks who got this book into readers' hands: Marissa Sangiacomo, Kejana Ayala, Brant Janeway, and Hannah Tarro. Hannah Tarro again because you took over publicity for *TYFS* after the acknowledgments had been written.

Claire, thank you for being my best living friend and birthday letter test subject. And also letting me steal your star sign for Jade and Jonah. I love you forever.

Thank you, Betsy, for every way in which you've supported me from that first draft of *TYFS*. I really feel like I'm on this publishing journey with you.

Nate and Anj, for letting me officiate (and all the other support!). Getting to celebrate your love was the exact push I needed to finish the final chapters of this novel.

To the Totani Survivors: thank you for loving me, typos, impostor syndrome, and all. Ava Wilder, there is no way I could have finished this book without trading those salute emojis back and forth for months. I'm so thankful that I get to do this extremely weird job with you. Kaitlyn Hill, you bring so much joy to the writing world for me from *Bachelor* live texts to "what are you hiding from my mother," which I still think about all the time. Samantha Markum, thank you for your entertaining hateration and enthusiastic responses to my work (both in our Tumblr eras and now), especially with this one. All of you are so immensely talented in ways I cannot describe. Bookstores are better with y'all's work on the shelves, and my life is better because y'all are in it.

Thank you to every fabulous romance author who has made this a real community for me in any way, big or small. Alicia Thompson, thank you for being in conversation with me in more ways than one. Thank you, Anita Kelly, for being all-around lovely—your warmth is felt throughout the romance community. Thank you to Clare Gilmore for exchanging books, kindness, and that gorgeous reel. Thank you to Jen Comfort for being hilarious and supportive (usually at the same time). Jo Segura for the long walks—it's always a pleasure and a relief to chat and hope and complain with you. Thank you, Regina Black, for the video calls that came just when I needed them most. Rachel Lynn Solomon and Rosie Danan, thank you both for sharing your veteran author wisdom (and Rachel, thank you for helping me take off my author event training wheels!) not just with me but with other debuts. I hope to be able to be as giving as you both. Sarah Adler, for always being willing to chat about publishing experience and expectations.

To all my nonpublishing friends and family (especially Simon, both brother and NYU correspondent): The way y'all have shown up for me this year has been nothing short of astounding. I am so very lucky.

And, finally, thank you to Patrick and Essi, the partner and the cat from my bio. Essi, sorry I wrote a dog this time. Patrick, I was able to make Nia and Kevin more real because of you. Thank you for ~~putting up with~~ taking care of me through this process. I love you so big.

ABOUT THE AUTHOR

Patrick Wilson

Rachel Runya Katz (she/they) is a contemporary romance author living in Seattle with her partner, their cat, and far too many houseplants. She has a Ph.D. in biomedical engineering, which is minimally helpful for this endeavor. Her books center queer Jews of color and their layered lives of joy, sadness, and love.